P Town is a 2016 Readers' Favorite Silver Medal Winner in the Contemporary Romance category.

Readers' Favorite gives *P Town* 5 stars and calls it an "unforgettable read."
"This book grabbed me from the very first page and kept me obsessively reading until the end. Author Howard Reiss has done a beautiful job in creating characters that his readers will connect with, relate to, and care about. If that isn't a hallmark of a great author, I am not sure what is."

--Readers' Favorite on *P Town*

IndieReader gives *P Town* 5 stars. "Beautifully written from beginning to end, *P Town* is endearing and inspiring."

--IndieReader on *P Town*

P Town won the 2016 Los Angeles Book Festival in the Spiritual category.

Readers' Favorite gives *The Laws of Attraction* 5 stars. *The Laws of Attraction* is "a very insightful and quirky legal thriller" where "nothing is what it seems at first." "The strange testimonies discussing the eternal soul and reincarnation, the various revelations about Susannah's past, and the way everybody's beliefs are tested all make for a page-turner." "This intelligent mystery" is a "guilty reading pleasure."

--Readers' Favorite on *The Laws of Attraction*

Howard Reiss is skilled "at making characters seem real and lovable in the space of a few pages or paragraphs."

--Readers' Favorite on *The Laws of Attraction*

Readers' Favorite calls *The Year of Soup* "a wonderfully insightful read" and recommends it to "anyone who loves mysteries, emotional fiction, and self-discovery." "Howard Reiss is able to deftly weave story into sustenance and create a plot that is beautifully original without straying too far from classic themes of this sort of genre." *The Year of Soup* is "a hands-down, great read."

--Readers' Favorite on *The Year of Soup*

BookBub calls *The Year of Soup* "a heartwarming read."

--BookBub on *The Year of Soup*

"*The Year of Soup*, as with his first novel *A Family Institution*, clearly establishes Howard Reiss' credentials as an especially gifted storyteller with a knack for creating fully developed characters and original storylines that engage the readers complete attention from first page to last. *The Year of Soup* is highly recommended and thoroughly entertaining, making it an appropriate addition for community library contemporary fiction collections."

--The Midwest Book Review on *The Year of Soup*

"*The Year of Soup*, mixes a fine stew of intelligence and wisdom, while also at times stirring in a sharp wit and a pinch of genuine, heartfelt charm and humanity."

--IndieReader on *The Year of Soup*

The Year of Soup received the Silver Medal for Best Fiction in the North-East Region at the Independent Publisher Book Awards in 2013.

"By understanding our family history we can understand our future. A frank novel of family and what binds us all through our troubles, *A Family Institution* is a choice pick for general fiction collections."

--The Midwest Book Review on *A Family Institution*

STARLIGHT SHINES FAR

by Howard Reiss

Starlight Shines Far
Published: June 2022
Printed in the United States of America
ISBN: 978-0-9995118-8-6

This book was published by Krance Publishing
Front cover illustration by Michael Witte
Back cover photograph by Daniel Silbert

To Ellen, Shira, Erin, Lucy, Gus, Alfie, and Millie, who help me see beyond the horizon and out to the stars

PREAMBLE

Stars are born in a cloud of dust. Currents deep within a cloud gather kernels of mass at its center. The kernels grow larger and larger until they create a sort of beating heart with their own gravitational pull. As the cloud is drawn inward, the center grows hotter and hotter. This hot core at the heart of the collapsing cloud is the spark that gives birth to a star. A star that will mature, grow old, and die like the rest of us, except it will take millions and millions of years. Much like us, the dust and debris left behind after the star dies and explodes provide the building blocks for the next generation of stars and planets.

Indeed, for all of life, for everything.

That was the first story Alex remembered his father telling him. His first memory really. It had to go way back before kindergarten. His father used to call it the story of the stars, and he told it to him often as they lay in the backyard looking up at the unbelievably starry nights they used to have back then, before the new strip mall and added streetlights dimmed nature's show forever.

His father could never pass up a starry night. Often it was already dark by the time he got home from work, and he would race through his dinner, ignoring the pleas from his mother to slow down and take his time chewing his food. She believed eating too fast and swallowing too hard were the causes of a lot of problems later in life—health problems—that and not getting eight hours of sleep every night were two of the things she always blamed for Alex's drug problems.

His father would always smile at her and nod in agreement while he continued to gobble down everything on his plate. Then he would pull the napkin from his collar, jump up, open the refrigerator to grab a beer, and announce to Alex it was time for the show. He never meant anything on the television like the other fathers; he always meant the stars.

His mother would throw her hands up in frustration, more mocking than serious, and young Alex, who was always standing nearby, waiting for the call, would rush in, ready to go. Sometimes that meant his coat, hat, and gloves were already on, and sometimes it just meant he had the binoculars around his neck.

Alex and his father would go outside, however cold it was, lie down on the grass, and stare up at the heavens. His mother rarely came out with them. She was always too busy cleaning up from dinner, although sometimes she did stand by the window, gazing out at them with a contented smile that was, in Alex's young mind, as bright as any of the stars.

She liked to say that Alex and his father were the only stars she ever wanted to watch.

Those were the best days for Alex—and his mother—the days before his father joined the stars and his mother began drinking.

His father loved to tell Alex star stories while they lay out in back. He had an unlimited supply, and Alex never grew tired of hearing them.

Alex liked to ask his father each night how many stars he thought there were in the sky. His answer was always the same, "too many to count."

His father would often remind Alex that while the points of light were indeed the stars of the show, he should not ignore the supporting players, which is how he described the darkness between the stars.

"Without them," he used to tell Alex, "there is no nighttime sky—just a blinding blaze of starlight."

The vast emptiness of space was there for a reason, his father would tell him. He said it was there for them to travel through, whether in our fantasies and dreams or one day in real life.

"The imagination may feed on the starlight," he told young Alex, "but the black emptiness of space is there for us to write on."

He called it a tabula rasa. His father was not an educated man, but he was intelligent and more knowledgeable about the stars and the night sky than anyone Alex had ever met.

His father used to encourage Alex to look for the pictures painted in the sky, nature's drawings he called constellations. He would outline them with his finger to help Alex find them. The Big Dipper was the easiest to see and the first one he pointed out. After that came the Little Bear, Orion the Hunter, Taurus the Bull, Canis Major—he called it the Big Dog—and a hundred others. He described imaginary planets only he could see that were covered with salmon-colored oceans, green skies, and giant black trees that Alex would often dream about.

His mother called his father a starry-eyed dreamer—which he was—and Alex wanted nothing more than to grow up to be a dreamer like him. Unfortunately, Alex stopped dreaming a long time ago, his dreams replaced with drugs, exactly the way his mother's dreams had been replaced with booze.

"We all come from the stars," his father would remind Alex after his mother called out his bedtime, "and we will all return back to the stars one day."

"Even Lucky?" Alex remembered asking once. Lucky was their dog. He was old and sick and spent most of the day lying on the floor, looking up at them with his sad, sleepy eyes.

"Yes, absolutely, everyone and everything," his father assured him, patting Alex on the head as he guided him back into the house.

"How about the kitchen table?"

Alex thought he was being funny, but his father did not take it that way.

"Of course, the table, the trees, the rocks…we're all made of the same stuff."

Once his father pointed to the handle of the Big Dipper—at an empty space between two of the stars—and told him that was where he came from.

"But there's nothing there. It's empty…just black," Alex pointed out.

Alex did not have his father's imagination, not back then and not now, despite his childish hopes and expectations.

"Don't be limited by your horizon, son," his father said, looking more serious than usual. He was a man who generally tossed around smiles as if he woke up every morning with a pocket full of them, as if they were little more than stardust. He took Alex's face between his hands after saying that and whispered, "It's just the limit of your sight. Not everything that's there, that you need to know or believe in will be visible to the eyes. That's why your imagination is so important."

Alex looked again at that black spot in the handle, squinting until his eyes were almost shut, trying hard to see something. He did not, not really, though he was not sure, and told his father he thought he saw a very faint star.

"Good," his father said. "I do as well."

His father was a mechanic who loved the heavens, as he sometimes called the starry night. A man with a high school diploma who never stopped reading astronomy books. A man who worked long hours six days a week fixing cars but had an imagination that was never confined by his work, his lack of formal education, or his vision—his horizon as he liked to call it.

He was a man with greasy hands who knew how every engine worked and how to fix it. He knew electricity and plumbing and could repair almost anything. He knew what things were made of and how they worked. He could talk about the principles of physics and chemistry as easily as the laws of nature, as if he had helped write them all.

He even talked about life on other planets, not in our solar system, but on planets orbiting faraway stars. His father was as sure of their existence as he was about the invisible electric charge that jumped from the distributor cap to the spark plugs when he turned the ignition key.

He was a stargazer and a dreamer, which is why his mother sometimes called his father her "dreaming man." He considered it a high compliment, and she always said it with love and admiration. For a while, Alex was her "little dreaming man." He loved it when she called him that.

His mother was a very different person back then, nothing like she is now.

Alex has changed as well. He stopped looking up at the night sky and dreaming a few weeks before his tenth birthday, the day his father returned to stardust, the victim of a terrible accident at the garage, followed by a fiery cremation, which he had made his mother promise she would do. He claimed it was the quickest way to return to the stars.

After his father returned to the heavens, stardust once again, Alex wanted nothing to do with the night sky, the stars, or his father's fanciful dreams, and he wanted nothing to do anymore with his own.

CHAPTER 1
GROWING UP

Alex's mother, Bonnie, met his father, Chris, in ninth grade. Chris was new to the school, having moved to Seattle over the summer. He had been living in the Philadelphia area, where his father was working in a plastics factory until his parents decided it would be much healthier for Chris if they moved near the Pacific Ocean to a place with fresher air and more open space.

Two days after they met, they had their first kiss. As far as Alex knew, neither of them had ever kissed anyone else before or after. At least not the lingering kind of kiss that follows you into your dreams, which is the way his father often described it, leaving his mother laughing so hard her eyes would fill with tears.

"It was a kiss," he would often tell Alex, "that shined as far as the stars."

"It was quick and wet," his mother would respond, continuing to laugh.

"Long enough," his father would add, laughing back, "to spark a love that reached across the universe—just like in the Beatles song."

They were popular in high school because Chris was full of smiles and could always find the humor in any situation. With a few words, a silly face, or a simple mime, he could change the mood of a classmate or even a teacher. He did the same with Bonnie and Alex, until one day he was gone—just like that—taking all the smiles and laughter with him.

After that, his mother's moods would overwhelm her. They did not simply take hold of her, they literally held her down. She would lie there on the couch, staring off into a darkness only she could see. Alex would retreat to his room, angry at his mother and angrier at his father for not coming home to lift the shadow off her, help her up, and make her laugh again.

Bonnie's talent in high school was listening. His father said she was the best listener he ever met.

"Since I was the big talker," he liked to say, "it was a match made in the stars."

As a young boy, Alex agreed. When he had something on his mind, his mother would stop whatever she was doing, take his hands in hers, and stare into his eyes. She would wait patiently for him to get it out, which was not always easy for him. She would listen to every word as if it was the only thing in the world that mattered.

She would scrunch up her face while she listened, crinkling the corners of her eyes as if there were a dozen little streams flowing from them, smile lovingly, and nod understandingly. His mother always seemed to know what he was trying to say even when he stumbled over the words and was not sure himself.

Alex's mother was the opposite of his father in many ways. She was sparing with her words. She made him feel better simply by hearing him out, by making room inside her for whatever was bothering him and readily taking on some of the burden. She was all about keeping both feet on the ground and moving forward, dealing with what you knew for certain, what you could see coming, and not worrying what you imagined might lie ahead.

She was not the type to worry about the things she could not see.

"Keep your eyes straight ahead," she often told Alex. "When you're looking forward, you can always see what's coming."

Unfortunately, that is not always true. The world is full of corners, surprises that come out of nowhere like flying tire irons, which means there are some things—deadly things—that you cannot see coming.

Alex's father liked to say he fell in love with Bonnie because she was "ninety percent common sense," and he needed her to keep him from flying off into space.

Alex's mother always chuckled when he said that, reminding him it was much closer to 100 percent than 90.

His mother always got right to the heart of the matter back then. She could not make people laugh the way Alex's father did, but she did encourage her friends to talk about the things on their minds— she used to say it was the best way to "let them go"—and usually she was right; all they needed was to hear themselves talk. She listened carefully to everything they had to say, never talked over them, never offered quick answers or judgments, and always had a few kind and thoughtful words when they were finished.

Unfortunately, unlike humor, which is tough and unyielding, a stone wall able to withstand the strongest of storms, Bonnie's talent for listening and feeling compassion for others required a certain level of contentment in her own life to function properly. She needed the calm, consistent hum of love and companionship to allow for the kind of patience and generosity necessary to listen to everyone else's pain and to see the world through their eyes, whether they be friends—former friends, which they would all become soon enough—or Alex.

A talent like Bonnie's is less a stone wall and more a pane of glass. It is fragile and easily shattered. All it took was his father's sudden death. The voice of her own life now cried loudly in her ears, too loudly for her to hear anyone or anything else. Her compassion and understanding were swept away in a raging river of tears and cries of *why me*. She took up drinking, and her alcohol-infused semi-consciousness made it impossible for her to move away from that window looking out from her own eyes. She lost the ability to see anything from anyone else's perspective or to talk about anyone other than herself. She could go on and on about the most meaningless things.

Sometimes, there did not have to be anyone else in the room listening.

Alex's mother never dated after his father died, but a few men did ask in the beginning. She found no solace in the fact that she was still attractive, and no solace in her female friends, who eventually gave up on her as well. She found no solace in Alex either. Perhaps because Alex looked so much like his father and had his sense of wonder and humor. At least he did before the accident, when she last looked.

After his father's death, it was a struggle for Alex to get through to her, and he eventually gave up. He realized he was on his own and had to bury his imagination out of sight so he could focus on his day-to-day living. There were no more nights out in the backyard, staring up at the stars. Alex was now earthbound, living in a place where humor had to be cynical and biting, the kind of humor only he could find funny.

As he got older, Alex became sullen and angry— much more so than his schoolmates—and avoided spending time with his mother or looking into her eyes. He did not want to risk the possibility that the old her was hiding in there somewhere and might peek out and get a glimpse of what he was becoming—not that she ever looked closely or was very good at doing that anymore.

Still, Alex was not going to take any chances, so he kept his distance.

They could sit in the same room together for hours, watching the television without saying a word, Alex absorbed in the show, his mother hiding behind a vacant stare and a wall of dark, starless thoughts she could only tolerate with massive quantities of alcohol. Liquor bottles became the voices his mother listened to. They accompanied her everywhere, whispering in her ear, resting beside her in bed, and snuggling in her arms like loving pets. They were her constant companions, always eager to listen to her endless monologues.

Alex tried befriending alcohol as well when he got a little older, but he could never find the kind of co-dependent, supportive relationship his mother did. He did not enjoy passing out or throwing up and found drugs to be far better company. They were always quick with an outstretched hand, far more dependable, and much easier to deal with the next day. All it took was more drugs.

This brings us to the present, with Alex sitting alone in his tiny room, not much bigger than a walk-in closet, staring up at the watered-down daylight passing through the bars of his dirty window. This was his third stint in rehab, and he was finding it just as annoying and meaningless as the prior two. Next time he might prefer jail. Of course, he might not have a choice, especially if he got the same judge who called this his third strike.

The way Alex understood it—the way it had once been explained to him by an older rehabber during his first stay—the main purpose of rehab was to help him figure out a way to slow down life and speed up forgetting. What the therapists did not get is that the drugs did the same thing, except they did it faster and easier. Unfortunately, they always wore off and required more. They were also expensive, the biggest downside as far as Alex was concerned.

He would not have minded if there was a way to do it without the drugs, but Alex had not found one yet, and doubted he could.

Perhaps it was possible for some people, but not for him. In the end, no matter what the therapists suggested and how hard he tried to make it happen, time never seemed to slow down, and forgetting still was impossible.

There was one surefire way to make both those things happen. Everyone in rehab knew it, and sometimes he wondered if that was not his best option. Alex always pretended to be horrified at the prospect of dying of an overdose whenever the rehab counselors brought it up. He did not want to give them any reason to hold him any longer than they could.

If he did not find another way soon, Alex wondered if it might be his only choice. The thought of dying did not frighten Alex all that much—in some ways it made the most sense— since even the drugs seemed to be losing their potency. The way he figured it, death was inevitable, it was part of nature, so there had to be a good reason for it. Since there was no way to avoid it—whether it was an accident at work, an opportunistic illness, a drug overdose, or simply old age—why wait until the last minute? Why not have as much fun as he can while he can?

Alex's father was not the least bit afraid. He had made that very clear when he talked about the stars. He believed all life came from the stars and returned to the stars in an endless cycle of birth, death, and rebirth.

"There are no endings," his father liked to say, "just transformations."

Sometimes Alex wondered if his father's death was really an accident or the result of some unconscious death wish on his part. He had changed a thousand tires over the years. Why would something go wrong that one time?

They made Alex take a poetry class his first time in rehab. He wrote haikus and the instructor always found some hidden message or meaning in his words that he never intended to put in there. The second time they made him take a drumming class. The teacher had them searching for the rhythm of the universe—their personal universe—because he said everyone's beat was as unique as a snowflake.

He told them that drumming was a way to take control of your life, a friend of sorts who could help suppress the drug urges and turn them in a different direction. Alex didn't believe it for a minute, but he nodded and pretended to search for his rhythm—the beat that would set him free—by closing his eyes and beating hard on the drum. At first, he tried to beat along with his own heart; later he tried to beat against it, as if he could drum it into submission.

This time Alex was assigned to a painting class. He was not any better at drawing than he was at poetry or drumming. There was nothing he felt compelled to paint. Not the bowl of fruit in front of the class, the trees out the window, or the emptiness he saw looking into his "inner self." He did not have his father's imagination. If he once did, it had abandoned him long ago.

Instead, Alex painted shapes, empty outlines of circles and stars. When the teacher asked him about it, he made up some story about trying to break the world down to its smallest components to help him understand it better.

"I think shapes are very elemental," Alex said, stepping back and rubbing his chin like he was contemplating something profound, "the elemental building blocks of life, if you know what I mean."

When you are always on the hunt for drugs, you get to be very good at bullshitting. What he told her was based on a line he recalled hearing once in an old movie, probably one of those black-and-white movies he used to watch with his father.

The teacher was fine with that explanation, as he knew she would be, nodding like she knew exactly what he meant and encouraging him to keep up the good work. He could have painted a severed head and she would have found something positive to say. They are trained to react with patients in a positive way. It was so easy to fool the therapists in rehab; all you had to do was look as if you were making a real effort and be very thoughtful about it.

He drew a few more shapes while looking around at the girls in his class. Girls and drugs were the only two things Alex really cared about. Since there were no drugs available, looking at the girls was the only option left. Fortunately, the prettiest one—probably one of the most beautiful girls Alex had ever seen—had been assigned to the easel next to his.

How lucky was that?

She looked about the same age, mid-twenties, and had long black hair. Alex was a sucker for straight hair when it reached down to the waist. Unlike the girls he met when he was getting high, her hair was clean and healthy-looking, reflecting the overhead neon light like a shiny new car. Alex leaned a little closer and took a deep breath. It had some sort of flowery scent fragrant enough to momentarily push away the awful paint smell.

She did smile at him when they were setting up. Alex was surprised that he smiled back instead of turning away, which is what he usually did when he was not high. It was as if she had locked her eyes onto his, and he could not move them away. She had the biggest, brightest eyes he had ever seen. They were sky blue and incredibly clear, untroubled, unlike everyone else in rehab whose bloodshot eyes looked as if they were recovering from an endless hangover. She appeared excited at the thought of painting—at least Alex thought so—which was the best he could do with what little was left of his imagination.

Alex glanced down at her arms and did not see any needle marks, so no shooting up. Her teeth were bright white, not yellow, which ruled out smoking a lot of dope and drinking. He figured she had to be a pill popper, maybe amphetamines or ecstasy. There were a lot of new club drugs even Alex did not know about. New ones seemed to come out every month.

Judging by what she was painting, Alex guessed she liked to hallucinate.

She was too pretty and seemed too content to belong in rehab, which made Alex wonder if she was a plant, some new young therapist embedded in class as part of her training. What better way to understand who winds up here than by getting an insider's view of the inmates?

He had no idea what to say to break the ice. Alex was better at that sort of thing when he was high. Besides, he knew a girl like her would not waste much time on him. He would not if he were her. Alex figured if she got really bored or had the slightest interest, she would make the first move.

She did have a strange name; Alula. They all wore their first names on badges like it was summer camp. Alex figured she must have been born with something plain like Sally or Jane and made up this new one to match the world she saw when she got high.

She had artistic talent for sure and one hell of an imagination, at least based on the landscape she was working on. She kept looking up as if she was being inspired by the stains on the drop ceiling or looking through it. Her painting was much more detailed than his and showed a lot more effort. It was a dark, starry night, like the ones Alex used to watch with his father, except her night sky had two moons on opposite sides of the canvas, each with a soft salmon glow in the reflection of a distant red sun.

Alex could not stop watching her work on her canvas. He had plenty of opportunity since painting circles at random—which was the only shape he was adding now—hardly required much effort or concentration. A ten-year-old could have drawn them just as easily.

Alex was amazed at how intensely Alula stared at her canvas and how gently and carefully she caressed it with the brush. She looked like a child when she leaned in close to touch up a spot, a young girl when she straightened up to make a broader stroke, and a mature woman when she stepped back to take it all in. Her expressions, indeed, her whole face, seemed to change from moment to moment.

It did unnerve Alex a bit to think his imagination might be returning after all these years.

Once she caught him staring at her painting—and her—and turned to smile and nod at him before going back to her canvas. He wondered if it was an invitation. He was not good at reading signals like that. He was usually wrong when he tried. Alex learned long ago to wait for the girl to make it clear, unless he was high. When he was high, he did not care about being rejected, especially since the girls, high as well, rarely rejected anyone.

Alex cleared his throat and stepped back as if to admire his own painting when all he really wanted to do was look at her from behind. She was curvy where she was supposed to be curvy with flat lines everywhere else. Her legs took forever to reach the floor, and she stood perfectly straight, her shoulders relaxed and confident, her head turned up, as if she'd been painting her whole life.

With all that, Alex found the back of her neck the most striking, demanding a painter's attention on its own, particularly the way the sunlight coming in from the window behind them illuminated her short, curly blonde hairs.

She had a perfect body as far as Alex could see, which he craved almost as much as he did cocaine.

He stepped back up to his canvas and drew another meaningless circle.

"So, you find shapes very elemental," she said with a soft chuckle.

"Eavesdropping?"

"Too close to avoid it."

"You tell them what they want to hear," Alex said, "and they move on."

He thought that was very clever, but Alula didn't laugh. She did not even respond. Instead, she leaned into her canvas and gently stroked one of her moons.

Alex went back to his canvas, making smaller circles this time. He wanted to appear as engaged as she was.

A few minutes later she spoke to him again.

"You don't talk very much, do you?" she said without looking up from her canvas.

"Not much to say."

He replied quickly before he had a chance to think about it because when he did, his words often got stuck in his throat, and when they did finally come out, they often sounded lame.

Alula added more shadow to her moons to give their topography more depth. They looked like twins. She had a natural talent for painting, particularly the way she used light and shadow, as well as an interest in it he did not have. Another reason Alex was sure she would grow tired of him by the end of the three-day class.

Alula added some faint stars in the distance, which magically added more darkness to the rest of her starry night. It was hard for Alex to look away.

"A world of your own?" he finally asked, trying to sound intelligent and funny at the same time.

Funny always worked with his father, except it came natural to him.

"Not anymore," she said, practically lighting up his face with her smile.

It was so bright, Alex had to look away at her painting.

"It's very good," he whispered after clearing his throat.

"Thank you."

If only he was high, Alex thought, he would know what to say next.

He would not have been surprised if this was the full extent of their conversation for the rest of the three-day class.

Alula looked over at Alex's canvas before turning back to add a few more small stars to hers. He liked the fact that she did not feel compelled to lie and return the compliment.

Okay, he thought, she had made up her mind. He was not worth the effort. Rehab was a solitary experience, and she preferred to keep it that way. He was fine with that. This was Alex's third time here, and he should know better by now. He sighed a little too loudly while he added some more circles.

Then she surprised him.

"How about if I ask you a question," Alula said without looking over at him, "and then you ask me one. Deal?"

Alex's initial reaction was to say no way, he did not like playing personal games like that, but then he thought why the hell not. She was beautiful, they were both stuck here, and he never had a friend in rehab, let alone a girlfriend. It would help pass the time if he could figure out a way to do it.

"A game of twenty questions, why not?"

He certainly was not engrossed in his universe of shrinking circles.

"I assume they're all yes and no questions," Alex added.

Alex knew he would not be any good at a game like this if the answers were too complicated.

"No, what makes you say that? It can be any question you want...but you have to give a truthful answer."

He sighed again, probably louder this time.

"Fine," Alex said, "go ahead and ask your question."

"Okay, my first question is very simple...why are you so unhappy?"

"Boy, you don't waste time on the easy ones, do you? Like how old I am or did I go to college. You get right to it."

"It's a fair first question," Alula said, still smiling, not the least bit upset or surprised by his reaction.

Alex was already disappointed because it sounded more like a therapist's question than one from a potential lover.

"Okay, here's the answer...because I'm back here again. This is my third time in rehab. Who isn't unhappy to be here?"

"I'm not talking about this moment. I'm talking fundamentally. What about this life makes you so unhappy?"

"That's two questions."

"No, it's not. You didn't answer the first question…my fault…now I've clarified it."

He thought it over while he stared at his last few circles. They were getting smaller and smaller. Eventually, they would become specks of dust invisible to the naked eye. Perhaps he did have some imagination left after all, at least when it came to shapes and sizes.

"Well?"

If he didn't answer, she would probably stop speaking to him. She might even ask to be transferred to a different easel on the other side of the room. Did Alex really think she would sleep with him because she was painting next to him in rehab art? She was way too beautiful and talented, even if she was trapped in here the same as him. At least they had that in common, and in Alex's world that was significant. This kind of confinement—like sitting around smoking pot—had to be conducive to quick intimacy.

Short and superficial was more than enough for him. It was all Alex ever experienced anyway.

Where could they do it if she were willing? They watched them every minute. There was no place Alex could think that offered any privacy.

Even so, having her next to him for a few days was better than having her across the room. She was nicer to look at than anything he could paint.

"I suppose because I have no burning passion or dream," he said. "Nothing I really aspire to become or accomplish…other than getting high. How's that for a good reason?"

Alula stared at her painting and covered her mouth while she thought it over. After a while she looked over at him and nodded. "That's a much better answer."

"I'm glad you like it," Alex said, picking up the brush and adding a few dots to his canvas.

"Now it's your turn to ask me a question," Alula said. "It can be about anything."

He thought it over. If this were a bar, Alex would ask her if she wanted to get out of here and go back to his place to get high. He could ask her if she would sleep with him, but how would that look after the serious, thoughtful question she just asked him.

"Take your time," she said. "Make it a serious one."

That made Alex angry. It was almost as if she was reading his mind or pre-judging his character, so he asked the next question that popped into his head.

"Is Alula your real name?"

"Yes. The last name is Borealis."

"Oh, come on, give me a break."

"It's true."

"You made the name up."

"No, I did not. Remember the rules, I'm required to answer truthfully."

"Yeah, right."

When she did not say anything more, Alex asked her what kind of name Alula was.

"It's the proper name of the constellation Ursa Major…the great she-bear. It's where the Big Dipper is located."

"You're named after the stars?"

"Yes."

"Your parents must have had a real sense of humor."

"We're all named after the stars."

"Your brothers and sisters?"

"Everyone on my planet."

Alex looked over at her and chuckled. Alula stared back, her eyes sparkling with good humor like she was happy to be finally telling someone, not because she was pulling his leg.

"Okay, then tell me how you got here. Where's your spaceship?"

"That's another question. It's my turn now."

Alex did not try to hide his exasperation. Such a beautiful girl in such a perfect body. Why did he always wind up with the crazies? Maybe because the ones he hung around with were usually hooked on drugs. Why get involved with another one? He was crazy enough as it was.

"Why don't you believe me?" Alula asked.

"That you're from Mars?"

"Not a planet in this solar system, one much further away."

"That's your question? Why don't I believe you?"

"Yes, that's my question."

"Well," Alex said, dipping his brush into the black paint and barely touching it to the canvas. They had to continue painting if they did not want the instructor walking over and intruding on their conversation. "I suppose because it's not true. How's that for a good reason?"

Alula did not appear the least bit insulted. She leaned closer to her canvas and added some faint stars meant to appear farther away. Sometimes when you challenge someone's fantasy, they get angry and lose it. Alex saw a fistfight once over whether this guy had left his body when he was high and flown over the city.

Alula continued painting with a steady hand, her lips parted slightly to give her tongue the opportunity to moisten them. Alex liked the way she did that. She looked so relaxed and content, more like she was at home than at rehab. She took a few moments before replying.

"Do you have the power to always recognize the truth?"

"I know bullshit when I see it."

Alula chuckled. "The truth isn't always visible…it often isn't. It can be the hardest thing to see sometimes…and the hardest thing to believe."

"The world according to Alula?"

"There's a lot of truth to be found in the imagination," she said, dipping her brush into the water and wiping off the white paint. "One of your poets said that."

Alex's father used to say something similar when they were lying out back looking up at the stars. He called it the truth of imagination.

Alex wondered what drugs Alula had taken to blow her mind like this, unless it was all an act, a way of getting attention and avoiding the disappointments in her own life. Maybe something traumatic happened to her when she was younger. Perhaps it was a lecherous uncle or some terrible accident where she walked away unscathed, but her parents were not as lucky.

This fantasy world had to be a lot better than her real one. It was one way of drowning out the past and keeping the present at a distance. Drugs were another. Alex figured the two together would work even better. He wondered if he should give it a try. Fantasies would be a lot cheaper than drugs, and they are not against the law. He could pretend to be a superhero—Chameleon Man, able to blend into any background. Invisible Man would be even better. There would be a ton of advantages to that, not the least of which would be his ability to score whatever drugs he wanted.

Perhaps rehab should be trying to cure his drug cravings with fantasies instead of poetry, drums, and painting.

It would take a lot of time and effort to become as good as Alula in terms of convincing herself it was true—if indeed she had reached that stage of delusion. She sounded fully invested in her fantasy.

"It's because I look and sound like you, is that it?" Alula asked without looking up from her canvas.

"That's part of it," Alex responded, thinking about the alien invaders in the comic books he read growing up who all had giraffe-like necks, multiple arms, large green heads, and bulging red eyes.

"What's the other part?"

"We are all here in rehab for pretty much the same reason."

"What's that?"

"None of us are particularly fond of reality."

Alex was pleased his response did not sound too insulting or dismissive. Even if she was crazy, she hid it well, and she looked even more beautiful when she turned to him with that big, bright, I-don't-give-a-damn-about-anything smile. Everything he said seemed to amuse her. Even rehab seemed to amuse her, probably because she felt at home with all the other crazies.

Sanity did not count for much in a place like this because most of the inmates came with their own large deficits in terms of common sense and normalcy.

Besides, Alex was not interested in her mind, and he was not looking for something long term; all he wanted was something different to think about in rehab this time. A sex partner—or even just a romantic interest—to compensate for the lack of drugs and freedom would make it a little easier and a lot more fun.

There must be a closet left unlocked somewhere, Alex thought, or perhaps they could get passes at the same time to go out for a walk and find some deserted spot in the woods surrounding the rehab center. There were cameras most everywhere, but they didn't try to hide them, which might give them a shot at finding a blind spot.

"You can't escape reality if that's what you're thinking, because it's not out there," Alula said, pointing over her shoulder at the window. "It's in here." She tapped her forehead. "And here."

She moved her finger down to her eyes. "And here." She rested her hand on her heart. "It's a matter of understanding, observing and accepting."

"Perhaps on your planet," Alex said with a chuckle.

Alula continued to smile. At least she had a sense of humor about it. Alex could not be the first person she tried this line on.

If she had told him that she was a pole dancer or one of those nude models who lay on a buffet table covered with sushi for people to eat off, he would have believed her. If she had told him that she cleaned the cages at the zoo or delivered the mail, he would have believed that too. She could have told him just about anything other than this outer space nonsense.

"Try looking at things through the eyes of other people," she said. "You'll be surprised at how quickly your reality can change."

"Drugs do the same thing, thank you very much. They're damn good at changing my perspective...and my reality. They make the world a much sunnier place."

Alex smiled because he thought he sounded rather clever.

"It doesn't appear to be working at the moment, does it," Alula said, dipping her brush into the black paint to darken the darkness around her two moons.

"Because they only work while you're using them...when you're high."

"How long does that last?"

Alex sighed dramatically for effect.

"Unfortunately, not long enough," he said, leaning in to paint a few dots at the edge of the canvas before putting down the brush to declare that he was finished. The last few dots were jumping off the edge of the canvas into oblivion, at least in Alex's imagination, but he had to admit it looked anything but finished. If the instructor asked Alex why he stopped, he would tell her that not everything is visible to the naked eye. He figured his father's words applied to art as well as the night sky.

He could not help smiling at that old memory.

Alex did not find painting any more engaging than poetry or drumming, not like being high, although doing it next to a beautiful girl—crazy in her own stary way—did make it more pleasant. He looked down at the glass of water on the table beside him, wishing it were filled with something stronger.

"It's my turn for a question," Alex said.

"Go ahead. May I borrow some of your blue?"

"Sure, I'm done...but I've never seen a blue star."

"That's too bad," Alula said, wiping off her brush and reaching over to dip it into his blue paint.

"Okay, so you come from Ursa Major?"

"Yes."

"That's a constellation filled with stars."

"Yes."

"What star do you live on?"

"No one can live on a star, not in this form," she said, touching her chest, exactly where he wanted to touch it.

"My ancestors are of the stars," she continued, "as are yours. We all become one again with the stars when our time comes to transform. Right now, I am of a planet...the same as you."

"What do you call your planet?"

"Now?"

"No, the one you came from."

"Home."

"No, what's its name? You know, like we call our planet Earth."

Alex chuckled as he listened to himself talk. He felt like he was eight years old again talking with his father. He used to say all kinds of crazy things when they were gazing up at the stars. Once he tried to explain to Alex how a light-year was not the only way to measure distance or time because there were different ways to travel. He said that a light-year could also be an instant because space and time were not fixed measures like inches and minutes, but relative measures.

Alex did not get it back then, the concept of relativity.

"Relative to what?" he remembered asking.

Alex wished he could remember his father's answer.

"Home is what we call it. It has no other name. We call a lot of things by their function."

"Then what do you call the place where you live on your planet...you know, the building where you sleep. You do sleep?"

"Of course. We call it a house. The planet is our home."

"A rather expansive view of things?"

"Compared to your narrow view, yes." Alula moistened her lips again with her tongue. She had such lovely lips, slightly upturned, red, soft, promisingly sweet. They were almost as expressive as her eyes. He had never noticed that about anyone else's lips before.

"Now, it's my turn for a question," she said.

"Go ahead, ask me whatever you need to know about the earth." He laughed when he said it and Alula laughed back. He would learn soon enough she was infused with good humor. Nothing annoyed her or made her angry. She would eventually tell him how she learned early on that she could not change the way people were on Earth, only the way she reacted to them, and smiles always worked best when it came to that.

She sounded a lot like a therapist sometimes.

"Why don't you look up at the stars anymore?"

Alex felt the breath catch in his chest. He had wondered about it himself over the years—he used to love lying on his back at night with his father staring up at the sky—but he did not need a session with an amateur psychologist to know the reason why he stopped. After his father died, it stopped feeling like he was watching a show; it felt more like he was searching the stars for him, which made him angry at them for taking him away.

His father used to tell Alex if he looked hard enough, he could find anyone and anything he had lost up in the stars, although that never worked.

"What makes you think I don't?" Alex replied unable to conceal his annoyance.

"I don't mean you in particular...I mean all of you. Your eyes are always straight ahead or looking from side to side, sometimes behind you, and often down, as if you think staring at that little phone keeps you connected when all it is really does is keep you apart...separate from each other and separate from the stars. No one seems to find the stillness and time they need to sit back and look up."

"I suppose because the stars are way beyond our reach," Alex said.

"A man's reach should exceed his grasp or what is heaven for."

"One of your *Home* poets?"

"No, one of yours...Robert Browning."

"What does that even mean?"

"It means that if you want to achieve anything worthwhile, you have to try...even if it may seem impossible."

Alex shrugged, and Alula continued.

"The stars are everywhere...even inside us." Alula reached over and touched Alex's chest, his heart beating faster as if it had a mind of its own. He had to sit down on his stool and take a breath.

"We are all the same... stars... planets... trees... rocks... animals... people. The calcium in your bones was once stardust... like the oxygen in the air and the hydrogen in the ocean."

"My father used to talk like that."

"Because he was of the stars as well," Alula said as if she knew who he was.

"He's dead," Alex mumbled.

"He's been transformed and enlightened. That's how we describe it."

"We call it dying."

Alula nodded. "We welcome enlightenment when our time comes." She dipped her brush back into his blue paint. "I like the way you mixed your blue. It's softer than mine, more meditative. I think I added too much magenta."

He wished he could take credit for it, but he was not paying attention. It was purely accidental.

"Well, enlightenment can't come soon enough for me," Alex said, picking up his brush and making a few imaginary dots when he noticed the instructor looking in his direction.

Alula added some more of his blue to soften her night sky.

Alex expected her to reprimand him the way the therapists did when he made a remark like that. He was always quick to assure them it was a joke. Otherwise, he was afraid they'd find a way to keep him here.

They never understand that simply saying it or thinking is not the same as seriously considering it. All it means as far as Alex is concerned is that he's prepared—like a lot of people—to trade pain for the absence of pain. But that's someday in the future when it becomes a real choice. They always write furiously in their notebooks after he says something like that, telling him in their deepest and gravest voice that it's not a laughing matter.

He would argue with them if it was not a waste of time. Everything can be a laughing matter if you want it to be. A good philosophy for someone accustomed to getting high to rely on during those moments when he is not.

It was true Alex had no real desire to kill himself—not yet— even though they had assured him during his first stint in rehab that taking drugs was "overwhelming" evidence to the contrary. He could have easily taken an overdose anytime if he really wanted to.

The drugs made the waiting around a lot easier. They helped pass the time, not much different than television and video games. Alex never saw the drugs as an endgame.

Alex's father spoke like Alula sometimes. Alex remembered when their dog Lucky died, and his father sat with him smiling and stroking Lucky's lifeless body. He told Alex his death was the most natural thing in the world and not something to fear. His father said he would welcome it when his time came, which Alex assumed meant when he was a very old man, not one day soon when he might subconsciously allow the tire iron that he was working with to fly off and smack him on the head.

Alex did not really believe he would let it happen and leave him and his mother like that, but he could never dismiss the possibility.

Alex never discussed any of this with the therapists; he simply nodded when they warned him about the dangers of talking the way he did sometimes, as if he completely agreed.

"I was just kidding," Alex told Alula in case she might be put off by his remark, and she smiled back like she already knew.

"I'm glad. We all transform when the time is right."

There were girls in Alex's experience who were attracted to this kind of talk, who moved closer the more depressed he sounded. They were the ones who had what one of his suppliers liked to call the mothering syndrome.

"The concept doesn't bother me," Alula added, sounding a little like his father, as she put down the brush and stepped back to look at her canvas. "Transformation and enlightenment are inevitable and a basic part of nature. I think it will be wonderful one day to rejoin the stars, just as wonderful as the journey there, which is important to enjoy and make productive and worthwhile."

"How do you do that?"

"You already know, you just told me; you find the right passion…the one that moves you to reach for the stars."

Alex thought she sounded like a Hallmark greeting card.

"And what if you never find the right passion…or any passion?"

"You mean if you choose the easy way out?" Alula asked, still smiling.

"Like taking drugs."

"Don't worry, you'll find it…even if it's the next time around."

Alex was afraid to ask what Alula meant by that. He didn't want to start yet another weird conversation about reincarnation. He had one of those a couple of years ago with this drugged-out girl who said she had been Cleopatra in a prior life.

"How about you?" Alex asked, hoping to take Alula's remark in an entirely different direction. "I could make you my passion on this journey through rehab."

She laughed, which he thought was a good sign.

"That's not what I was getting at…but it is a good first step." Alula chuckled to herself as she leaned forward to examine her canvas more closely.

Alex took her response as another positive sign and stood silently watching her. He stared again at the little hairs on the back of neck as they continued to glow in the sunlight. He liked the way she held her shoulders, still and calm, perfectly straight, as if contented with life, even in rehab.

He looked back at his uninspired painting. He could have done better. He should have tried harder if only to impress her.

"Your turn or mine?" he asked, afraid the awkward silence from the beginning of the class might be returning.

"Yours," she said.

"Okay, here's an easy one…how old are you?"

"Eight."

Alex coughed out his surprise.

"That's also bullshit. You look my age…mid-twenties."

"Home takes three of your years to orbit our star."

"So that means you're old… seventy-five by the time you turn twenty-five."

Alula smiled again, bigger this time, while nodding in agreement.

"How long do you live?"

"We don't use words like live and die."

"What do you use?"

"I told you, emerge, enlighten, transform."

"You sound like caterpillars."

"In some ways I think we are."

"Okay, I get it, you emerge, become enlightened, transform, and then get to do it all over again."

"More or less."

"You never die?"

"Nothing ever ceases to exist," Alula said. "We are all made up of the same elements...planets, stars, rocks, soil, trees, animals... us... nothing ceases to be."

"You transform."

"Exactly."

Alex sighed. He glanced down again at her perfect body and wondered if it was worth the effort. What if she were riding the downslope of the bell curve and would get even crazier? What if she started talking in tongue and whirling in circles? Besides, how much of a chance did he have in rehab, where they were watched every second?

"All right," he said, "let me ask the question differently. How long have you been here on Earth?"

"I arrived here with my parents when I was four."

"Twelve Earth years ago?"

"Yes."

"Why did you come?"

"My parents are settlers. Our planet is small, it has limited resources, so every five or ten years, they ask for volunteers to settle on other planets."

"Earth?"

"And about a dozen others scattered around the universe."

"Are there a lot of inhabited planets?"

"More than you could count."

"People like us?"

"The ones we settle on for sure. Most of the ones we know. But there are countless solar systems and planets we have yet to explore."

"It sounds like you people on Home get around."

Alula nodded.

"Does that mean you'll be returning soon?"

"There's no going back once you settle."

She did not look upset at the thought of it. She did not wipe away a tear or stare up and out the window with longing the way they always do in the movies. Instead, she put down her brush, put her hand to her chin, and stepped back from her painting.

"That's it, I'm done."

"It's really good," Alex said. "A beautiful...and very strange starry night."

"Because it's Home, not Earth. Different sky."

"And two moons."

"The moons are beautiful," Alula said. "They are almost identical twins. They orbit each other as they orbit Home...it's like a celestial ballet."

They stopped talking when the teacher came up behind them to look over their canvases. She smiled at Alula's canvas and whispered, "Very imaginative...great detail...your perspective is wonderful. It's as if I'm standing there looking up."

She covered her mouth with her hand while she examined Alex's canvas.

"Painting is a good way of expressing what you see or imagine you see. It can reveal a lot about yourself...especially to you," she added, repeating something she told them at the beginning of the class.

"It's true," he replied with a quick glance at Alula. "I feel as if I'm always traveling in circles."

"For the next one," the teacher said, clearly not amused, "I'd suggest trying something a little more personal and expressive. Perhaps a fantasy like Alula's or a dream."

"You don't think shapes are personal and expressive?"

He loved putting the rehab therapists on the spot because he knew they were not supposed to be too confrontational or dismissive. They were supposed to be as supportive as possible, which should be all the time in Alex's opinion when it came to a stupid painting or poem.

"I do. Don't misunderstand me. I like what you've done for your first attempt. There is a certain consistency and predictability to it...the way the circles trail off in size until they jump off the canvas. Those little certainties in life are what we are all searching for whether consciously or subconsciously. Repeating shapes and patterns...I get it...but for the next class, I would like you to try something a little different, something less predictable, with more color...something that might better reflect what's going on in your life...what has brought you to this moment."

"That's a tall order."

"Just let it happen; don't overthink it."

"At this moment in my life, I think I'm more comfortable with shapes," Alex said, pointing at his canvas.

"Then by all means continue with shapes, but they don't all have to be symmetrical. Perhaps some lines as well...curved and straight. And some color. Ever see a Kandinsky?"

"No."

"He was a Russian painter who filled his canvases with shapes, lines, and colors. There is no wrong or right way to paint. It is all about expressing yourself, the way you see the world, and yourself in it. If shapes are what do it for you, then by all means use them."

"I'll think about it tonight and see what I can come up with for tomorrow," Alex said. He had no intention of making any more of an effort on his next painting than he had on this one. He planned on focusing his attention and effort tonight and tomorrow on Alula. He would learn a hell of a lot more about himself and his place in the world that way.

"Great. Different angles and planes will also give the painting more depth. You will be surprised at how much fun it can be when you really get into it...like your neighbor here. This class always turns out to be everyone's favorite."

Alex gave her his best I-got-it nod. He was barely listening at the end.

"Try to visualize something tonight. See what pops up in your imagination."

Alex stood there as still as a statue as she patted him on the shoulder like a good boy before walking over to the next pair of inmate artists.

"I guess she liked yours a lot more," Alex said with a smirk.

This was his third time in rehab, and he was used to disappointing the staff. They never thought he tried hard enough or really cared. They were not totally wrong, but they were not totally right either.

"It doesn't matter," Alula said. "The only person who needs to like what you do is you."

"You sure you don't work here?"

Alula chuckled and said, "It's my turn to ask a question."

"Go ahead, but don't expect an imaginative answer."

"I try not to fill my thoughts up with expectations."

She had a cute comeback for everything, Alex thought, which could eventually get on his nerves.

"What's your question."

"What do the drugs do for you?" Alula asked.

"You don't know?"

"No."

"Then why are you here? To dry out?"

"Dry out?"

"Too much drinking."

He pantomimed taking a shot of something.

"No."

"For what then?"

"For the experience," Alula said, sending Alex into a small coughing fit.

"The experience of what...being in rehab?" It took him a few moments to get the words out. "You're kidding, right?"

"No, the experience is part of it, but the main reason...the real reason I'm in here is to meet you."

It took Alex a lot longer this time to find his words. This was getting way too weird, way beyond ridiculous. He felt like a character in the theater of the absurd.

"Give me a break," Alex finally said. "What is it really? Painkillers? Uppers? Downers?"

Alula shook her head slowly from side to side, her big smile replaced by a smaller one.

"You just checked yourself into rehab like it was some kind of spa vacation?"

"Not a vacation, a learning experience...and an opportunity to connect."

"With a druggie?"

"Not any druggie...with you."

"Me?"

"Yes."

"Okay," Alex said with as exasperating a sigh as he could muster. It was a waste of time trying to understand her, and he did not see the point in continuing to try. "The answer to your question is the drugs make me feel good."

"That's it?"

"How many things do you know in life that always do that?"

"Chocolate always makes me feel good," Alula said. "So does coffee, music...watching the yellow sun light up the sky in the morning and paint the dusk red and purple. There must be more to drugs than just feeling good."

"They also help you forget."

"Forget what?"

"The things you don't want to remember."

Now she was really beginning to annoy him, perfect body or not.

"Forgetting is the opposite of learning," Alula said. "Everything instructs us, even the darkest of moments."

"Maybe under the red sun."

He meant it as a joke, but it sounded dismissive and mean.

"Accepting...sharing...listening to the birds...studying a flower...finding a passion...time...all work as well when you pay them attention...and there are no risks or side effects."

"Now you definitely sound like one of the therapists."

"Maybe they know what they're talking about."

"I'm sure there are a lot of things that work," Alex said, trying to sound like one of the therapists himself. "It comes down to a choice like anything else as to what works best for you and what you're most comfortable with."

"Drugs?"

"There's no disputing that they are faster and dependable. I know what's coming after I take some."

They are a lot more dependable than people, Alex thought.

"But they're temporary...fleeting...they never last for very long."

"You can always buy more."

"Seems sort of monotonous…like going round and round in circles," Alula pointed to Alex's painting, "which is perhaps what your circles represent."

"Perhaps…or perhaps they represent completeness…the fact that I don't need anything or anyone else."

"No one can do it alone…no one should."

"I think I read that once in a fortune cookie," Alex said, hoping to lighten up the conversation and bring it back around to them.

"You know, Alex," Alula said with as kind a smile as Alex could ever recalled seeing on anyone in rehab or anywhere else for that matter. It seemed very different from her amused smile. "You are not alone in the Universe; no one ever is…not on Home, not on Earth…not even when you're by yourself and high on drugs."

It was the first time she had said his name. She said it like they were old friends or lovers. Alex could never buy that kind of part-of-everything philosophy of life, but he liked the way Alula said his name.

"Good concept in the abstract," Alex said, "up there with God and religion. But not much help in real life…but it might explain some of the voices I hear in my head from time to time."

That brought back her amused smile.

"Even humor is a better choice," she added.

"It's my turn for a question."

"Go ahead."

"Do you have religions and rules on Home? You know, like the Holy Trinity and the Ten Commandments? You know what those are?"

"Of course. I've been here for almost twelve Earth years. I try to learn something about my new planet every day."

"Just making sure. What kind of commandments does Home have? If we have ten, I suppose you have a hundred by now."

"Home has no commandments and no religions. They have six words, words we all learn as children, the words we live by, the same six words for everyone and everything."

"I can't wait to hear them."

He thought about asking if one of the words was abracadabra, but she looked so intent and sweet, Alex decided for once in his life not to be a wise-ass and keep his mouth shut.

"Eyes Open. Hearts Open. Minds Open."

The words hung up there for a while like the dialogue in a comic strip. Alex bit down on the inside of his lip to stop from saying something stupid or laughing out loud.

"That's it?" he asked after gaining control over his baser instincts. "That's the magic recipe from a civilization a million years ahead of ours?"

"How much more do you need?"

"How about thou shall not kill?"

"It's in there. Eyes Open. Hearts Open. Minds Open. No one who lives by those words would ever hurt another."

"Your God is a God of few words."

"They are much more than words. It is who we are. They are part of us."

Alula pushed her hair away from her eyes. She had the bluest eyes Alex had ever seen. Bluer than the sky, bluer than the ocean, a blue that deserved to be its own flower. They were as round as her two full moons and filled with a kindness—and sweetness—Alex was not accustomed to seeing. You do not get much of a chance to look into eyes like that when you spend your time chasing drugs and getting high.

"My father calls it the music of the stars," she continued. "He says when he looks up at the night sky and listens closely, he can almost hear the stars whispering them."

Alex wondered if she had any idea how beautiful she was. Probably not. If she did, she would not be telling him about whispering stars or pretending to be from outer space. She would not be talking to him at all.

"They are not words sent from a God, not the way you think of God as an entity to worship, a being or consciousness up in the heavens who you beseech to intercede on your behalf. It's a reflection of the nature of the universe…the DNA of being…as basic as oxygen and water."

Alex nodded as if he understood, even though it sounded like new age mumbo-jumbo to him.

"The universe…call it nature if you want…is always," Alula said. "It never ceases to be, and there is always something we can learn if we open ourselves up to it. We are all part of nature, so what better teacher."

"Not much you can learn from a rock in my experience," Alex said with a smile, so Alula understood it was a joke.

She smiled back, the sparkle in her eyes undiminished. She was not done answering yet.

"One of your poets said that consciousness is not required to exist or to teach, which is very true…just ask the stars."

Alex took a breath and let the air out slowly. Alula might be crazy, but she was not stupid. She could not possibly be making all this up on the spur of the moment. She must have given her fantasy universe quite a lot of thought over the years. As fantastic as it all sounded, the concept made some sense. It was consistent with her overall theme.

There was nothing wrong with keeping your eyes, heart, and mind open. Theoretically, of course. It was another story when it came to the real world. If she thought anyone could go through life practicing that mantra every minute of every day, she was indeed mad.

Still, Alex had no doubt he would be thinking about what Alula had said later tonight in bed. Sleep did not come easily to him these days—not without the drugs—so he always had a lot of time to think.

It was hard for him, for any red-blooded American boy, to dismiss a girl as pretty as Alula simply because she had a few screws loose. Alex knew some of his own screws could use a tightening.

"It's all in the stars," Alex said absentmindedly, responding to her last remark by repeating the words his father often used when Alex could not understand or appreciate what he was trying to say.

"Exactly."

Alula looked pleased with herself, as if she had made another convert to her new age religion of the stars.

"That's all for today," their art therapist called out from the front of the room. "Leave your canvases where they are. I will collect them and hold them for you until you leave. Please clean off your palettes and wash your brushes. Think about what you want to work on tomorrow. Try for something personal, if you feel comfortable with that, perhaps something from your childhood. You'll be working on this second piece for the rest of the week."

Alula started cleaning up while Alex stood there watching her.

"See you," she said when she was done, quickly walking off, as if they had just spent a few minutes sitting side by side in the waiting room of the dentist's office making small talk about the weather.

They segregated the sexes at rehab, except during classes and meals, so if Alex wanted to see Alula before the next class, he would have to look for her at dinner.

CHAPTER 2
THE FIRST AND ONLY

If you want to calculate the odds that the earth is the first and only repository of conscious, intelligent life, you need to consider the number of stars in the observable universe, about twenty billion trillion, and the age of the universe, estimated to be thirteen billion years old. Then you need to consider why with all those stars and after all those years the ingredients required for the recipe for life would only get mixed together in the right proportions one time and on one planet—Earth.

You could say it was God or some omnipotent, omniscient force who picked Earth for some reason, but then you would have to ask yourself why that God—if he or she was pleased with the result—would not want to sprinkle a few seeds on some other planets as well. Why not scatter them all around the universe? Why would God ignore the trillions of other planets in similar orbits around their own stars? Why leave everything else barren?"

Was creating Earth too exhausting? Or were we that disappointing? Even if we were, why not try it again a little differently the next time? Do a better job by filling the planet with flowers, butterflies, and kindly elephants? Forget the humans. See how it goes without them. Or make everyone the same light shade of blue, the same height, and the same weight. Give everyone the same intelligence and see what happens.

The varieties and possibilities are endless.

How could one living planet ever be enough for a limitless universe...God or no God?

If you are not a big believer in the guided hand—the deity—and prefer instead to believe it was random luck that created the spark necessary to start the evolutionary march on Earth, then the universe should be teeming with life, because what happened here millions of years ago had to have happened on a thousand other planets over the course of billions of years.

In that case, it would appear to be a statistical certainty, which, in fact, formed the basis for Greg's thesis.

Gregory Underwood, III, Greg for short, calculated the odds of there being no other sentient life anywhere else in the universe. It was the theme of his PhD thesis in astronomy entitled, *They Are Out There*. The number he advanced as the odds against Earth being the only planet with life was one in 10^{303} or one in a centillion, which he concluded amounted to a mathematical certainty the universe was teeming with life.

We simply had not found them yet because they were too far away, or they had not found us.

Greg went into astronomy because he desperately wanted to be part of the big reveal. He wanted to be around for the greatest of all discoveries—the moment when he could tell everyone who ever doubted him that the earth was not alone.

His math was impressive, he defended it well, and Greg's thesis was accepted. He was awarded his doctorate, appointed an instructor, and a few years later promoted to assistant professor at the University of Washington's prestigious Department of Astronomy. The approval of his thesis and his initial hiring did come over the objection of one of his readers and the oldest professor in the department, Professor Ronald McNamara, who was not impressed by Greg's statistical approach to extraterrestrial life or his conclusion.

"I cannot tell you how many times I have heard that same tired old argument," Professor McNamara said to Greg when he appeared before the five members of the faculty selected to question him on his thesis and then vote on whether to accept it. There were three members from the Department of Astronomy, one member from the Mathematics Department, and a lone representative from the Humanities, a retired professor of nineteenth-century English Literature. The vote was four to one with Professor McNamara being the only dissenter.

As the professor explained to his fellow panelists when they questioned him about his negative vote, it was not because he felt the paper was poorly written or reasoned, but because he felt Greg should be seeking his doctorate from the Mathematics Department, not the Astronomy Department.

"Astronomers require proof; they don't deal in probabilities," Professor McNamara told his fellow panelists during their deliberations. "There has to be life out there because there's life down here—really? That's the best he's got?"

He was no kinder to Greg when he appeared before them.

"The problem with your argument...which I have to call specious...is it assumes there can never be only one of anything. If the odds are one in a trillion that the primordial soup will spark when the conditions are optimal for the formation of a living cell, those odds remain the same every second of every day on every planet in every corner of the universe. When you look at it from that perspective, it's amazing we're even here...mathematically speaking...and the odds of anyone else being out there are and will always remain...excuse the pun...astronomical."

Professor McNamara smiled at his own joke.

Greg did his best to refute Professor McNamara's argument, but he had to admit the professor did have a point, and Greg did feel a little intimidated since the lowest grade he had ever received, a B minus, he got in Professor McNamara's class on detector physics, measurement extraction, and planetary surface processes.

Besides being the oldest member of the Astronomy Department, Professor McNamara was a vocal denier. He did not believe there was intelligent life out there anywhere. He believed the earth was a freak, an outlier, the one-in-a-trillion lucky lottery winner. He believed the study of astronomy had one true purpose, and it was not finding extraterrestrial life. It was the study of the universe to better understand its makeup and origin, especially the physical laws under which it operates.

The professor thought that the real goal was to find suitable planets to relocate to before our sun goes supernova. He was pessimistic about that as well because he believed we would exhaust the earth's resources and destroy its climate long before that kind of space travel became possible.

It did not much matter because Professor McNamara believed there would come a time in the future, perhaps one or two billion years from now, when the universe would stop expanding and start contracting, returning once again to a dense ball of lifeless matter. In the end, he liked to tell his classes, the universe will return to stardust and us along with it.

Neither he nor his classes were popular, but they were required if you wanted to major in astronomy or earn a master's and PhD.

Fortunately, the other four faculty readers were impressed with Greg's math, as well as his conclusion, and thought he defended it well enough to earn his doctorate. Since there was an opening in the Astronomy Department for someone with a mathematical bent, his timing was perfect.

Now that Greg was a member of the faculty, albeit not yet a full professor, he had a more collegial relationship with Professor McNamara. Greg hoped to prove him wrong one day by becoming the astronomer to discover conclusive proof of life—conscious, intelligent life—on another planet. Greg's specialty was searching solar systems using radio telescopes and other devices to look for other planets in life-sustaining orbits around distant stars. The more planets he could find, the more likely it was that life would have taken hold on one of them, and the more likely it would be to pick up some sort of transmission—a mathematically based signal—that would confirm it.

Greg was sure he would find that elusive proof one day—even if he only stumbled upon it—and receive worldwide acclaim, as well as the Nobel Prize, which would secure him a place in history alongside Galileo and Copernicus.

Greg's good friend on the faculty, Amber Garrigan, joined the Astronomy Department a year ago as an instructor after earning her master's and doctorate at the University of California in San Francisco. They were the same age, but she had to take time off after college to earn enough money to continue her graduate studies. Greg's parents were wealthy, his father was an accountant at a big firm in Chicago, and he never had to worry about money. His father thought studying astronomy was a complete waste of time. He had wanted his only child to follow in his accounting footsteps and liked to joke at the office that his son should be searching for intelligent life on this planet instead.

Amber was also a big believer in other life out there—not just basic life as Greg proposed, but civilizations, some more advanced than ours—waiting to be discovered or searching to discover us.

"With the universe over ten billion years old," Amber was fond of saying, "it wouldn't surprise me if we were the new kids on the block."

Recently, their friendship had evolved into something more engaging and enlightening, the words Greg used when his dentist asked him if he was serious with anyone. He had been hoping to set Greg up with a cousin of his who was killing it as a Realtor. Greg begged off, but he would have declined even if he had not been dating Amber. As a matter of principle, he didn't go on blind dates, and he avoided businesswomen after an MBA student in grad school had compared stargazing with navel gazing.

To Greg's thinking, what he and Amber had was something like pre-love or the preamble to love if there was such a thing. It was like a mathematical proof where you start with an inferential argument evidencing certain stated assumptions that if followed to their logical conclusion lead you to the correct answer or in this case love.

When he and Amber talked about the stars now, they were often lying side by side in bed, looking up at the ceiling or through the ceiling in their imaginations to the deepest reaches of outer space.

A shared love of the stars seemed to Greg like more than enough to sustain a relationship.

Alex spent a couple of hours outside in the late afternoon on a guided hike with ten others to the flower garden at the edge of the woods. Gardening was another one of the programs offered to the rehab patients. He had a choice this time between painting and flowers, but he had no desire to get down in the dirt, so he chose art. They were starting a knitting class as well. If he got a fourth shot at rehab, which he doubted after what the judge had threatened, he would take knitting over gardening.

Alex did not know any of the others on the hike, which was not unusual. Most people kept to themselves at rehab. He always did. Alula was the first person he had ever talked up. He was assigned a buddy for the walk, Hank, a sixtyish rail of man who smelled of alcohol, as if it had gotten into his blood and now oozed out of his pores in place of sweat.

"First time here?" Hank asked.

"Third."

"This is my sixth…signed myself in. Alcoholic. I dry out, stay dry for as long as I can, sixteen months once when my daughter and granddaughter came to live with me after her marriage went bad. Once they moved out, I fell back off the wagon." Hank shrugged. "My father was the same way. This kind of thing is in the genes if you ask me. Why should I beat myself up about it? It's not my fault. The docs don't like it when I talk like that, but that's the way it is. So, what's your story?"

"Drugs. It was either here or jail. I'd just as soon keep taking them."

"Know that feeling."

They stopped talking when the group leader called for their attention to tell them about the plants they were passing. Alex looked down at the flowers, but he was not really looking at them or listening. He had no interest in plants, except for the kind he could smoke. He was thinking about Alula, wondering why she was here instead of a mental institution. Rehab was for substance abuse, not fantasy addictions. He figured she had to be lying about that as well. She was probably into hallucinating. How hard could it be for her to deny it if she could lie about coming here from another planet?

Alex figured she was not hard core like he was, but one of those eggshell types who get off on LSD once or twice and wind up with their reality cracked. Maybe her parents found some of the pills in her room and sent her here because it was too much for them to handle. Dating a guy like him would be the worst thing for her, but only if it became a long-term thing. A couple of tumbles in the sack before they each went their own way would not do her any harm— him either.

Alula had the best body he had ever seen up close—like she had stepped off the pages of a fashion magazine—and he did like talking with her. He did not feel the least bit self-conscious when he did. He was not thinking every second about what he should say next or kicking himself for what he did or did not say. He had never experienced anything like that before. Certainly, not when he was sober. He also liked that she was funny and seemed genuinely happy. The girls he came across were usually sad and as desperate as he was to score.

There was something kind and understanding in her eyes, especially when she looked at him. It was sort of encouraging. He really liked the way her smile seemed to be connected to everything else—her eyes, her lips, her cheeks, her forehead, her neck, even her shoulders. It did not seem as if she were counting the minutes until she could get away from him like most of the girls he met, at least the ones who were not high or eager to get high.

What if she was a little crazy? Anyone who slept with him had to be a little crazy. If she thought of herself as an alien from another planet, she should be eager for a new experience with a drug-obsessed Earthling. On one hand, it did not seem right trying to take advantage of Alula's craziness like that. On the other hand, how different was it from what he did with girls when they got high?

His conscience never got in the way then.

Alex laughed to himself, and the others on the tour turned around to look at him. Even the tour leader paused for a moment, wondering what was on his mind. She knew it could not be something she was saying about the flowers.

Alex's father used to say no one ever makes a mistake by trying to follow a dream. His father was full of cliches. Many of them neither he nor his mother had ever heard before. He said he picked them up reading. His father was a voracious reader. He liked to say life was all about learning something new every day.

Why couldn't Alex consider sleeping with Alula his new dream?

Two young people hooking up was perfectly natural. Young men and women had been dreaming about it for eons. It was more hormonal than anything else. Alex figured that if it were not with him, it would be with some other crazy addict.

Eyes open. Hearts open. Minds open. His father would have liked that motto. Alula would indeed have to be from another planet to believe living like that was possible here on Earth. Alex was willing to bet her parents were drugged out most of the time or major alcoholics, and she had spent most of her time in her room hiding away from it.

Creating an alternate reality had to be the easiest way to deal with them while she was growing up. Every kid had their own way of coping with a broken reality, whether it was keeping to themselves, getting into trouble and taking drugs like Alex, or making up stories. A fantasy was a lot cheaper than drugs, a lot less dangerous as well, and unlike a high it can last forever.

What Alex did not understand was how she could still believe it. From the way Alula talked and looked at him it, appeared she did.

How else could she stick to her fantasy like that and appear so content and confident while she did. No one in rehab—or on the street—was ever that insistent and happy. None of his drug friends could keep up a lie for long.

"I smuggled in some hooch," Hank said, interrupting Alex's reverie, "if you're interested."

"Sure," Alex said, perking up.

"I'm in W2. Where are you?"

"E4."

"You have privileges?"

"No."

"Too bad."

Without privileges he could not leave the east wing for anything other than meals or therapy. He would need a good reason to get a pass, and a cocktail party was not one of them. The only time he was not watched closely was at dinner, and he planned on looking for Alula tonight. He wondered if she would be surrounded by a half-dozen other guys on the make. There were plenty of weirdos in rehab who would eagerly pretend to believe anything she said to get into her pants. Some were even weird enough to believe her. She could have her own cult following soon, all horny males promising to return to Home with her if she slept with them.

After Alex got his tray—some unidentifiable, pasty white fish with brown rice and roasted vegetables—he stood there scanning the room. There were always enough tables to eat alone if you wanted to, which is what he always did and was about to do when he spotted Alula sitting by herself at a table in the far corner. There was one chair across from her, pulled in tight in case anyone had any ideas.

Alex's father would have called it kismet. He was a big believer in fate. Maybe not fate in the traditional sense like something preordained, written down in some heavenly book, but more like coincidence helped along by Mother Nature. Alex's father thought attraction began on a molecular level, some sort of subatomic attraction he said that went back to the beginning of time. His father would come out with the funniest things sometimes which always made Alex and his mother laugh.

His father never got mad when they did. He just laughed along with them.

Alex walked over to Alula's table, hoping she was saving the seat for him.

"Mind if I sit down?" Alex asked, startling Alula, who was staring down at her plate like she was trying to identify what was on it. She had not touched a thing yet. She did not look like much of an eater.

"Not at all," she said, putting down her fork and smiling up at him, "but that's your next question, so it's my turn."

Alex laughed as he put down his tray and sat down.

"I saw you walking in the garden earlier."

"Where were you?"

"Talking with one of the therapists. I saw you through her window."

"Talking to her about your planet?"

"No, you're the only one I've told that to...ever."

"Why me?"

"Because we have a special connection."

"That's nice to hear."

"I watched the way you were walking," Alula said.

"What did it tell you?"

"You're carrying around a lot of sadness...and anger. You need to let it go." She raised her hand, which she held in a fist and then opened it as if she were setting a butterfly free. "You'll be able to fly when you do."

"You mean like a bird?"

"You know I'm speaking figuratively. Why let past moments hold you down."

"Doesn't everybody?"

"Not like that and not for so long. Eyes open. Heart open. Mind open. It reminds us how important it is to release negative feelings to the stars."

"Just like that?"

"It takes some effort sometimes and a strategy. It's something we learn and practice when we're young. We call it releasing or letting go. It's our way of life."

"Not mine, unfortunately. I like to think of myself as a clinger. I hold tight to things, especially the bad moments."

Alula gave him a gentle, understanding smile and a little nod.

"You don't have to let go of the memories, just the negative feelings attached to them...the feelings that weigh you down. The memories will help turn the bitterness into something much sweeter...if you let them. Holding on to the emotions too tightly prevents learning and interferes with hope."

"Thank you, doctor," Alex said, looking around for an empty table. He was tempted to get up and eat by himself. He was not sure a tumble in the sack was worth this kind of analytical crap.

"You sure you don't work here?" he asked instead.

"Yes, but I wouldn't mind it. I think I could help."

"Okay, what's your question?" Alex asked, picking up a forkful of fish and stuffing it into his mouth.

"Tell me a story," she said.

"That's not a question."

"It's a request...the same as a question."

"About what."

"Something that happened to you growing up. Not something with your family but with someone else...a friend or a stranger. It's a good way for me to learn more about you."

Alex thought it over while he stuffed some soggy vegetables into his mouth. He noticed Alula was eating her vegetables and rice, but not the fish.

"Why do you want to learn more about me?"

"I told you, we have a lot in common."

"Like what?"

"We're in here together for one thing," Alula said.

"True."

Alex was hoping for something a little more romantic. If it were going to happen, it would have to be quick. No one stays in rehab for very long. They might kick her out soon or transfer her once they realized she was crazy as opposed to addicted.

"There's a reason for that," she said.

"For what?"

"Our being together...finding each other."

"Are we talking kismet?"

"I always liked that word."

"One of my father's favorites," Alex replied. "He had his own definition of it. The dictionary says it means fate, and fate presupposes a God with a big black book with everyone's future written down inside it."

Alula laughed.

"My father thought of kismet more as an invisible force, a kind of gravity that pulls certain particles together…certain stardust and the people made up of it."

"I agree with him," Alula said. "We are all made up of stardust, you know that?"

"Yes, I've heard," Alex said, his father having told him the same thing a thousand times before he died. "But if we're all made up of stardust, why should there be any special attraction between two people?"

"Because there are different kinds of stardust from different places in the universe…just like there are different kinds of stars. You and I contain much of the same stardust…from the same star in a distant galaxy."

Alex tried not to choke as he swallowed down some rice. Alula kept doubling down on her fantasy, he realized, although his being included in it had to be a good sign.

"Time for my discovery story," Alula reminded him.

"What am I supposed to have discovered?"

"Something about yourself…or others."

Alula went back to eating her vegetables. No doubt they did not eat living creatures on her imaginary planet, which would leave out his father since he loved hamburgers. Perhaps he was more eager than Alula to adopt to the ways of his new planet. Alex chuckled at the thought, and Alula looked up at him and smiled like she was in on the joke.

Alex had the feeling that if it took him five hours to come up with his story, she would sit there patiently waiting. Unfortunately, they only had one hour for dinner.

He was not going to tell her anything about his father or his mother. There was not much to tell. He died early, she took to the bottle—probably a familiar story to most everyone here. His father was also obsessed with the stars and had his own star stories…so what. Lots of people looked up at the night sky when his father was a kid, before cable TV and smartphones were everywhere, and the Internet took over everyone's imagination.

His father used to tell Alex he hoped—*expected* was the word he used more often—that one day the two of them would travel together among the stars. What little kid wouldn't wish for something like that as well?

Alex thought about telling Alula some drug stories since he had a lot of those. Unfortunately, most of them were gross, and all he ever learned from those were who and where to avoid. He wondered if learning to be invisible in a room or walking the streets without being noticed could count as a good story.

Alula pushed her tray away, rested her elbows on the table, her head on her hands, and waited eagerly for Alex to begin. In that instant, a pretty good story popped into his head. He wondered why it had not occurred to him earlier.

"I was about thirteen," Alex said, "a couple of years after my father's accident. There was this old library near our house surrounded by a high black metal fence. You know, the kind with pointy spikes on top to keep people out."

"I don't," Alula said.

"No need for spiked fences on your world?"

"Why would a library ever close?"

"Well, this one did, and it was dark, so no one was around. Wily was a year older than me and said he had this great idea. We climb the fence, break in through a window, take some books...the big, expensive kind and maybe a few dictionaries, and sell them."

"Not read and return them."

"That's not what he had in mind."

"And you?"

"I was young...angry...ready to go along for the ride...any ride really. The wilder the better."

Alula nodded, her index finger resting against her lower lip like she was trying to understand it.

"Go on," she whispered.

"Wily went first. It was a hard fence to climb because it was tall and smooth. It had been recently painted, so it was slick from some rain earlier in the day. When Wily got up near the top, his foot slipped. He didn't fall to the ground because he was already half over, but he got stuck on one of the spikes. He struggled and it went deeper into his shoulder. He couldn't get off it, and I could see the blood beginning to drip down."

"What did you do?"

"I stood there for a second watching. He looked like a fish on a hook. I thought about running away because I didn't want to get into any more trouble. I'd been getting in more than enough at school."

"But you didn't, did you," Alula said like she already knew Alex well enough to know the answer.

"No, but I thought about it."

"Instead?"

"Instead, I ran over to the next block to the pizza place to get help. The fire department came with a ladder and lifted him off. He had passed out by then. An ambulance took him away."

"What happened to him," Alula asked.

She looked totally engrossed, as if she were a little girl listening to a bedtime story and could not wait to hear how it all turned out.

Alex thought about embellishing it a little, making up a conversation with one of the firemen about how his quick thinking had saved the day, but the way Alula was looking at him made it hard for Alex to consider anything other than the truth.

"They took him away. He was in the hospital for about a week. He didn't hang with me after that; he kept to himself."

"What an incredible story," Alula said, clapping her hands together and turning a few heads in the dining room.

Alex could not imagine anyone getting that excited over absolutely nothing.

"Incredible? I don't think so. I ran for help. Big deal. Barely interesting at best."

"What did you learn?"

Alex shrugged before he smiled. "I learned to be careful climbing sharp metal fences, especially after it rains."

Alula smiled back. "And that you care about others and won't abandon people who need you…even when you're scared and could get into trouble."

"I don't think running to the pizza place took an act of courage."

"You could've run away."

"If we'd already broken in and were on our way back over the fence with a pile of stolen books, I'm sure I would have."

"I don't think so. Don't sell yourself short. You were young, immature, and angry, but your heart and eyes were still open."

"I suppose two out of three isn't bad."

"The way I see it," Alula added, ignoring his wise-ass comment, "if you can care enough to help someone else in trouble, you can care enough to help yourself."

Alex sighed. How did he not see it coming? The little moral she found at the end of the fairy tale.

"That was then. Now I'd have to run and leave him hanging there to avoid jail."

"Cute," Alula replied, "but I don't believe you."

Alex stuffed some food in his mouth and looked out the window. He would give anything for a big, fat joint.

"On Home," Alula continued, "libraries are always open. You take whatever book you want and return it when you're done."

"Do your houses have locks?"

"Nothing is ever locked, and there are no fences."

If you are going to live in a fantasy world, Alex thought, you might as well make it a lot better than the real one. He would do the same thing if he had the inclination.

"My turn to ask a question," Alex said.

"Go ahead."

"Is every girl from your planet as pretty as you?"

"Why waste a question on that? What you see is simply a form, stardust in a different shape and color. It doesn't define who I am."

"Still nice to look at."

"Instead of focusing on the outside, you need to be looking inside at the things that really matter."

"Unfortunately, I don't have x-ray vision."

"Eyes Open, Heart Open, Mind Open. You can see deeper if you try."

"Can you see inside me?" Alex asked.

Alula nodded.

"What do you see?"

"The stars."

"What else?"

"Kindness, passion, beauty, happiness…all hiding there behind the dark curtain."

Alex let out the breath he had not realized he was holding. "Who in this place is happy? No one, not one single person, not even the staff...except maybe for you."

Alula knitted her eyebrows together like she was trying to figure something out.

"Are people from Home ever unhappy?" Alex asked.

"We have feelings like all creatures, but we recognize they are transitory, and we don't let the negative ones grow roots. We have a long, cyclical view of our experiences in this form. We don't let moments hold us down. We learn to let them go."

"It's a nice world you've created," Alex said. He was getting tired of playing this game, regardless of the prize he was hoping to win at the end. "Let go of everything bad, huh? What's the point of pretending anyone can do that?"

Just then the dinner bell rang. Everyone was expected to finish eating within the next five minutes and return to their rooms.

"I'm not pretending," Alula said, putting her water glass back on the tray. "The real question is why you only believe in the things you can see...and ingest?"

"Because drugs are reliable, I told you that. I always know what to expect, and they never let me down."

"But they do, all the time. They abandon you a couple of hours after you embrace them. They get up from the bed every time and leave you in the middle of the night."

"But they never go far or leave for good. They're always ready and eager to come back."

"You wouldn't need them if you opened your eyes, your heart, and your mind," Alula said, still upbeat without any of the frustration or disappointment he was used to hearing and seeing on the therapists, his teachers, or anyone else who ever tried to help him.

Alula stood up slowly.

"It's still my turn," Alex said. "That wasn't my real question."

"Okay, go ahead." Alula stood there holding her tray.

"My real question is the same as yours: tell me a story everyone on Home hears when they're young."

"Like a bedtime story?"

"Yes."

"I'll think about it overnight," she said. "See you in class tomorrow."

With that Alula walked away.

That night Alex lay awake in his narrow bed, his arms folded behind his head. He was not the least bit tired. He was thinking about his father's star stories. He was the only other person Alex had ever known as obsessed with the stars as Alula. He had not thought about his stories in a long time.

Alex used to have this dream about his father from time to time—the same one—where they would be lying in the backyard together, and his father would be telling him a star story he had never heard before. When he finished, Alex would turn to tell him how good it was—the best story he had ever heard—except his father wasn't there. It turned out he was not lying beside him but whispering the story into his ear from a star directly overhead, which winked at him as soon as Alex realized it.

He always felt good when he woke up from that dream. It had been years since he last had it.

His father often told him stories about the stars as they lay there in the backyard. Stories, he said, which had been told since ancient times. Alex remembered almost all of them. Like the one about the Pawnee, who believed the world was created by Tirawa, who made the stars to hold up the sky. He put the brighter, bigger stars in charge of the clouds, the wind, and the rain. When some of the smaller stars became jealous, they stole a sack of deadly storms and emptied it onto the earth. His father also told him that the Pawnee believed the first woman was born from the marriage of two stars and the first man from the marriage of a star and the moon, which would mean everyone was indeed made up of stardust.

The Blackfoot tribe had a story about six young brothers. People were unkind to them because they were orphans and always dirty and ragged. After a while, his father explained, the brothers no longer wanted to be people. They thought about becoming flowers but were afraid the buffalo would eat them. They thought about becoming stones, but stones could be worn away over time and broken. They could not be water because water ran off, or trees because they could be burned by lightning and cut down. In the end, they decided to become stars because stars were beautiful and because starlight always shines far, so the six brothers rose to the sky and became the Pleiades.

Maybe his father was a little crazy like Alula. Maybe Alex was attracted to people like that because he was crazy as well. His father used to call people like him and Alex stargazers. Even though Alex had not stared up at the sky in years, he still loved the stars.

"What's your bedtime story?" Alex asked the next day as they settled in front of their new canvases.

The instructor had just finished reminding them that they had new canvases in front of them. "Clean slates, fresh starts, the same as every day." She urged them to paint something new. "Something that brings up different memories and different feelings."

"What are you going to paint?" Alula asked Alex before responding to his question.

"I'm sticking with geometry, but I'll add some different shapes and colors."

He was not interested in searching his subconscious for something dark and revealing like the dream he had last night about his mother tossing his father's ashes into the wind and having them blow back into her eyes, which was pretty much the way it happened, except in his dream some of the ashes did not just blow into her eyes—some of them also blew into his mouth.

"I like the idea of different shapes and colors," Alula said.

"You?" Alex asked. "More stars?"

"Home, but this time a landscape perspective."

Alula dipped her brush in the black paint, drew a thin line across the bottom of the canvas, and Alex could immediately see the ground. She was very good.

"I have a story for you," she said as she started filling in Home's landscape. "A story needs a name, so I'll call it 'Everything Must Change.'"

"Cheery."

"It is…and very true. Even stars change over time. It's a very old story told to all the young children on Home. It goes back to the beginning."

"The big bang?"

"The beginning of us. The universe has always been. There has always been energy and mass; then came the stars. We are much more recent."

"Nothing about God creating the world in seven days."

"We are all creatures of the stars."

"Astrolatry?" Alex asked with a chuckle.

"Not quite," Alula responded before adding, "you are not nearly as uneducated as you like to pretend."

"Not when it comes to the stars. I know a lot of cultures over the years have worshiped the stars. Old cultures, thousands of years ago…some even believed a different god lived on each star."

"Suggesting what?" Alula asked. "That you have evolved beyond worshiping the stars to worshiping a bearded old man sitting on a throne high above the clouds?"

"One god, instead of many," Alex said with as much skepticism as he could muster. "It's certainly a lot simpler."

"There always seems to be a lot of fighting over who's found the right one."

Alex nodded. He couldn't argue with that.

"On Home, we respect what has been, what is, and what will be. I suppose you might consider it a form of nature worship. The purposefulness of nature is what we honor. The supreme good on Home lies in harmoniously aligning with the stars and with the nature of the elements that flow from them. It's about appreciating the essence in form and matter, and we don't limit that to consciousness. Unconsciousness is as much existence on Home as anything else. It's just another form of stardust."

"I don't call anyone or anything God," Alex said. "I gave up on that concept a long time ago."

"Which means you're a lot closer to me than you think."

He would like to be.

"You believe in mass and energy, don't you?"

"You got me there," Alex said. "I can honestly tell you that I believe in those two concepts without reservation. Now, how about your story?"

"Sure, but we should be painting while I tell it to you. Otherwise, she's going to separate us."

Alex thought that was another good sign. He picked up his brush, dipped it in some red paint in Alula's honor, and painted a five-pointed star on the top of his canvas. Then he dipped his other brush in black and painted a small circle with two identical squares orbiting around it. She would have to admit he was pretty good with freehand shapes. He felt more comfortable drawing them than he did anything else.

After painting a few more shapes, he looked over at Alula's canvas. With a few lines she had raised a mountain range in the distance.

She had a great eye.

"As I was saying," she whispered, without looking away from her canvas, "on Home all things matter…mountains, plants, stones, Homebodies, the soil…we are all made of the same stardust. We all exist. We are all part of the cosmic consciousness."

"How is a stone conscious?"

"How do you define consciousness?"

"Thinking and feeling."

"We define it differently…we define it as existing…as having a shape and a form."

"Pretty expansive, wouldn't you say? That would include a speck of dust."

"Exactly. We are taught to see all things that way and respect them. We all belong to the stars," Alula said as she added trees and rocks to her landscape. Today, she was standing on her fantasy planet looking out instead of up.

"Because we are all made of stardust, I got it," Alex responded as he added a green triangle and a yellow pentagon to his geometric solar system.

Alex realized how much he sounded like his father, even if he did not say it with the same conviction as his father used to.

"Isn't it rather remarkable that you look like us, and your planet," Alex said, pointing at the trees and mountain, "looks a lot like Earth?"

"Which means I can't possibly be from another planet."

"Exactly."

"Is it so impossible to believe that our forms, evolving over millions and millions of years from the same stardust, could turn out the same?"

"It is if you grew up reading comic books. The creatures from outer space always had multiple heads and green scales."

Alula laughed.

"You look very different from a duck," Alex added.

"Because I'm not a duck. Evolution has many branches and many leaves."

"Any ducks where you come from?" Alex asked, trying for sarcasm.

Alula smiled back at him.

"Yes, there are ducklike creatures across the universe."

"Okay, stardust is stardust. I'm still waiting for your story."

"Before us—we are called Homebodies like you are called Earthlings—before Homebodies the universe was a stew of dust and clouds."

"Infinite?"

"How can there ever be a beginning or an end? There is always a before and after? The horizon is just the limit of our sight."

Alex's father used to say the same thing.

"Before us, when the universe was a stew of dust and clouds, there was a collision of particles that fused together and grew as more particles were drawn to it."

"Creating a gravitational pull and a star," Alex interrupted. "I've heard the same story before. My father used to tell me it."

"Because your father was a Homebody. I told you, we've been settling on Earth for centuries."

Alex dropped his brush. The teacher looked over to see if he was all right, and he waved to her as he picked it back up.

"So, you're saying my father was an alien like you."

"Yes."

"How would you know that? You never met him. You don't know anything about him."

"He knew my father back on Home when they were children. Your father settled first with his parents. My father came years later with my mother. Your father helped them after they arrived."

"I don't believe any of this. You do realize that?"

"You will soon enough."

"No, I won't, no matter how high I get."

Alex chuckled at his own joke.

"You're half Homebody. That's our gravitational pull."

"And my mother?"

"No."

"Why didn't he find another settler or wait around for the next batch of spacewomen?"

"Love."

Alex painted a series of concentric circles to help him calm down. How could he get upset over this nonsense? What if it were the same story his father used to tell him, so what? His father probably got it from the same book her father had. What he really needed now was a cold beer and some pot, not a new wormhole to chase Alula down.

"I thought you said you didn't die. My father certainly did."

"That is an Earth word; death is their concept, not ours. We do not have the equivalent on Home. We don't consider transformation and enlightenment an ending…or a dying…not the way you use the word like there's nothing afterwards…like it's the cessation of existence. Our form may change, but the matter remains. It may scatter, some of it may convert into energy, but it is still us. The atoms stay connected to each other, no matter how far apart they drift. Your father is now…"

"Yeah, yeah, of the stars, you said that before."

His father used to say the same thing whenever Alex asked about his father and mother.

"A lot of good it did me or my mother," Alex added.

"The good it does is for him and the universe…for you too if you could open your heart and mind."

"This is your childhood story?" Alex asked. "How the stars came to be?"

"How everything came to be. Everything springs from the stars. Their story is our story."

Alex sighed loud enough to turn the teacher's head.

"It's the story my father told me," Alula said, "and his father told him…and your father told you."

Alex stood as still as a statue. He refused to breathe, let alone shake his head in acknowledgment. Yes, it was strange she knew the same story, but life was full of odd coincidences. Maybe her father and his were once members of the same religious sect.

"Maybe we should just paint for a while," Alex said, picking up his brush and moving closer to his canvas.

Alula smiled and nodded before turning back to her painting.

She was good, Alex thought, there was no denying it. Alula would make a great saleswoman because she could convince you she believed in her product whether it worked or not. Alex shook his head slowly from side to side at the thought of his father on a spaceship traveling to Earth from another planet. He imagined him—the adult version, not the kid—standing there holding onto the overhead bar like he was riding the bus to work.

You would think an extraterrestrial would be better prepared so he would not wind up repairing cars, even if his father said he loved the job. Sure, he had an unusual interest in the stars, way more than the fathers of any of his schoolmates. He talked about them with longing, as if they had once been lovers or close friends. But he also rhapsodized about the workings of the car engine.

If Alex checked the Internet, which he was not allowed to do in rehab, he would probably find a children's book about the birth of the stars with the same story—word for word.

Alex wondered if Alula was one of those carnival-types who can pick up on a few cues and practically read your mind. He tried to remember if he had mentioned anything to her the other day about his father and his star stories. Alex was pretty sure he had not, but he was so focused on her "form" he doubted he would remember if he had.

Alex also wondered if there was some recognized alien syndrome in the psychology textbooks for people who create fantasies like this to deal with trauma. Perhaps all the bad news in the world these days was enough to crack someone like Alula—one of those people with an ego like an eggshell. Who would not want to be from another planet, one that was not filled with violence, hunger, and despair? Why live in a world that seemed to be driving full speed toward a cliff when you could pick one with two dancing moons?

"Why would my father marry my mother, instead of another Homebody?" Alex wondered out loud while he colored in some of his shapes. "Wouldn't it have been easier if he had?"

He felt like an idiot simply asking the question.

"A lot of settlers prefer it. It's a good way to start fresh and quickly come to belong, particularly when you arrive at a young age like your father did. Besides, you know what they say."

"What's that?"

"You can't help who you fall in love with. Love is everywhere in the universe, and while the attraction may start on a subatomic level, there is no controlling where it goes from there. There are always intangibles… an alluring mix of stardust from other galaxies."

"That doesn't sound very romantic…more like you're dusting for love."

Alula laughed.

"I suppose it is in some ways," Alula said. "It starts with an unconscious attraction…stardust to stardust…an attraction that goes back billions of years."

"Like being married in a prior life?" Alex asked with a chuckle of his own.

"It's just the foundation…stardust is a basic part of love, but it's not everything."

"I'm glad to hear that."

Alula went back to her painting.

"Did he tell my mother?" Alex asked.

"I don't know."

"Didn't he have to? Aren't there rules about this sort of thing?"

"No."

Alex scattered some stars around his canvas. It looked like a geometric fantasy world. Alula's painting was much better. It was a mountainous sci-fi landscape with a red sun in the sky and a rainbow of plants—pinks, reds, blues, silvers, and blacks. It could have been from the cover of one of his old comic books.

"Black plants?"

"The most fragrant on Home."

"If any of this were true," Alex said, "why didn't my father tell me?"

"He talked to you about the stars, didn't he?"

Alex nodded.

"Whatever else he wanted to tell you…and when…was up to him. He was probably waiting for you to get older and better at keeping secrets."

Alula had an answer for everything. She knew exactly what to say to draw him in.

"A lot of people are fascinated by the stars," Alex responded. "It doesn't make them extraterrestrials."

"No, it does not."

"Okay, here's my next question."

"It's my turn," Alula said. When she saw the frustration on Alex's face, she changed her mind. "But I'll pass while I think it over."

"Good," Alex said, unclenching his jaw. "Do you have any unusual talents, like a superpower? Isn't that what's supposed to happen when you come from a planet with a red sun?"

"Like Superman?"

"Maybe the guy who created Superman was a Homebody."

"I wouldn't be surprised," Alula said before turning back to her canvas.

"Answer my question."

"We can travel the universe faster than the speed of light...that's pretty super. You have a long way to go before you figure that out. Most of your scientists think it's impossible."

"I mean some personal power," Alex said. "You know, like moving objects by waving your finger or bending steel rods."

"I can read minds."

"You're kidding."

"No, sometimes, not always."

"Like you can hear someone else's thoughts, not guess what they're thinking?"

"Hear their thoughts," Alula said, leaning closer to her canvas.

Alex started coughing, his saliva having gone down the wrong pipe. The teacher walked over with a cup of water. He took a sip while she looked over his shoulder.

"I like the different shapes and sizes," she said, "and the colors. I also like the different eye levels and sight lines. There's much more depth today than yesterday."

"I feel deeper today."

She made a little frown behind Alex's back before moving over to Alula's painting.

"Interesting. You have a wonderful sense of perspective. I like your trees and the colors as well. The way you use shade is very good, very natural. It makes everything pop. You've got real artistic talent."

"Thank you."

"Why only sometimes?" Alex asked after the instructor had moved away.

"It requires a close, personal connection and a great deal of concentration. It gives me a headache if I do it too much."

"Okay," Alex said, putting down his brush and turning toward Alula, "what am I thinking?"

"It's not a game."

"I thought so."

He wondered if he could request a transfer to the gardening group. This was getting way too bizarre, and he was not getting anywhere on the other front.

"I wouldn't," she said.

"Wouldn't what?"

"Be scared off. Give it a chance. Who knows what might happen between us?"

Alex stared at her. Of course, she had to know what was on his mind from the moment he started talking to her, especially from the way he looked at her at times, like a man dying of thirst. His expression would have given him away.

"Written all over my face, huh?"

"Absolutely."

He wished he had some idea what she was thinking.

"Who decides who has to leave?" Alex asked. "Is there a lottery? Is there a Department of Space Settlement?"

"It's voluntary."

"Why would anyone want to leave a perfect planet like Home?"

"It's considered a noble thing to do."

"Why?"

"Because it's a small planet with limited resources, and it's necessary to keep the population manageable. Plus, there is the urge for adventure, to explore and learn about the universe. Wouldn't you like to travel through space?"

Alex nodded. Who wouldn't?

"Why not put a limit on children?" he asked.

"That's been in place for thousands of years. No one has more than one. At this stage in our evolution, it's all we can conceive."

Alex always wondered why his parents stopped at one. He assumed it was either bad luck or him. Maybe it was his father's idea. Just thinking about it made Alex shake his head back and forth in disbelief. How could he be buying into this nonsense?

"Home sends out settlers every five to ten years," Alula added. "To different planets, not just Earth, and there are always more volunteers than there is room. Space travel has always been a focus for us. We always knew there were others out there, long before we ever met any of them."

"We only believe in us," Alex said.

"Part of your problem. As a species, you need to believe in something greater than yourselves."

Alex shrugged and drew some more stars. They outnumbered the other shapes on his canvas.

"Now it's my turn for a question," Alula said.

Go ahead, Alex thought. *If you can read my mind, ask me if I want to sleep with you.*

"It's not going to be the question you want," Alula said. "We believe there needs to be a strong spiritual connection besides the basic elemental attraction before there can be a meaningful physical one."

"Home etiquette?"

"Common sense."

"Go ahead, ask your question."

Alex knew she did not have to be a mind reader to guess his intentions.

"If you could stop taking drugs just like that," Alula said, snapping her fingers, "would you?"

The answer he always gave the therapists when they asked the same question was yes, of course. It was the answer they wanted to hear before they started explaining to him how he could make that happen with their help. In truth, he was never sure. Until something came along that made him feel better, he would stick with the drugs. It felt like a way of life by now, and Alex figured it was not hurting anyone but him.

If it shortened his life, so be it.

"If I had something else to replace it."

"Like what?"

"Alcohol, fried food, marathon running, it doesn't much matter," Alex said, "because I have an addictive personality. I need a passion to get through the day, let alone a life."

"Not just a passion…a burning passion."

"Yes," Alex said. "The hotter the better. Got something or someone in mind?"

"How about astronomy?"

"Meaning?"

Alex put down his brush and sat down on the stool.

"Become an astronomer. Study the stars. Prove to the earth it's not alone."

"I barely graduated high school."

"You know a lot about stars. More than most college graduates. You don't need a degree to be curious and learn…or to teach."

"Another fantasy," Alex said with a chuckle. "I once loved the stars, but that was years ago."

"A passion like that never burns out."

"Maybe," Alex said, looking over at Alula with his best flirtatious smile, "but I had a different kind of burning passion in mind."

"I gather, but you know what they say?"

"What's that?"

"There is a time for everything…a season for every activity under the heavens."

Alex knew where that came from, Ecclesiastes. "Turn, Turn, Turn" was one of his father's favorite songs.

"Patience has never been one of my strong points."

"Work on it," Alula said, turning back to her canvas. "All things evolve if you give them a chance."

There was not much time left in today's class, and they did not say much more until it was time to go, at which point all they did was exchange goodbyes.

He looked for her at dinner that night, but she was not there.

Alula did not show up for class the next day either. Alex's new partner was a high school kid awash in pimples who talked nonstop about himself and his friends while he painted rainbows and trees.

It seemed Alula had been cured or perhaps she really was a voluntary commit and had checked herself out. Maybe they realized she had come to the wrong place for a space travel delusion. Maybe she beamed back up to Home. Unfortunately, Alex knew they would not give him her address or telephone number because of the privacy regulations.

Two weeks later Alex was released, his drug cravings satisfied for the moment. He got back in the early afternoon and found his mother pretty much where he had left her, sitting at the kitchen table staring at an empty bottle of scotch. She looked up and nodded as if he was returning from buying a cup of coffee, instead of a month in rehab.

"Are you going out again?" she asked, looking Alex up and down to make sure there was nothing different about him.

"I don't know, why?"

"I need some scotch...and there's no food in the house. Take some money from my purse."

"How about nice to see you. How was the rehab?"

"Same as before?"

"No, this time I met an alien there who told me Dad was from another planet."

His mother chuckled. "Buy some salty snacks while you're at it."

"Like what?"

"Potato chips, the sour cream kind, and some frozen pizza. Maybe some canned soup. And something you might feel like eating."

Alex threw his bag into his room, took some money from his mother's wallet along with her car keys, and went to the store. He drove around first looking for some of his drug friends. He did not see anyone, which did not surprise him since they were like the stars—they did not come out until dark. He planned on scoring something one of these days soon, although he was going to stick to pot for a while. The police rarely hassled anyone over that.

Alex wanted to stay away from anything harder for a while, for as long as he could, a resolution which was a first for him. He wondered if it was because of his conversations with Alula or simply because he didn't want to wind up in jail. The judge had promised Alex that he would be headed there the next time he appeared in front of him.

For the next two weeks Alex lay low, getting high at home while looking for a job. His mother made it clear she was running low on money. What she had gotten from his father's accident— quite a lot at the time—might last her for the rest of her life, she explained, but not if she had to continue supporting him.

"You need to find a job and a life," his mother said, holding tight to her glass.

It was the first bit of proper parental advice she had given Alex in years.

He found a job as a barista at a local coffee shop on the other side of town and moved into a small studio apartment upstairs. Alex could not explain it, but he found coffee, beer, and pot more than enough for the time being. He did not feel the compulsion as he always had in the past to move on to something higher and harder.

Maybe the rehab took this time, although he doubted it. If Alex had to guess, he would say it was the books on astronomy he was reading after work. They were not quite the burning passion he always had in mind when he was talking with Alula, but the books did keep his mind occupied. He had been to the library twice already to take out books on the stars. He would spend hours at night studying the star charts, and it always amazed him how familiar it all seemed—how much he remembered. He was even more amazed at how much he did not know.

Another month went by, and Alex found he liked being a barista and was pretty good at it. He liked working the espresso machine and making the cappuccinos and lattes. The beans had to be good, which they were, but they had to be freshly ground, and he often felt a little high just breathing in the aroma.

The key to a great latte and cappuccino, Alex discovered, was how he steamed the milk. As the foam rose, he needed to lower the pitcher and tilt it to create a vortex. This way the milk stirred itself. Then he tapped the base of the pitcher firmly on the counter to compress the foam. How he poured it was equally as important. He needed to start at the center of the cup and then continue in a circular motion out toward the rim.

Alex liked the rush in the morning, at lunchtime, and in the late afternoon. It kept him busy, and the day seemed to fly. The slower hours in between gave him an opportunity to drink his own latte and read some more. He usually brought one of the astronomy books with him to look through during his break. It reminded him sometimes—just a little—of lying in the backyard with his father looking up at the night sky.

His coworkers were all friendly, and some of them started calling him the star-man, which made Alex laugh. It was the nicest thing anyone had called him in a long time, much nicer than any of the things he was called in the drug world.

He loved the smell of the shop, particularly in the morning. It was more than the coffee and the freshly baked muffins; it was the customers as well. They smelled fresh and clean, some minty, some flowery, some like spring days, as if they had all just stepped out of the shower, which they probably had. He got to know most of them, not by name but enough to smile, nod, and engage in some friendly, meaningless chitchat while they waited for him to make their order. Alex liked the fact that there were no heavy conversations, no sudden reveals, and no feigned intimacy.

No questions like Alula's that required serious answers.

Alex could not stop thinking about her, probably because he had never met anyone like Alula, down to earth and together, while deranged at the same time. The drug world had plenty of deranged Earthlings—Tellurians as he read in one of his books—but no one like Alula, calm and well-balanced, sweet, and beautiful; a woman who radiated happiness along with her sensuality and bizarre fantasies.

The way she loved the stars was crazy—and crazier still that she believed she came from one a couple of hundred light-years away—but there was something about her that made Alex feel relaxed, content, and more in the present, as the therapists were always urging him to be. Maybe it was the things she said that reminded Alex of the things his father used to whisper as they lay side by side on their backs looking up at the stars.

Near the end of his second month back, while Alex lay sprawled out on his bed, high on grass, watching some idiotic reality TV show about eight girls trying to get this one guy to propose, he began to feel the urge again. The urge he had been expecting would eventually find its way back up to the surface, demanding something stronger, higher, and longer lasting; something with a more burning passion attached to it than weed. It took longer this time to rear its ugly head, but Alex knew he did not have the strength to resist it for long.

He never had before.

It felt as inevitable as the spring.

At that very moment, as if the universe were indeed reading his mind, there was a knock on the door. He was hoping it was this customer who had been flirting with him at the coffee shop, a twenty-one-year-old with long eyelashes and dark straight hair crowding around her face. He had mentioned to her the other day that he lived upstairs and had plenty of pot.

Her eyelashes fluttered in response.

Sex was always more exciting after a joint or two, and it had been over three months. He could not remember a dry spell this long.

Alex would not have been disappointed if it was one of his old drug buddies—who he had been avoiding—popping in with some real stuff. They would not expect him to pay at first, not until he was securely back in the fold. They were good businessmen.

It turned out to be neither. It was the UPS man with a late delivery of a rather large package.

"I didn't order anything," he said.

"This is the address. You Alex?"

"Yep."

"Sign here."

There was a return address, but it was not a person; it was a company, Celestron, which advertised itself as the largest manufacturer of telescopes on the planet. Inside was a large, high-resolution, and clearly expensive telescope.

There was no card or note.

Somehow Alex knew it had to be from Alula, but why would she send it, and how did she find him?

The telescope came in a trunk so it could be carried anywhere. He set it up in the apartment and pointed it out the back window. It was the first quarter moon, the best time to observe it because it was less bright. The glare from the sun's reflected light did not obscure its topography the way it did during the half and full moon.

His father had taught him that.

The first thing Alex looked at was the Maria, the dark patches once thought to be parts of a big ocean, but which were simply flat plains of lava. Then he focused on the line of light and darkness called the terminator because the features near the light stood out in bold relief, so were easier to see. He used to look at the terminator with his father through the small telescope he had growing up. Once again, after all these years, Alex got to see the long shadows cast by the mountains in the late afternoon, just as mountains do on Earth.

He could see the moon a lot clearer now than he could back then. There was no comparing his old telescope to this one.

Alex spent an hour examining the Copernicus crater, one of the moon's largest. After that, he looked at Venus in its crescent phase and Jupiter's four Galilean satellites, Callisto, Ganymede, Europe, and Io. Alex was surprised at how much he remembered and had learned over the past couple of months.

By the time he pulled himself away from the telescope, it was almost three in the morning.

It was the best present he had ever received.

The next day he found himself whistling as he steamed the milk for someone's cappuccino and wondering what he might be able to see in tonight's sky. Alex thought about taking the telescope to a park away from all the building lights, but he figured it made sense to become more familiar with it first.

That night he turned his attention to deep space, starting with the Pleiades, slightly north and west of Jupiter. They were visible to the naked eye as the Big Dipper, but through the telescope dozens of invisible stars popped out at him. He looked at two of the closest star clusters, one about one hundred and fifty light-years away and the other a little over three hundred. They were the clusters familiar to most amateurs, which is probably why Alula picked that area of the sky for her fantasy planet.

Alex spent a lot of time staring at the Sword of Orion. It was one of his father's favorites. He liked to point out how the Orion Nebula hung like a sword below the Belt of Orion. He told Alex it was like a stellar nursery where new stars were being born all the time. It was about thirteen hundred light-years away, but his father would describe it with such detail, it seemed as if he could see it up close or perhaps once had.

Alex never asked his father how or why he knew so much about the stars, but he did not doubt a single thing he told him. After all, Alex was just a little boy, and little boys believe almost anything their fathers tell them. As he got older, Alex figured it was because his father was always so curious and such a voracious reader. He also had the biggest imagination of anyone he had ever met, until Alula.

Perhaps that sort of delusion—being from outer space or belonging there—is more common than one would think.

It would really be something if Alula and his father had learned about the stars firsthand during a space tour they gave to the settlers before they embarked on their journey. The very thought of it made Alex laugh.

He looked for—and found—the quadruple star he had recently read about called the Trapezium. It was part of an alignment of young stars unusually close together. The book said most astronomers believe they were drawn together by a nearby black hole. Afterward, Alex turned to Cassiopeia, an easily visible white patch in the sky called the Andromeda Galaxy. It was the closest large galaxy to ours, about 2.5 million light-years away. He focused on the fringe of the galaxy where the darkness contrasted with the light.

When Alex was not busy looking through the telescope, he was devouring more books on astronomy, all the star books he could find in the library. He even started skipping his nightly pot to better concentrate on the sky and his reading.

Two weeks after the telescope arrived, Alex got another delivery. It was a book called *Far Out* by Michael Benson, which was a collection of astronomical images from observatories around the world, as well as some from outer space—outer space being the Hubble Telescope in orbit around the earth.

Alex looked at the photos. caressing them gently with his fingertips, before trying as best as he could to find the spot in the sky where they were taken. As good as his telescope was, it did not have the power to see that far out or with such detail. It was another night when he did not fall into bed until after three.

The stars never felt indifferent or cold to him like one poet had written in a poem Alex remembered reading his senior year in high school. To the contrary, he felt as if the night sky wrapped around him like a warm blanket. He was not overwhelmed by its immensity as the poet wrote but drawn to it. It made Alex feel as if the stars had a purpose for him, as if they were reaching out to him.

Alex had not felt like that in a very long time, not since he was a child.

He knew the book had to be from Alula as well, and he wondered in the morning as he descended the stairs to work if she would show up one day—still claiming to be from another galaxy—to help him move forward with his life. The thought of being with her made anything seem possible. Alex knew he could never find his way alone, any more than his mother could.

Fortunately, Alex did not have to wait long to find out. About a week later he looked up after making a latte for one of his regulars to see Alula waiting in line. She ordered a large cappuccino and sat alone in the corner waiting for his break.

"Thank you for the gifts," he said, walking over with a latte for himself.

"My pleasure."

"That telescope was pretty expensive," Alex said, having looked the price up on the Internet.

"Well worth it."

"Independently wealthy?"

"We come to Earth well prepared."

"Cash?"

"Diamonds."

"Apparently not my father's family."

"They started sending the settlers out with a lot more by the time my parents left."

"Increased cost of living?" Alex said with a smile, as he looked around to make sure no one was listening to their conversation.

Alula chuckled and Alex moved his chair closer to hers.

"Do you live around here?" he whispered.

"No."

"Where do you live?"

"Nowhere at the moment."

"What does that mean?"

"I thought I'd stay with you."

"Reading my mind?" His smile felt as big and bright as the Super Pink Moon.

"Trying not to."

"My thoughts are more on the stars these days, thanks to you."

"I'm glad because I'd like to talk more about that with you."

Alex gave her his key, hoping she had more than talking in mind, and said he would be up as soon as his shift ended. Unfortunately, it was his turn to stay late and close the coffee shop.

When he finally got upstairs, he found Alula looking through the telescope.

"What are you looking at?" he asked. He knew the answer before she had a chance to respond, as if he were reading her mind. Maybe that's the way it was done. You got to know someone and stay focused enough in the moment that you could anticipate what they were about to say.

"Ursa Major," he said, answering his own question.

"Yes."

"Can you see it?"

"No, Home is way too small. I can't even see Alcor; it's too far away."

"Alcor?"

"Our red star," Alula answered, "but I can see where it should be."

"I brought up some dinner."

He had a bag with leftovers from the coffee shop. Two sandwiches, one all veggies, one ham and cheese, and a couple of yogurts with granola and fruit.

Alula picked at her veggie sandwich and said she would save the yogurt for breakfast. Her mind was clearly on something else.

"Want some wine or grass?"

"Wine maybe...a little later. I want to talk first."

"About what?"

Alula put her hands together as if in prayer. Alex figured it was one of two things: either she was about to come clean about her fantasy, which is what he hoped, or she was about to double down on it and ask him to return with her to Home. Maybe they were sending a fleet of spaceships because their scientists had determined the earth was getting too warm too quickly and it was poisoning its atmosphere with pollutants.

Alula was hesitant, he could see that.

Alex bit down hard on his cheek when he realized it could be something terrible, like she had a terminal illness. It always seems to happen that way in the movies.

"I think it's time for me to go public."

Alex cleared his throat, stood up, and started cleaning off the table. He was relieved and disappointed at the same time. He was glad it was not the worst he had imagined, but he was hoping it would have been something more intimate, or at least more normal.

Maybe an apology and the truth about why she created this wild fantasy.

Alex quickly rinsed the dishes in the sink and put them out to dry. He did not want her to see his face since she seemed so good at reading it. He did not want her to see how disheartened he was and how reluctant to follow her down this rabbit hole by continuing to humor her and pretending she was about to make some momentous decision.

"You understand what I'm saying?" she asked.

Alex dried his hands, turned around to nod, and sat back down across from Alula.

"What do you think?" she asked.

"About announcing you're from another planet?"

"Yes," Alula said. Her hands, still clasped in prayer, were now up in front of her mouth.

Alex took a moment to rub his eyes to make it look as if he had to give it serious thought.

"What do your parents think? What about the others?"

"The other settlers?"

"Yes."

"It's a personal decision...up to each of us to decide."

"Isn't there some kind of rule against it?"

"No, it happens eventually. There's only one hard and fast rule."

"What's that?"

"We can't help, you know, science wise. No sudden leaps forward. It's not as if any of us could help with that. My parents were agricultural workers back on Home. They never send out scientists as settlers."

Alex nodded like it made perfect sense. In a way he supposed it did.

"And we are discouraged from revealing ourselves if it's too early in a planet's development...which is not the case with Earth. Earth is on the brink of discovering it's not alone. Speeding it up a little is necessary, if you ask me, if we are to change the destructive course that we're on. I'm hoping for your support...and help."

Alex was not sure how to respond or whether he even should. Instead, he got out the bottle of red wine he had taken from his mother's house. Alula watched as he filled two glasses and handed her one.

Alex made a toast. "To the stars."

They clinked glasses and looked over at the telescope before taking their first sip.

"I don't know how to answer that question," Alex finally responded.

"It's happened before on other settled planets. I think it's time for the earth to know it's not alone. It will help people be nicer to the planet and take better care of it. It's not going to last much longer the way we treat it."

"How long is not much longer?" Alex asked.

"A century or two. It may sound like a long time, but it's not. It will seem like tomorrow. Knowing we're not alone might help the world's leaders come to their senses and change their priorities."

"If you think that's possible, then I know you're not from around here," Alex said. He meant it as a joke, but all it got from Alula was a nod and a little smile.

Her smile, however small, seemed so familiar and comforting, as if Alex had been seeing it his whole life. Did it really matter if she had this small crack—like a damaged eggshell—if he felt like a better person when he was around her? Alex did not want to see her hurt and embarrassed, and he figured he could talk her out of it—out of her delusion—given enough time. First, he had to talk her out of going public.

"Going out on a limb like that can be very risky." Alex spoke slowly, using his deep, serious voice. "Dangerous really. You might be surprised and disappointed by how some people will react…a lot of people actually."

"That's okay. I can't be any more disappointed than I am now about the way we are headed."

"The climate?"

"Among other things."

"Why not get involved in one of those organizations that work against global warming?"

"I can accomplish more this way."

"No one is going to believe you. They will think you're off your rocker, which means you won't accomplish anything, except become the butt of all the late-night comedians' jokes."

"That doesn't bother me."

"And you won't be the first person to claim they came here from another planet."

"What if the others were also telling the truth?" Alula asked.

"That's exactly my point. No one believed them back then; why should anyone believe you now?"

"Times are different. Science is different. So are the possibilities. There is the Internet, artificial intelligence, and wristwatch telephones. No one would have believed any of that fifty years ago. I can tell the world things it doesn't know, which couldn't be verified back then but can now, things which will make it impossible for them not to believe me."

"Impossible, I don't think so. Even facts don't convince people these days. They don't believe three-quarters of the things they hear, and not half the things they see. We have become a world of doubters and deniers."

"I don't think that's true," Alula said, still smiling. "At least I hope not."

"Even if they do believe you, how is it going to change anything. All you will do is make people afraid. It's not going to make the world pay any more attention to the health of the planet than it does now."

"Aren't you the pessimist."

"That's because I was born here."

Alex followed that remark with a big smile to make it clear he was joking.

"Ha ha," Alula said with an equally big smile.

They both took a moment to sip some wine.

"We won't know for sure," Alula added, "unless we try."

He liked Alula's use of "we," but what Alex really wanted to say was that if she could not convince him, how could she possibly convince anyone else. He had never met anyone so sure about something as nutty as this, and he had spent quite a lot of time with drugged-out, crazy people. Some of Alex's old drug friends had the weirdest opinions about life and the world of do-gooders. One of them believed certain drugs gave him magic powers like the power to become invisible, but only when he was alone and at unpredictable moments.

He sounded normal now compared to Alula.

Instead of telling Alula what was really on his mind, which was unusual for Alex, he put his hand to his chin and nodded like he agreed and was trying to come up with the best way to reveal it.

After a while, Alex got up and refilled their wineglasses. Perhaps a relationship would help Alula let go of her fantasy. It would be good for him as well, Alex thought, because when he was with her, his drug cravings seemed to diminish. Maybe this was what falling in love was all about, wanting to be a better person. It sounded like as good a definition of love as any he had heard before.

"Okay, assuming some people do believe you...or most everyone does...it's still going to get pretty ugly. A lot of the world will panic, particularly the politicians and the generals. They'll think the world is in danger. The aliens in the movies are always coming here to take over the earth. I remember one where they came to turn us into food."

"Science fiction," Alula said. "That kind of thing doesn't happen, not when a society is advanced enough for interstellar travel."

"There's always a first time."

"A cliché."

"Aren't clichés based on ancient wisdom?"

"Not always, not in this case."

"This country has grown up on science fiction. A lot of people will believe it's possible...and likely."

"Once they get to know me...and you, they'll calm down. We haven't come to hurt anyone or take anything, just to live here like everyone else...and learn."

Alex dragged his hand through his hair. He felt like pulling some of it out.

"What can you possibly learn from us?"

"Why do you study your ancients?" Alula asked. "No age has a monopoly on knowledge. We can learn from the smallest insect and plant. It's just as important to learn from the past as it is from the present...from our differences, as much as our similarities."

"Do you report back to Home about the things you learn?"

Alex hoped the answer was no. One delusion at a time was all he could handle.

"Of course not. We have no way of doing that. Once we settle, all contact ends. What I'm referring to is learning on a personal level. There's nothing more important."

With that pronouncement, Alula sat back and picked up her wineglass. Alex drank along with her. At least she seemed normal when it came to some things.

"So, what do you think?" Alula asked.

"About going to bed?"

"No."

"About going public?"

"Yes."

"I don't know."

"I want you with me," Alula said. "I need you standing there alongside me. After all, you are half Homebody."

"As you keep reminding me."

"You and I were meant to do this together...to be together."

"Because it's in our stardust?"

Alula nodded before looking down at her hands. They were long and slender, almost like a pianist. His father had long fingers like that. He used to say it was what helped make him such a good mechanic.

His mother's hands were shorter, her fingers stubbier. His were somewhere in between.

"Can I think it over?" Alex asked.

"Sure, but don't take too long. I really do believe time is of the essence...we don't want to be too late."

"Because of global warming?"

"As well as all the hunger and disease...the wars...people are fighting the wrong battles."

Alex nodded. If only two people could make a difference. If that were true, the earth would have been repaired a long time ago.

"Besides," Alula added, looking up with the sweetest grin on her face, the opposite of what Alex would have expected given the serious nature of their conversation, "I'm ready to settle down and mate."

Alex took such a big gulp of wine it was hard for him to swallow it down.

"It's my time," she added.

"Is that the way it's done on Home? You reach a certain age and pick someone to mate with?"

Alula laughed. "More or less…it's expected at our age."

"I guess I'm the only available half-breed around." Alex meant it to be funny, but it didn't come out that way.

Fortunately, Alula already seemed to know Alex well enough to know how he really meant it.

"There's a lot more to it, of course," Alula added. "I have known about you since I was a little girl. My parents always talked about you and your father…and I just knew it."

"Knew what?"

"That I would feel it."

"Feel what?" Alex asked.

"What I didn't feel with the other boys I went out with in school."

Alex knew what Alula was saying, but he wanted to hear it. He had not heard it since he was very young, since his father's death. The longest Alex had been with the same girl was about three months, and that was senior year in high school when they both wanted to make sure they had a date for the prom. The love word never came up. It was all about the sex, which was important back then, as it is now, but the hormones were the only ones speaking up during that relationship.

"You know what I mean," Alula continued. "You and I share the same stardust. It's a good foundation, but there must be more…a gravitational pull…a spark like the kind that gives birth to a star. Don't you feel it?"

"Like in the story."

Alula nodded.

"When it is love," Alula continued, "it creates the same beating heart that draws you into it and becomes hotter and hotter, but instead of creating a star, it creates a new heart by expanding the old one…so you're able to believe all things, hope all things, and endure all things. Can you feel it?"

Alex nodded. He did feel it. He felt it the moment they started talking in the art rehab class. It was as good a definition of love as Alex had ever heard.

"I knew it the moment we stood side by side in painting class," Alula said, as if she were reading his mind. "It was in the first breath I took of you…it was as if I were standing at the center of a flower."

"Like love at first sight?" Alex asked. The words did not sound nearly as cynical as he had intended.

Alula was dragging him into her fantasy, and as much as Alex wanted to be with her, it did feel strange, not like the kind of love that would last forever the way it did in the movies, but more the kind of love that crashes and burns when it flies to close to reality.

"I know you felt it too," Alula said.

"Because you were reading my mind?"

"Because I was reading your eyes and your heart."

Alex could not remember the last time he felt choked up like this. Probably his father's funeral.

"Love is in the open eyes, the open heart, and the open mind," Alula said sweetly, reaching out to touch his arm, "but it's also in the chemistry of quantum physics, which says that two particles are always more dynamic than one."

"I've never heard it put quite like that before."

"It's from a famous poem on Home called 'The Chemistry of Love.'"

They both took a few minutes to sip their wine and gather their thoughts.

What Alex was feeling was very different from what he usually felt when he was getting high with a girl. It was not so much below the belt, although there was some of that as well; it was a sensation much higher up. Somewhere between the shadow of his heart and his soul, a line Alex remembered reading once in an Earth poem. A place he never thought existed, at least not inside him.

"We are perfectly compatible," Alula added, "because our stardust came together when our star was born and will be rejoined after we transform."

Alex liked being compatible with someone like Alula, even if it was only in her delusional world. He would not agree that they were "perfectly compatible." He liked drugs and burgers. She would not touch either one. His goal in life—until now—was to remain invisible, and hers was to stand naked before the world.

He wondered if he could convince Alula to wait until they grew old before letting the world in on her fantasy, or at least make the announcement in an anonymous letter to the editor, or on some website where it would sink quietly out of sight.

"You can't be cautious with love," she said, as if she really were reading his mind. "Love makes you brave. It encourages you to take chances. I could never be afraid of telling the world who I am with you standing beside me."

"What about your parents? Won't they be upset? Won't the announcement affect them?"

"I've already discussed it with them. They understand how I feel. They prefer to remain unidentified."

"They must have a good reason for that."

"They're in a different place, a different stage of enlightenment," Alula said. "I'm sure your father felt the same way. I don't."

"The press will find them."

"No, they won't. We have different names. My past is untraceable. We have been very careful about it."

"They'll put you in a mental institution."

"I'm sure they'll give me a psychiatric examination. I'll pass it easy enough."

"Or dissect you under a microscope."

"Not until I transform."

"The people who believe you won't leave you alone or they'll panic...the others will think it's a big hoax."

"Doing the right thing is never wrong...and it's never easy." Alula reached over again to touch Alex's hand. "My mind is made up. I will do this with or without you. I'd much prefer to do it with you."

The way Alula said it left no doubt. It was going to be very difficult for Alex to change her mind.

"You know," he said a bit sheepishly, "I did feel it as well...the chemistry."

It was the boldest declaration of love he had made in a long time, maybe ever, including when he was high and tended to say whatever he needed to say to get what he wanted.

Alula smiled.

"But I worry about you and the bad things that could happen."

"Because you still don't believe me," she said, "not really. I know that. You can't hide it from me."

"Reading my mind?"

"I don't have to; it's in your eyes."

"If I'm having difficulty believing," he said, "think how hard it will be for the rest of the world."

"Yet the world is full of people who believe in an omniscient and omnipotent consciousness who watches over them from someplace up in the heavens and listens to their prayers."

"Not this one."

Alex poured himself some more wine. Alula's glass was still more than half full.

"What can you offer as proof?" he asked. "I mean real proof...perhaps a spaceship hidden somewhere in the mountains or a teleporter."

"Like on *Star Trek*?"

"That would be perfect."

"Nothing like that. We get dropped off and they leave. We have clothes, diamonds, identification, basic stuff we need to get started, that's it."

"Can you get back in touch with Home if something goes wrong...you know, Earth to home base? Please send some photographs of our red sun and two moons so we can save the planet."

Alula laughed.

"These days I doubt a photograph would do," Alex said. "They can fake those like most everything."

"No communication is possible. That could change once the earth accepts it's not alone. Home monitors a lot of planets to see when it would be appropriate to open up a dialogue."

"Like sending ambassadors and arranging tours?"

"Something like that."

Alex took another gulp of wine.

"Why not let it go and enjoy your time here on Earth with me? Isn't that what they intended? The reason why they sent you here without any proof? We'll figure it out eventually. We're always sending probes into deep space."

"At the rate they travel, the earth will be long gone before they reach anyone."

"Long gone?"

"Uninhabitable."

If only Alex could convince Alula to keep her fantasy a secret between the two of them. He could easily live with an eccentricity like that. He had had a lot of experience. Addicts are filled with them, as was his mother.

"No one will ever believe you," Alex said softly.

"I do have a way to prove it."

"It has to be more than a mind trick. There are psychics in carnivals trained to pick up on every expression and cue to make it seem as if they're reading your mind."

"That wouldn't work anyway because I can't always do it and certainly not on a big scale, not with an audience. There has to be a personal connection that creates a heightened state of…"

"Awareness?" Alex interjected while Alula looked for the right word. He almost said arousal.

"Emotion. Emotions are the best transmitters of thought. It only works one on one, and they have to be close by."

"What's the other way you have of proving it? If you could disappear and reappear on the other side of the room, that would work."

"And it would be fun." Alula chuckled.

Nothing Alex said, none of his doubts, seemed to bother her. He envied her natural calmness and certainty. The only one he ever knew like that was his father.

"It would be telekinesis," Alula said, bringing him back to the moment.

"You mean like levitation? Spinning a pencil on the table without touching it?"

"Not that. There are all different kinds of telekinesis from molecular manipulation and transmutation to bending quantum strings and manipulating reality."

"You can do all that?"

"No, I can do what you would call organic manipulation and only on a very limited basis."

"What does that mean?"

Alex picked up his wine and leaned back against the chair. She was either super-bright or had done a lot of reading to make her delusion sound so real.

"I can regenerate and manipulate my own cells...we all can...which is why we never get sick, not for long, and rarely transform before our time."

"No one on Home dies?"

"Transforms...not from illness, from accidents sometimes, but mostly old age. All organic cells eventually wear out."

"I suppose that's one reason why Home is wildly overpopulated."

Alex topped off Alula's wine and tossed the empty bottle into the recycle bin. This was getting weirder by the minute, even if he was getting a little buzzed and beginning to enjoy it.

"There's more to it," Alula said.

"You're descended from the gods?"

"From the stars."

"Right."

"It means we also have the power of psionic healing...within limits of course."

"Of course. What is psionic healing?"

"The power to heal others. It has to be someone I can touch...and there is a limit to what I can do."

"For example?"

"I can't regenerate an organ or heal one that's been badly damaged."

"Can you heal me?"

"You're not sick."

"Not according to the counselors at rehab. They keep telling me addiction is a sickness, no different than diabetes."

"It is," Alula said, "but it's not the kind of thing susceptible to organic manipulation. It's way too dangerous to fool around near the brain or the heart. It works best with cuts and infections...broken bones, burns...things like that."

"Makes sense," Alex said to make Alula feel good, although it did not, not to him. "Can you show me with something small?"

"Like what?"

Alex extended his left arm and pointed to a raw spot just above his wrist.

"Got a pretty bad burn here about a month ago from the steamer."

Alula reached out to examine his arm. She turned it over and pushed up his sleeve.

"You've got more than one," she said. "I see an older one here and another there. I count three."

"One of the hazards of the job. Being a barista is dangerous work."

"Which is why I need someone like you by my side in this quest."

They both chuckled. Alula held tight to his arm when he tried to pull it back.

"Hold still," she said, closing her eyes.

Alex watched her face to see what she would do next. He imagined her mumbling some magic incantation, but all she did was squeeze her eyes tight, suck in her lower lip, and slow down her breathing.

He remained perfectly still and quiet, keeping his eyes glued to Alula's face. He doubted he could have broken her concentration if he had let out a scream.

About twenty minutes later she opened her eyes.

"There, that wasn't so difficult."

"There what?"

"Take a look."

Alex snatched his arm back to examine it more closely. The burns were all gone. There were no scars, no discolorations; it was as if they had never been there. Even the one from last month, the biggest and most discolored of the three, had disappeared. He could hardly think over the sound of his heart drumming in his ears.

He walked over to the lamp to get a better view. He tried to feel the burns as if their disappearance might be an optical illusion. They had a raised goose-bumpy feel before, but now all he could feel was smooth skin.

"*They're gone*," he exclaimed, looking back at Alula as if he had to convince her as well as himself.

"Yes, all gone," Alula said, looking very pleased. "I haven't tried anything like that in a long time…it's exhausting."

Alula slumped back against her chair.

"If I had a broken bone, could you fix it…just like that?"

"If it wasn't displaced...a hairline fracture, yes, but it would take more time. It would be much harder with a bad break. I suppose it's still possible. I've never tried anything like that."

"How about old age...can you get rid of the wrinkles...un-age the cells?"

"No, we can't turn back time... Aging is natural; it's different from an injury or a burn."

"If I were killed in a car crash and you were there, could you...um...bring me back to life?"

"No. If you had not already transformed, it would depend on the extent of the damage, and how quickly I could get to you. Getting rid of a burn is easy. Fixing a broken leg is harder. Internal bleeding maybe if it were only one small tear because I would need time to repair it before you bleed out. Multiple injuries, major internal damage, there's not much I can do...and I can't just add blood if you've lost a lot."

"Have you ever tried to save someone?"

"No."

Alex took a deep breath and let it out slowly as he continued to stare down at his arm.

"Now you believe me."

Alex nodded. What else could explain it?

Alula clapped her hands. She was as excited as a young child on Christmas morning. Then she leaned her head back and closed her eyes.

"I always get so tired afterwards."

Alex watched her resting for a bit, an extraterrestrial who looked as American as apple pie. It made him wonder if he was being a bit too hasty—still—and too unimaginative. What if there was another possible explanation?

"What if that doesn't convince them?" Alex asked. "What if they consider you one of those idiot savants. You know, one of those people born knowing how to play the piano or instantly able to tell you the square root of any number."

"That is a talent, not a power. No one on Earth is born with the telekinetic power of organic manipulation. It took a million years for it to develop on Home."

It made sense, though it sounded like something one of the characters in his old comic books might say.

"Did my father have that power as well?"

Alula nodded.

"Why didn't he save himself?"

"Probably not enough time...too much bleeding. If he lost consciousness, he couldn't have tried. But that would mean he didn't suffer."

No matter where you came from or whatever powers you might have, Alex realized, there's no way of getting around bad luck.

"Are you okay?" Alula asked, opening her eyes wide and reaching out for Alex's hand.

"Show me again where Home is?" he asked, pulling her up and leading her over to the telescope.

Alula showed him the dark area in the handle of the Big Dipper, pointing out again where Alcor was located.

"It's much too faint to see," she said, "except through one of the giant telescopes."

Alex tried squinting, but all he could see was black, empty space.

Alula did point out a faint star he could see through the telescope and told him Alcor, Home's sun, was about two finger widths to the left. It was all relative since one finger width probably translated into a million light-years.

Alula explained that there were trillions of stars and planets, most of them invisible to the biggest telescopes on the planet, including the Hubble Telescope orbiting the earth. Alex had no trouble believing that, because his father used to say the same thing, reminding him he had to use his imagination if he wanted to see what others could not.

Over the next two weeks, Alex and Alula lived together and slept together without any concern for Alula getting pregnant since she said she ovulated once a year and it would not be for another eight months. They spent every evening looking at the stars, Alula pointing out things that were not in any books, things no astronomer on Earth knew anything about. Dark patches of space that hid countless stars and planets—many of them inhabited—and wormholes which one day would help Earthlings travel the universe, provided they were still around.

There was no way Alex could know for sure if anything Alula said was true, whether it was about the planet Rhoanna, where the inhabitants spoke with their fingers and eyes and could jump great distances because of the low gravity, or the sun in the Mamoona Galaxy that changed color every ninety days from red to yellow to a bluish black and back again to red.

How could he doubt someone who could erase the burns on his arm in an instant, even though every sci-fi comic Alex had ever read and every sci-fi movie he had ever seen featured some Earthling who had been exposed to a burst of gamma rays or some other toxic radiation, giving them strange powers.

CHAPTER 3
AN INTERSTELLAR ROMANCE

Alex still had to work to pay the rent and buy food. He did keep off drugs and cut back on the pot now that Alula was around. He did not feel the same urges, not the irresistible ones. Alula felt like the burning passion Alex needed. He did wonder sometimes if it could also be the result of some organic manipulation on her part, assuming there really was such a thing.

Alula did not work. She preferred to explore the city and observe the people. She did not worry about money because when her parents settled here, Alula told him, they were given an ample supply of local valuables—in this case diamonds—much more than had been given to the settlers when Alex's father came to Earth with his parents. Alula's parents had done very well and could afford to be generous.

Alex figured his father's family must have used up their allotment, so they did not have anything to spare when it came time for his father to marry and start his own family. His mother did not have any diamonds lying around the house; otherwise, she would not be worried all the time about making ends meet.

"How should we let the world know?" Alula asked one day after dinner, a vegetable chili she was fond of making. She liked to cook, but she refused to make anything with "animal flesh."

It had not come up in a while, and Alex was hoping Alula might be changing her mind now that she was finding domestic bliss with her stardust mate. Love changes people's dreams and aspirations—and in Alex's case, his cravings—at least they did in the movies and the novels he read in high school.

Going public was not going to be good for their relationship, Alex was sure of that, which might explain why his father never told his mother. She was not very good with secrets or keeping her thoughts to herself, certainly after the accident. Perhaps his father was worried what she might say after he was gone. What if his power was a little different from Alula's? What if he was prescient when it came to his own transformation?

"Any ideas?" Alula asked, snapping Alex back to the moment.

"Let's brainstorm," he answered, shaking his head as if to loosen some cobwebs.

Alex stood up and walked over to the window.

"Okay, here's one...you could go on the *Jerry Springer Show*."

"Be serious."

"*Oprah?*"

"We need to do this right," Alula said. "We'll only get one chance."

Alex stroked his chin the way the actors on television do when their characters are faced with important decisions. He loved the way Alula looked at him—so hopeful—as if being a native-born Earthling would help her come up with the best way.

"Okay, how about doing something spectacular...you know, like going into a children's hospital and curing everyone."

"It's not that simple. It only works one on one, and it would take a ton of time depending on the reason they're there...assuming it's even possible."

"Right...probably too dramatic anyway," Alex added. "The whole world will start beating down your door after something like that."

Not counting the government, which would be eager to take her apart to see how it worked.

"How about a letter to the editor?" Alula suggested.

"They'll never print it."

"I could offer to come in and give them proof...like the kind I gave you."

"Too small, too slow, too hard to control."

Alex covered his mouth with his hand while he thought it over some more.

"The first step is always the hardest," Alex said.

"And the most important," Alula added. "What if I post something on Facebook?"

"And get a couple of thousand likes? You'll get lost in all the other fake news."

Alex thought about making a joke like suggesting she dress up in a spacesuit and announce it with a bullhorn in the middle of

Discovery Park, but it was clear Alula wanted a good idea, not a funny one.

About a half hour later, Alex came running out of the bathroom.

"I got it," he announced. "We do it through a university… through their astronomy department. That will give it more legitimacy."

Alula jumped up and threw her arms around him. "Perfect."

"To get their attention, you need to point out something in the stars that they don't know. Something they can verify. Maybe some sort of new solar radio wave, something they've never detected before."

"With their primitive equipment, not likely."

"Can you help them build something better?"

"No, scientific discoveries have to come in their own time. It's one of the cardinal rules of settling. I couldn't help them build anything anyway, even if I wanted to. I know the stars and planets, the ones we learned about in school, but not the science behind any of the equipment."

"Won't revealing yourself and the existence of all these alien worlds speed things up and cause problems?" Alex asked.

"It's a different kind of knowledge. It's not a sudden scientific leap forward; it's a recognition of what is…what most astronomers already believe… which is why they're always looking and listening."

Alex opened a couple of beers and handed one to Alula.

"What could you show an astronomy professor to convince him…or her…using just the equipment we have now?"

Alula stared down at her hands while she thought it over. She did that a lot. After a while she shook her head and shrugged.

"I don't know. I need a few days to think it over."

"Take a few weeks or a month. You've waited this long."

What Alex really wanted to suggest was that she take a few years or a lifetime.

Alula looked lost in thought.

"You guys have been here for hundreds of years, right?" Alex asked.

Alula nodded.

"Why haven't any others revealed themselves before now?"

"They may have tried, I don't know. Before television and the Internet, it was a lot harder to be heard. Or maybe the time didn't seem right...as urgent as it does now. A planet needs to progress to a certain stage of development before it's ready...and willing...to know."

"Is that in the travel manual?"

"It's part of what we learn when we prepare to settle."

"When did the earth reach that stage?" Alex asked.

"When it reached for the stars."

"Airplanes?"

"Satellites...trips to the moon and back...rockets exploring the solar system and beyond, even if they do take forever."

"It's hard to believe we're ready to join the cosmic community considering the way we treat the earth and each other."

"All the more reason it's important now," Alula said.

When Alex did not respond, Alula added, "It's true, you are far from the most peaceful and considerate beings in the universe."

"Are we the worst?"

"No, there are places that still have slaves and others who have already reduced their planets to a cinder...but you're doing a pretty good job of poisoning this one, that's for sure."

Alex stared at Alula over the rim of his beer. She was not only the most beautiful girl he had ever been with, but she was also the smartest, the first one with a real purpose other than getting high and having fun.

"If climate warming makes the earth uninhabitable, would they move all of you to another planet?"

"No, when you settle here, you're here for good...or bad."

"Do you think knowing we're not alone is really going to change anything?" Alex asked. "Because I don't."

Alex had been a cynic and pessimist since he was ten, and he didn't see why he should change now.

"I think knowing you're not alone will always make a difference, whether individually or as a species. Learning what can happen and what has happened on other planets will change a lot of people's perspectives."

"I find it hard...as a half-Earthling...to imagine how knowing about you will put an end to pollution, war, and hunger."

"It won't, it will take time, a lot of time, but I think it can help shift the conversation and transform the thinking. You wouldn't be the first planet to come to its senses and pull back from the brink."

"Of planetary suicide?" Alex said without any of the emotion those words warranted.

"More like negligent planet-cide. No one intentionally wants to end all life. A quarter of the people think it's a hoax, and another quarter think science will figure a way out in the nick of time because it always has. You know, discover some magic machine to scrub the atmosphere clean and reverse the warming."

"Is that possible?"

"I don't know; almost anything is possible when it comes to science. How else could I be here? But that kind of science is probably way too far in the future to be of any use. There will come a moment, an instant really, when it'll be too late even for science."

Over the next couple of weeks, they talked about it constantly. Alula was trying to come up with something, some irrefutable proof that would convince an astronomer she had to be from another planet. As far as Alex was concerned, he would be very content if all they ever did was talk about it. He was very happy the way things were. His life was far better than he could have ever imagined, and he was sure it would all change the day Alula went public. It would be impossible for them to live a normal life together after that. Perhaps it was the reason why his father kept silent, even from his own wife and child.

Alula believed this was a critical moment in the earth's evolution, when people either moved past their differences, which she called small, embracing the similarities instead, and joined hands to preserve life and reach for the stars. She did not deny coming out would test their relationship, but doing nothing would probably destroy it. She couldn't love herself if she did nothing, she explained, so how could she love someone else any more.

"We have to try," Alula said. "We can't just sit by and watch it happen. Without truly believing we're not alone and the whole universe is watching, I don't know if the earth can find the will it needs to do what has to be done."

"Otherwise, we're doomed?"

"It seems that way. We must try to make it a better world, a more sustainable world… if we are going to procreate."

Alex could feel the blood suddenly rush to his face. The drug-addicted Alex would never have considered adding another human to the planet. He never gave any thought to the future, not beyond his next high. The Alex in love would be very content to live a small, drug-free life if he had Alula, a good barista job, and a telescope. He would prefer to move to the middle of nowhere, to a place that had the same hauntingly dark, starry nights he remembered as a child.

However, this new Alex, the one whose love of the night sky had been reenergized, also carried around a new belief—however shaky—that he was someone special and had the stuff of stars in his DNA. He had a new more expansive view of the universe and his place in it and did not walk around all day the way he used to, feeling as if he had been shortchanged and was owed something. He was concerned about others and woke up inspired by the morning sunlight streaming through his window and glad to be in the moment, words he had heard often enough in rehab, but which never made much sense before.

He wanted to do the right thing. The new Alex was not going to stand in Alula's way.

"Listen," he said one night as they lay in bed wide awake, "I was checking the Internet, and the University of Washington has a pretty well-respected astronomy department."

It was also within walking distance of his apartment.

"It won't be hard to pick a professor to approach," he said. "We can pick one and go from there…once you come up with something really good to convince them. Something you know but shouldn't, something they don't but can confirm."

The next day as he was climbing the stairs after work, Alula stood in the doorway wearing one of her big, bright smiles.

"I got it," she said, "something really, really good."

"It has to be better than good…it needs to be astounding."

"It is, one that a girl without a formal education and no access to a world-class observatory could never discover on her own or know…unless she was from another planet."

"Something they can verify?"

"Absolutely, with a little help."

"What kind of help?"

"It can't be done with one observatory. They'll need at least three."

"But we have the science?"

Alula nodded before explaining about this dwarf star Earth's astronomers were very familiar with.

"They call it Trappist-One and it's relatively close. About forty light-years away."

"We're like neighbors."

Alula smiled.

"Yes, but it's only visible through a telescope, a substantial one, not like ours, but what the astronomers don't know yet is that there are seven Earth-sized planets orbiting around it."

Three of them were rocky, Alula explained, not gaseous like Jupiter, and were in orbits that could support life. She said the third and fourth planets were temperate with water and an atmosphere and did have life.

"Like us?"

"No, they are where Earth was perhaps a million years ago."

"Dinosaurs?"

"On one."

Pointing out previously unknown planets, three of which are in the habitable zone of a star, Alula explained, would be a game changer.

"Like Columbus discovering America," Alex added.

"He really didn't discover it. It was already there…just like these planets."

Alula laughed and Alex laughed along with her.

"The sun is red there as well," Alula told him later that night, "and their atmospheres have a salmon tint to them."

"How come?"

"Because of the way the particles in their atmosphere break up the light. I saw photos of them in school before I left Home."

"Too bad they didn't let you bring a schoolbook along with you."

"That would have been nice…and way too easy."

"How can our astronomers verify the planets," Alex asked, "if they can't even see them with a giant telescope?"

"Because you don't have to see them to figure out that they are there. That's the beauty of astronomy…there are lots of ways to see things without using your eyes."

Alex's father used to say the same thing.

"If they look where I tell them to look, their light sensors will pick up the interruptions…like little eclipses…as they orbit the star. It won't be hard for them to figure out they're caused by planets in orbiting Trappist-One."

Alex paced around the room. Now that it was about to happen, he could not help getting excited, the way he did years ago when his father talked about the stars and pointed out things in the emptiness of space that Alex used to think were in his imagination.

"Can you show me where the star is through my telescope?"

Alula turned the telescope to the proper coordinates. It was black, empty space, but Alex had rediscovered enough of his imagination since meeting Alula that when he squinted, he swore he could see a pinprick of light.

"By using the global network of ground-based telescopes," Alula said, "the astronomers can confirm everything…the planets, the sizes, the orbital times, and the distances from the star. One is in an orbit almost identical to the earth. It's the kind of discovery that should make the front page of every newspaper."

Alex sat down and folded his arms across his chest. It all sounded so exciting, something he might have even brought up with some of his drug friends, but he also knew the discovery would pale in comparison to the announcement about Alula. The possibility— or probability—of life on another planet was one thing; a visitor here from one of them would be "as different as chalk from cheese" to quote another one of the clichés his father was fond of using.

"It'll still be small potatoes compared to you," Alex said. "You'll be the big discovery…the one everyone wants to talk about."

"I hope so."

"I think we should proceed slowly. Perhaps we shouldn't put both announcements out there at the same time, you know, sort of let the world stick its toe into the water to get used to the temperature before we push it all in."

"Meaning?"

"Let our astronomer announce the discovery of the planets first. Give the world a little time to get accustomed to the thought of other life out there before they get to meet one. A month or two later, our astronomer holds another news conference to introduce you and tell the world that you were the one who pointed out the planets."

"No way," Alula said, "I need to be there from the start...at the very first news conference. They'll want to know how our astronomer picked Trappist-One, and the answer has to be the truth...the whole truth."

"It could be dangerous," Alex whispered.

"It won't be so bad."

"You haven't seen as many science fiction movies as I have. They never end well...not for the aliens."

Alex took out a beer and collapsed on the couch beside Alula.

"It's called science fiction for a reason," she said, "the operative word being fiction. They'll want to interview me... examine me, you too, so what."

"Are you completely the same, you know, inside?"

"Mostly the same."

"Mostly? What's not?"

"My organs are reversed," Alula said, "same organs, different sides of the body."

"*Really?*"

"They operate the same...it's not a significant difference."

"Am I like you?"

"No, you take after your mother."

"How do you know?"

"I've looked."

"With what, your x-ray vision?"

"Telekinesis...I can sense where your organs are."

"Seems like an invasion of privacy."

"Do you mind?"

"No, that's fine," Alex said with a chuckle. "You can do anything you want to me."

Alula leaned her head against his shoulder.

"I am afraid they'll never let you go once they get hold of you," Alex said. "They'll want to keep an eye on you. Me too, I suppose. We will never be alone...never have a normal life together."

"We've already discussed this," Alula said. "We'll make the best of it, take it one day at a time. Are you getting cold feet?"

Alex shrugged before shaking his head slowly up and down.

"It'll be all right," Alula said, lowering her head to his lap and smiling up at him. "In the beginning it might be difficult, but we'll get used to it."

"Difficult is an understatement."

"Maybe some others from Home will come out of the closet. We are all over the world. I bet most, if not all, of the second and third generations are like you and have no idea. Still, there are a lot of recent settlers who do know."

Alex had nothing to say in response. Alula was right, they had discussed all this ad nauseum.

"Things will eventually calm down, and if they don't, it won't matter," Alula added, "because we will always be together. We'll just find a new normal."

Alex stared out the window. There was no going back now. He chuckled softly at the thought of their having a normal life.

"What's so funny?" Alula asked.

"Us having a normal life."

Alula laughed as well.

"It's all relative."

"Like time and the speed of light?"

"Exactly."

They fooled around, which they did most every night now as if they both knew they had to enjoy each other as much as possible while they still could. Afterward, they lay on their backs in bed exhausted but not sleepy. Neither of them could ever fall asleep on their back.

"You know," Alula said, "there's always a price to be paid for being the first."

"I get that, and I'm not saying you shouldn't do it...we shouldn't do it, but I'm still thinking it should be a more gradual process. You know, one step at a time. Each step with the same purpose and effect."

"Okay, I'm listening."

Alex sat up. Alula had not given him this much of an opening before.

"Here's what I suggest. We let the world know right off that you exist...we exist...and that you're the one who provided the astronomer with the information about the planets, but you don't attend the first press conference, and our astronomer doesn't identify you but promises the world will get to meet you a little later."

"How long is a little later?"

"I don't know…a month…six months…a year, until things calm down and the world is ready."

"How will we know when that is?"

"I haven't thought that far ahead yet."

Alex wanted to say a lifetime, their lifetime, but he knew how Alula would react to that answer.

"If the purpose is to let the world know it's not alone," he added, "isn't that accomplished once they know you're the one who provided the information, that you're living here on Earth and will soon introduce yourself to the world?"

Alula's head shook slightly—side to side at first and then up and down—as if she were debating it with herself.

"I'm still listening," Alula said, looking at him with her eyes wide open.

Alex kissed Alula on the forehead and jumped out of bed. It was the first time she had not dismissed his concern and caution out of hand. He paced back and forth in front of the telescope while he organized his thoughts.

"Okay, here is what I'm thinking. We contact one astronomer at the University of Washington with the planet information, but we start off anonymously. Maybe through a burner phone or a one-off email address I set up that can't be traced or at least it won't matter by the time they do. We tell him who you are and where you're from. He verifies the planets, and when he…"

"Or she."

"Or she announces the discovery, she tells the world about you but without revealing where you are living or your name or even what you look like except that you've assured her you look exactly like us. She can promise the world it will get to meet you in person."

"When?"

"When the time is right?"

Alex didn't mean it to come out sounding like a question, but it did.

"And that will be when?" Alula asked back.

"When the dust settles, and the initial panic dies down."

"There has to be a time limit."

"I don't think we should set an arbitrary limit," Alex said.

This time Alula's head shook only from side to side.

"One month, three months…a year…however long it takes for things to calm down, because there will be a worldwide panic at first, I guarantee you that. It is the safest way to proceed. All I'm asking is for you to consider it."

Alex jumped back into bed and put his arms around Alula.

"*Please.*"

Alula stared at him, narrowing her eyes like she was trying to see inside him.

"Okay," she finally said after what seemed like an eternity to Alex.

"Okay, you'll consider it, or okay, we can do it my way?"

"Okay, we try it your way, but only if we agree to an outside time limit, and it can't be one year, not even three months. I won't wait that long. The planets are not enough. I'm the only one who can turn the probability of extraterrestrial life into an actuality."

"Agreed," Alex said, excited to have moved the needle this far. "We play it by ear, depending on the world's reaction. We wait thirty to sixty days before your press conference."

"Not a day longer."

Alex took a deep breath before nodding.

It would be enough time for them to move somewhere safe while they waited and watched the world's reaction. Alex was confident he could get Alula to stretch sixty days to ninety days and maybe longer if the circumstances warranted.

"As long as they know I'm here from the very first press conference," Alula added, "and that I am the source of our astronomer's discovery. It can't be about some astronomer stumbling across a few likely planets."

"Absolutely not. Our astronomer gets to speak to you, even meet you. He…or she…gives you all the credit but promises to keep you anonymous until we're ready."

"You think that's possible?"

"I don't know, but it's worth a try. What do we have to lose?"

"They'll come searching for us right off the bat," Alula said.

"Like we're America's most wanted. But you'll be stepping forward long before they find us, and hopefully by then the world will have gotten used to the idea. Maybe some of the other settlers will come forward as well."

Alula snuggled up against Alex, and they both stared out the window at the black, starless night. The dark clouds seemed low enough to reach out and touch.

"I did picture myself standing beside our astronomer at the press conference announcing the discovery of the planets," Alula whispered.

"I know, we're just tweaking the plan a bit to be on the safe side."

Alex listened to a couple of men stumbling down the street. They were talking too loudly for this late hour, and their words were slurred, too hard for him to make out. Alex was sure they were coming down from a high and searching for food. He remembered nights like that. They seemed far in the distant past now.

"I'm okay with trying it that way," Alula repeated, "but if there is any doubt or any problem, I'm not going to wait sixty days to step forward…whatever the risk…with or without you."

"With me," Alex said, "absolutely with me."

Alex squeezed Alula tight and closed his eyes. He tried to clear his mind and will himself to sleep, but he did not feel the least bit tired. When he looked over at Alula, her eyes were open and fixed on the ceiling.

"I have an idea," he said.

"What's that?"

He jumped out of bed and opened his laptop.

"Let's get started; we've waited long enough. Let's look over the bios of the astronomy professors at UW and pick out one we think can be trusted."

They stayed up until two in the morning, reading the bios of everyone in the astronomy department at the University of Washington in Seattle. They settled on Amber Garrigan, a senior instructor of Astronomy, Earth, and Planetary Sciences. The primary area of her research was active galactic nuclei, which Alula explained was the study of the compact regions at the center of some galaxies where the luminosity was much higher on the electromagnetic spectrum.

"Meaning it's not being produced by the stars," Alula said.

"What produces it?"

"Dense matter at the center of the galaxy gathered by a black hole. They're the most persistent source of electromagnetic radiation in the universe. They can be very helpful in discovering distant objects."

Alex nodded, although he did not completely understand it, not yet anyway. He was determined to get more books out of the library to bring himself up to speed.

The next day they bought another laptop, a used one, and Alex set up a phony email account under the name Taurus, another star, and they started off with a very simple email:

> *Ms. Garrigan,*
>
> *I have information concerning the location of 7 planets less than one hundred light-years away, three of which are in orbits that would support life and two of which do have life.*
>
> *Are you interested?*

Her response took three days, which surprised Alula but not Alex. He said it would take her at least that long to decide whether to answer it or delete it. He was betting on the trash can. Alula was confident she would eventually respond.

"True scientists know discoveries can come in the strangest ways and from the strangest places."

When Professor Garrigan did respond, she was very succinct.

> *Who are you and how would you have obtained this kind of information?*

Alula wanted to lay all her cards down right away. Alex convinced her to proceed more slowly.

> *The information is based on personal knowledge. I prefer to provide it anonymously at first to give you time to verify it. Once you do, I will be happy to provide you with more information about how I came to learn about it and who I am. Still interested?*

This time the response came back a couple of hours later.

Sure, why not. Let me hear what you have.

Not surprisingly, she sounded very skeptical. She probably thought it was a student prank or a joke by one of her colleagues. Even though Professor Garrigan was young and relatively new at it, she could not imagine astronomers got approached like this very often, if ever. Still, she was a scientist and dreamer, the way Alex imagined most astronomers to be, and she was not prepared to leave any stone unturned.

The next day Alula emailed her the name of the star, Trappist-1, and how Amber could confirm the existence of the planets and their orbits. Alula was sure she already knew how to do it, but she wanted to show off her knowledge to help convince Professor Garrigan she was not crazy. Based on their location, Alula wrote, she would find that three of the planets were in orbits appropriate for water and an atmosphere. Indeed, one was almost identical to Earth in size and orbital distance from its star, although only two of the planets supported complex organisms.

Alula did sound crazy when she made a statement like that, but they both figured Professor Garrigan was already intrigued, so they had nothing to lose.

Amber Garrigan did not contact them for almost three months. Alex and Alula knew she had to be busy with her teaching and other university obligations and could not afford to waste too much of her time trying to verify what she had to assume would turn out to be a wild goose chase.

"And she will need help," Alula reminded Alex, "because there is no way she can verify any of it on her own. It's not possible with only one observatory."

Alula explained how she would need three large telescopes in different locations around the world to measure and triangulate the interruptions in the starlight to identify the planets and their orbits. Even then, it was not the kind of thing that could be verified overnight.

"It will take a few months at a minimum," Alula said.

When Professor Garrigan finally did respond, she remained very succinct.

Confirmed. Who are you and how did you know?

Alula and Alex had talked at length about their reply, and it was already prepared. They wrote back almost immediately.

While I am not from one of those worlds, I am from
another planet that orbits a star in Ursa Major.

This time Amber's response took a couple of days, longer than Alex expected. Perhaps she was concerned about continuing down this path alone. Worried about the stability of the person on the other end—the risks really—though there was no denying her mysterious correspondent had known what the world did not know about the planets orbiting Trappist-1. It was not the kind of discovery an ordinary astronomy buff could have made alone.

Amber's response was brief.

Where in Ursa Major?

Amber was giving Alula a little test. How much did Alula really know?

The Big Dipper. A star invisible to the naked eye in
the bend of the ladle's handle. One barely visible to
your telescopes. A red dwarf companion to a larger
star.

Amber responded immediately.

Alcor?

Alula's answer was just as quick.

Yes.

If Amber had been a fish, she was now securely on the hook. She wanted to talk. She wanted to meet. She invited Alula to come to her office. Alula explained she wanted to keep out of the spotlight for the time being. No name and no address, but she would agree to meet Amber someplace public if she promised to keep her existence a secret until she was ready to go public and she came alone.

Amber eagerly agreed.

If you live in Seattle, Starbucks is the obvious choice.

CHAPTER 4
THE UNIVERSITY

Amber and Greg were having dinner. They started dating last semester, and it had become more serious over the break. The new semester found them spending three or four nights together each week, sometimes at her apartment and sometimes at his. Greg was a city boy from a rich family in Chicago, an only child who decided at the age of ten he wanted to be the one to discover—and prove—we were not the only children in the universe. Amber was a farm girl from the Midwest who fell in love with the dark, starry nights. They did not have a lot in common, but what they did have in common—their love of the stars—was central to both of their lives.

After dinner, while they sat around drinking their coffee, Amber said she had something interesting to show Greg. She got up from the table and pulled out a folder from her bag. Inside was a single sheet of paper.

"I got this email a couple of days ago," she said, taking it out and sitting back down to read it to him.

Greg's first thought was it was an offer of an assistant professorship or professorship somewhere, and he felt a tightness in his chest. A lot of schools wanted to expand their astronomy departments, and when it came to science, women were suddenly in big demand as part of the push for more diversity. While Greg did not object to it in principle, it did unfairly limit his own opportunities. He deserved to be a full professor somewhere, and he resented the idea that an inferior astronomer, at least one with less experience, should get a position simply because of her gender.

Of course, he would never say that to Amber. He knew by now to keep those kind of opinions—politically incorrect to some—to himself. He had not always been so circumspect, which might account for his relationship failures in the past. Women were far too sensitive to the inequalities they perceived—imagined, really—in the academic world. It was way overblown to Greg's thinking.

It had been this way for a thousand years, and as far as he was concerned, there had to be a good reason why.

Greg realized that he had to be careful now because he and Amber were just beginning to know each other—really know each other—and he could feel things settling into a very comfortable routine. He valued the little consistencies in life; he considered it a sign of maturity—hers as well as his—and he liked knowing he did not always have to eat and sleep alone. He needed someone like Amber to help support him on his way to full professor and eventually head of the department. Department heads needed wives to host cocktail parties and sing their praises.

Amber was his first real girlfriend in quite some time, and he had been worrying about it since there was not one confirmed bachelor heading an academic department at UW.

Most of the women Greg had dated in college and grad school found themselves put off by the second or third date. They complained he was not much of a listener, which was not true. He was a very good listener, or he would not always have gotten such good grades in school, as well as earning a master's and a doctorate. What they really meant was that he was not very good at pretending to be interested in their mundane problems and opinions. Women could talk endlessly about absolutely nothing.

His mother was a good example, and his father was always quick to point out to her when she was talking nonsense. Of course, what you can say when you are already married is very different from what you can say when you are still dating.

Greg was a scientist and did not have time to waste on their hurt feelings, their perceived insults, and their disappointing intimacies. He considered himself above that sort of thing, and as an instructor—and now an assistant professor—he preferred talking about the stars, the planets, and the certainty as far as he was concerned that we were not alone.

It was not his fault the girls he attracted could not appreciate it.

The first question he always asked a woman was whether they believed—truly believed—in extraterrestrial life. If they said no or were unsure or even indifferent, there was no second date. It was rarely his choice. Greg had not had a second date in quite some time, not until Amber joined the Astronomy Department as its first instructor. With Amber, Greg did not have to ask since he already knew she had the same heavenly obsession he did and was just as confident that there was life on other planets.

Few women he had dated in college or grad school were worth the effort when he looked at them in the cold, clear light of hindsight. Amber was an exception, which is why he had to suppress some of those instinctive remarks his other dates found objectionable. Even if Amber was not the knockout he always dreamed about, she was attractive in a nerdy kind of way, enough to be an acceptable girlfriend and wife, and, importantly, she was familiar with and admired his statistical analysis of the stars and his mathematical proof of extraterrestrial life.

She was not a follower of Professor McNamara's philosophy of dead space.

Amber was a scientist—an astronomer like him—who loved talking about the stars, so Greg's lack of interest in most everything else was not as noticeable, at least it didn't seem to bother her. He crossed his fingers and prayed it was not a job offer, especially a full professorship, which would be better than his position.

Amber read him the email.

"Ms. Garrigan, I have information concerning the location of seven planets less than one hundred light-years away, three of which are in orbits that would support life and two of which do have life. Are you interested?"

Amber read it without any of the sarcasm or humor it deserved, and Greg expected. He smiled not because he thought it was funny—he suspected it was a joke for which she was about to provide him with the punch line—but because he was relieved it was not a job offer from another university.

"Have you ever gotten anything like this?" Amber asked.

"You're kidding, right?"

He was shocked Amber looked a little disappointed by his response. Did she think he was that naïve? Did she really expect him to respond seriously to that kind of nonsense? He was even more shocked she managed to ask the question with a straight face.

"It's a prank, Amber, come on, you have to realize that."

Greg sensed from the look on her face he might have spoken a little too harshly. Perhaps he should not have used "come on" the way he did. Maybe it did sound a bit dismissive, like he was talking to one of his students, but it was hard for Greg to believe Amber thought this bit of nonsense was worth reading to him or interesting.

Greg decided he had better cover it up with some kinder words.

"You know what I mean," he said with a chuckle. "You're the new kid on the block. It's obviously one of the grad students pulling your leg, maybe even one of the other professors. That kind of thing goes right in the round filing cabinet under your desk. And I wouldn't ask anyone else in the department about it because you'll just be giving them a good laugh at your expense."

Greg felt as if he had recovered nicely by demonstrating his sensitivity and compassion. He thought Amber would smile back and nod, but she just sat there, her face wiped clean of expression.

Like a little child, Greg thought to himself, who had drawn a stick figure with a crayon and expected her father to drool over it like it was a Picasso. Women were too damn sensitive when it came to things like this. If you did not immediately love their new dress or their silly hat, it was as if you'd slapped them in the face.

When Greg saw the pout beginning to spread, he realized he had to tread more lightly from now on, certainly until they were married. In a strange way courting and marriage were a little like training a dog. If he could do it right, using subtlety mixed with positive reinforcement, he could get her to change over time and become more understanding and appreciative of his comments and suggestions, but he had to lead her there slowly.

Women needed time when it came to adapting to a man. He saw it very clearly growing up.

Greg put on his best professorial smile, almost a fatherly smile, and nodded while he searched his memory for something that might relate and not sound too patronizing.

"I remember once getting a handwritten note in my office mailbox; it was shortly after I started as an assistant professor. It said the math in my thesis was all wrong and the odds were half of what I had concluded. I spent a good part of the next day checking and rechecking my calculations, which, of course, were spot-on."

Greg forced a chuckle. He was making it all up, but he expected it was what Amber needed to hear in order to let go and move on.

When she didn't respond or smile back, he continued with the story.

"It was unsigned, so I had no idea who sent it. A few days later I received a second note…the handwriting identical… This time the author said he knew the math was wrong because he had run in through a top secret government computer. He signed it with a strange name that had to be thirty letters long, all of them vowels."

Amber was still wearing a pout, although it did appear to be shrinking. Greg knew he had to wrap up his little story quickly if he wanted to have any chance of resurrecting her good mood before it was time for bed. He had been looking forward to a roll in the hay.

"It was clearly from one of the students in my intro to Astro-calculus class who thought he was being funny. You know what they like to call us?"

He waited for Amber to ask, which she did.

"No, what?"

"Stargazers, they call us stargazers…particularly the business majors taking an astronomy course as a lark… They say we're too full of dreams and fantasies to look where we're going. For them it's all about money and things."

That got a little smile and Greg felt relieved. He was better with little children when it came to this kind of thing, but he felt as if he was improving with women as well now that he had Amber to practice with.

He waited for Amber to say something else, but all she did was stare back down at the email.

Woman had too many expectations, and most of them were too high. His father used to say that about his mother all the time.

"Listen, Amber, I'm one hundred percent certain it's some business jock taking your intro to the stars class to fulfill some science prerequisite, pulling your leg because you're the youngest…and prettiest instructor he's ever had."

Amber gave him a little closed-lipped smile.

Greg reached across the table and took the email out of Amber's hand. He chuckled as he read it again to himself.

She needed to develop a more critical eye—and a more cynical one as well—if she ever hoped to make assistant professor. He thought about warning her again about not showing it to anyone else so she wouldn't become the butt of every joke at next month's faculty cocktail party, but he thought better of it since he had already made that clear enough.

"Listen, when the earth finally discovers it's not alone," Greg said, "it's not going to be through an email. An advanced civilization will have a much better game plan. Something well thought out, like breaking into the broadcast of every radio and television station on the planet."

That was from an old science fiction movie. Greg decided not to point it out and sound too pedantic.

Amber nodded, a little chagrined perhaps. Greg could not be sure because Amber was not looking directly at him but out the window. Women were very gullible, which was why they were so often—and easily—taken advantage of. Greg had been hoping Amber, as a scientist, would be different.

"You don't believe it, do you?" he finally asked, unable to contain himself. "You're not taking this seriously, are you?"

Greg pushed the email back at Amber.

"No, of course not," she said, snapping back to attention, looking at him with those unblinking eyes, the ones Greg saw sometimes when she was getting annoyed. In this case it was more likely due to embarrassment.

In Greg's opinion, emotions all seemed to overlap and merge into one when it came to most women, making it hard sometimes to tell them apart.

"I'm glad," Greg responded.

If Amber was taking it seriously, Greg would have to question her maturity and common sense. He wondered if he would have to be the one to end it this time. He wanted a relationship with a scientist, not another sentimental woman chasing her own silly dreams and fantasies. He wanted a quiet, thoughtful, and somber wife who believed in the scientific method, and recognized his quiet strength and, most of all, her own nonsense.

"Whoever he is," Greg added, "he probably has a crush on you... Now that's something I can believe."

"I suppose so," Amber said, "but I would think he could come up with something a bit more romantic."

"Like spending thirty dollars to get a star named after you?"

Greg thought that was funny and expected a chuckle in response, a soft moment to end the tension and turn the page. Instead, Amber carefully returned the email to the folder and put the folder back into her bag.

"I'd forget about it if I were you," Greg said.

Amber nodded.

"And ignore it."

Greg thought the point worth repeating.

"I know it sounds silly," she whispered, "but I've got this funny feeling about it."

"Funny feeling? Is that one of those women's intuition things?"

Greg pushed his chair back from the table.

Greg did not believe women had any more of an intuitive sense than men; less in fact when it came down to it because women were too emotional, and emotions cloud judgment. Greg believed—like his father—that calm reasoning and clear objectivity were the best foundation for intuition.

Amber frowned and looked away again.

"Come on, Amber, what are the odds a visitor from another planet picked your name out of the university directory for an email announcing the earth has company?"

"Probability is your specialty, you tell me. Even if the odds are infinitesimal, aren't you the one who says that still means it's possible...anything's possible?"

Greg sighed a bit too loudly. It was a figure of speech, a starting-off point for an academic discussion; it was not something to take seriously. Greg believed in math and statistics, not random, improbable, dumb luck. He refused to buy a lottery ticket for that reason or to ever entertain those flights of fantasy all the other boys had growing up, as if there was a real chance that they could become professional baseball players and movie actors.

In Greg's opinion, "anything is possible" was the last refuge of the uneducated and unprepared...the ending point of a hopeless argument. It was tantamount to closing your eyes.

"Possible in this case is a million light-years away from probable," Greg said.

Amber got up and walked over to the window to stare out at the campus. There had not been a moment like this since they had started dating. Greg did not mean for it to get out of hand like this, but he was not auditioning to be her father, and he wasn't going to bless her every utterance.

Still, Greg realized he had to calm her down if he wanted to preserve the evening.

"I'm just trying to be helpful," he said.

"I know, I'm sure you're right."

"I am…totally."

Greg was happy to see her scientific mind beginning to kick in, and even happier she was willing to concede the point.

His high school girlfriend, the only girl he went out with in high school, used to complain that Greg was not the least bit sentimental. His response was always the same—so what? Sentimentality just got in the way. He saw it often enough with his father and mother. His father was a very successful accountant who knew what was important in life. His mother was always talking about her childhood and her dreams as if any of it mattered anymore.

In the future, Greg remembered once telling her—shortly before they broke up—people would be matched by computers, and sentimentality would be a thing of the past. He thought it was a clever remark; she did not. Everything would have a statistical certainty to it, he went on to explain. You would know things based on their probability, not your feelings.

The future he foresaw back then was happening now. Life was no longer about intuition or hunch; it was about algorithms and artificial intelligence. AI was nothing more than automated reasoning, advanced decision-making that filtered out the fiction of intuition and the other emotions that led to mistakes and disappointments.

Amber sat back down at the table and sipped her coffee.

"Not much time wasted in a short reply," she said after a minute. "What do I have to lose?"

Greg felt like kicking himself. He should have known better. Press a woman too hard not to do something, even a bright woman, and she will do it out of spite.

"Do what you think best," he replied. "Just be careful. I wouldn't be going to any secret rendezvous."

Amber nodded.

At least the last thing she said—what do I have to lose—was true. Not much except a little dignity and self-respect, clearly not two things she valued as much as he had thought.

Greg would be the first to admit that the world's knowledge sometimes advanced in strange and unpredictable ways, like mold growing on a piece of bread or a lightning strike. But those were accidents, and that was then, not now. We lived in a digital world where accidental discoveries were a thing of the past. Discoveries these days required meticulous research and the assistance of massive computers.

There were no more loose stones to overturn.

Greg chuckled.

"What's so funny?" Amber asked, trying for a little smile.

Greg was relieved. He liked that about Amber. She did not remain annoyed for very long. She let it go, as his father so often told his mother to do. Amber had to know he meant well and what he said was for her own good.

"I was just thinking," he chuckled, "what if the email came from Professor McNamara? What if he was really from another planet, here for an extended stay, pretending to be a disbeliever to put us off the scent? Maybe it's time for him to beam back home, and he's decided to reveal the truth before he goes, picking you because he hates me."

"I suppose that's one possible explanation," Amber said, her smile growing. "Sometimes he hardly seems human."

Greg laughed, longer than her remark deserved. They could both let it go now. He would not even bother asking her next week if she had replied. He hoped she would tell him if she did, unless she felt a little embarrassed when the response from her alien came back asking for a naked photo so he could see what Earth women looked like under their clothes.

They did not see each other the next five days because it was Greg's turn to staff the university's observatory, which was located outside Vancouver in the Canadian Rockies. He called Amber as soon as he returned, and she invited him over for dinner, which he was happy about because it usually meant spending the night.

Even though he had promised himself, he could not resist asking the question.

"Did you ever respond to that crazy email?"

Amber did not answer "of course not," which was what he was hoping, or tell him with a sheepish grin he was right about it being a prank. Instead, she blushed bright red.

"You responded, didn't you?"

Amber nodded.

"And you heard back?"

She shook her head again.

"What did your space buddy have to say? Did he ask for a photo?"

"I promised to keep it confidential."

"It's too late for that," Greg said. "I already know about the first email."

He was pretty sure she was teasing him and would tell him one of her students had confessed to sending it.

"I could use your help," she said instead, "because I can't do this alone."

He could hear his gulp echo around the room.

"Do what?"

"You have to promise first to keep everything secret and not say a word to anyone without getting my okay first. I mean it, not a word to anyone else unless we first discuss it, and both agree."

"Done."

It felt like one of those childhood promises you readily make because you know you can break it anytime without feeling the least bit guilty.

"I'm serious," she said. "I gave my word."

She lowered her voice to a whisper and raised her eyes, which looked a little bloodshot. If Amber was one of his students, Greg would have thought she'd been up partying all night.

Greg raised his right hand as if he was being sworn in. "I promise, Scout's honor."

"Were you ever a Scout?"

"No, okay, I triple promise."

"Even if you disagree with me," Amber said. "Even if you think I'm making a big mistake and letting my emotions get in the way of science...even if you think it's for the greater good."

"Jesus," Greg said, restraining himself from telling Amber that it was beginning to sound as if she had joined a cult. "You're making me a little worried. Have you met our little visitor from outer space? Does he have antennas instead of ears?"

"I'm serious, I want a real promise, a serious promise."

"As serious as death, how's that."

Amber frowned.

"Yes, absolutely...not a word without your approval. I swear on every star in the sky. What more can you ask of an astronomer?"

"Let me get it," Amber said, going into the bedroom and coming back with her folder.

She handed it to him. Greg opened it and quickly read the follow-up emails; then he read them again, slower this time.

"Trappist-One," he said, rubbing his chin while he looked up and out, one of the new habits he had consciously developed over the past year because he thought it made him look more professorial. "I know that part of the sky pretty well. It was one of the areas we observed over the weekend. At least this guy knows some astronomy."

"It's not he, it's she."

"If you ask my opinion," Greg said, "I still think she's making it all up, leading you on a wild goose chase. If there were planets orbiting Trappist-One, don't you think someone would have discovered them by now?"

"They're not visible...even through the Hubble."

"As I well know, since someone would have seen them by now if they were."

"Which is why no one knows about them."

"Assuming they exist," Greg added with a sigh.

Amber ignored him.

"We need three observatories in different locations around the world to look for interruptions in the starlight, and from that we can determine the orbits. She is right about that, which means she knows her astronomy. I haven't heard of anyone focusing on Trappist-One like that. I looked in the journals and couldn't find any papers on it."

"Probably because no anomalies or planets were found."

"In that case, there still would be a paper with the findings so the rest of us could cross it off the list."

"If they carried the study through to conclusion," Greg said, "and didn't just give up."

Amber stared back at him, shaking her head slightly from side to side.

"If it's never been studied like that," Greg added, "how could she possibly know?"

Amber swallowed hard. "Exactly."

"She undoubtedly read something somewhere and is sending you off on a wild goose chase."

"What if she's telling the truth?" she whispered.

"That she's from another planet?"

"I have a funny feeling about this."

There she goes again, Greg thought, *with this woman's intuition crap.* There were a few biting retorts on the tip of his tongue, but he thought better of it. First, Greg was hoping for a good night in bed; it had been almost a week since the last time. Second, if he played along this time, when it turned out there were no planets and it was all a big hoax, Amber would think twice about challenging his judgment again. He would have the upper hand forever, just like his father did.

"Okay," Greg said, "tell me what you want me to do."

"We need to line up three observatories to search for any interruptions in the light."

"Asteroids can do the same thing."

"Won't be as large and regular as planets."

Greg sighed and nodded at the same time.

"We will need time, three months at a minimum, to learn what we need to know from the interruptions," Amber added.

"Assuming we find any, which I highly doubt."

"Of course."

She was acting like a little girl on Christmas Eve, Greg thought, who was destined to be disappointed by her gift. Greg knew well what that felt like.

"If we are lucky," Amber said, "we may have some answers before then."

"Unlikely."

"Unless the timing is right, which might be why she chose to contact me now."

"Aren't you the optimist."

Amber shrugged. Most women were optimists in Greg's opinion, whether they had reason to or not. Greg would not call himself a pessimist but a realist like most men.

"This is going to take observatory time away from people who could put it to better use," Greg said, "and screw around with their current schedules. You know they are booked six months in advance."

"I've got a few contacts I can ask for a favor, and I'm sure you have more than me."

"You're willing to do all this based on a couple of emails?"

"Just think about it," Amber said, her eyes sparking. "No one has ever done a study like this for Trappist-One. Think what it will mean if we find planets there."

"And if we don't?"

"It's still worth investigating. We can write a paper about it."

Greg wondered how long he could go on saying "I told you so" after Amber found nothing.

"You're committed, right? You're going to help?"

If Greg said no, which was what he wanted to say, he figured he could kiss this relationship goodbye, just as it was beginning to fall into a comfortable and reliable routine. Who knew when—or if—he would get another opportunity like this. Women like Amber had not been beating down his door lately. In fact, it had been two years since Greg had any kind of relationship, and it seemed like forever since he had one lasting this long.

It did not sound like too high a price to pay, and there was always the what-if factor. What if there was a sliver of truth here somewhere? What if they did discover planets orbiting Trapppist-1 and what if...what if?

"Greg?" Amber called out, interrupting his reverie. "You are going to help, right?"

Greg bit down on his cheek. He hated going against his natural instincts.

"Yes, of course, but if we try to put this through a formal budgetary and scheduling process, it could take years. We'll have to piece it together and do it on the cheap during off-hours. We are definitely going to need some favors."

Amber leaned forward and gave Greg a quick kiss.

"I've got a former classmate in New Zealand," she said, "who works at the observatory there. She must get some personal time. I'm sure she'll help."

"I know someone in Chile who owes me a favor," Greg said.

"With the UW observatory," Amber said, "that's three."

They sat for a while in silence, Amber chewing on her lower lip while she imagined the possibilities and Greg thinking that her kiss was a good sign for tonight.

Greg opened the folder again and reread the emails.

"How could she possibly know any of this," Greg asked.

"Exactly," Amber said, letting go of her lower lip.

Truth be told, Greg could feel a little flutter in his own chest, despite the best efforts to tamp it down. It felt as if his heart were more gullible than his head, although history does show that science can be very strange sometimes, both unpredictable and counterintuitive. Discoveries do not always come when you expect them or from where.

What if this really was the first contact Greg had always dreamed about? What if this was the one-in-a-hundred-million winning lottery ticket? What if some naïve space traveler, ignorant of the earth's ways, clicked on the Internet and placed her cursor on the first university and name that popped up?

Still, it didn't make any sense to Greg—why Amber of all people? She was at the bottom of the food chain when it came to the astronomers on the department's web page. She was also the least credentialed with fewer publications than anyone else. Why not pick someone like him, someone whose doctoral thesis was intended to prove they were out there? Someone with more gravitas than Amber had or likely ever would.

"We also need to check for gamma rays and examine the stage of the star," Greg said, snapping himself out of it. "It could be expanding. Either one could eliminate the possibility of life…certainly as we know it."

"Absolutely," Amber replied, "we have to look into that as well."

"What if it's true," Greg murmured without much emotion, even though it was a statement that deserved an exclamation point.

Amber reached her hand out to squeeze his. "I know, I haven't slept well in days."

Later that night, after what Greg thought was the best sex that they had ever had, he lay there wondering how long he could keep it a secret if the planets did turn out to be there and their emailer did turn out to be of the heavenly variety. Some promises cannot be kept—should not be kept—for all kinds of valid and compelling reasons.

The first person he would tell and rub his face in it would be Professor McNamara. He had spent his entire career denying the likelihood of life existing anywhere else but Earth. He had been less than collegial in his treatment of Greg since he joined the department. He was not a big believer in math. Greg once overheard him call his probability analysis "wishful thinking."

After McNamara, the whole world needed to know. As a scientist, Greg owed it to mankind. He had no doubt Amber would eventually come around and agree that he was right. The timetable for something as important as this should not be dictated by some female instructor at a public university.

Once they announced that an extraterrestrial had provided the information about Trappist-1—and produced her for the world—they would be able to write their own ticket to any university in the country. Princeton would be nice or somewhere farther away from the urban lights, like Dartmouth in New Hampshire. As a married couple, now the world's most famous astronomers, they would be able to demand all the research money they could ever want.

Their own observatory would not be beyond the range of possibility.

It could also mean a Nobel Prize.

It would prove to Greg's father that studying the stars was not a complete waste of time and money, as he so often said. Too bad he wasn't alive to see it. His father's two-pack-a-day habit did him in at an early age, and his mother was not far behind. In her case, the doctor said it was all those years of secondhand smoking.

CHAPTER 5
The Meeting

Three months later, Alula, Alex, and Amber met for coffee. She came alone as promised—Amber had not even told Greg about the meeting—and she seemed a lot more excited and nervous than Alula.

"You look and sound exactly like us," Amber whispered, as if she still could not believe it, although she had been assured of that fact and could not be too surprised considering they agreed to meet at Starbucks.

"There is life throughout the universe," Alula explained, "much of it like us, which is why we've been able to settle here. We've been coming to Earth for centuries."

Alula told Amber about Home's small size and its settlement program.

"When we left there were twelve planets in the program."

Amber's chin practically hit the table. "It's hard to fathom," she said, "considering how long the earth has thought it was alone."

Fortunately, they had a table by themselves in the corner, and by keeping their voices low, they could avoid being overheard.

"So, you do believe her?" Alex asked.

"I don't know any other way Alula could have known about the planets orbiting Trappist-One."

"We learned about them in school. It's the only solar system we know of where the planets have no moons. Of course, there are countless solar systems Home has not yet discovered and explored."

Amber nodded as if she already knew that. "We're still working out the orbits and their distance from the sun, but three of them look promising."

"They are."

"That's great," Alex said, picking up his coffee while he looked around.

"Still," Amber added, "I do have a test of sorts."

Alula smiled. "An oral exam?"

"You're not insulted?"

"No, not at all. Ask away."

Amber took a notepad out of her bag and asked Alula a dozen questions about the stars. Questions only a PhD in astronomy or a space traveler would know. Alula got them all right. She answered each one without a moment's hesitation, as if the questions were no more challenging than an elementary school multiplication table.

"Why me?" Amber asked.

"Random," Alex answered. "We were looking for an astronomer at a nearby university and found you on the Internet."

"Serendipity?" Amber whispered to herself as if she could hardly believe her luck.

Alex explained who he was—half Homebody—and how he and Alula met.

Amber smiled. Everyone likes a good falling-in-love story, especially one written in the stars.

"It's so strange," Amber said, "to realize how much your world can change in an instant...for the good. It's always for the bad in the movies."

Alula and Alex both shook their heads in response.

"What are your intentions?" Amber asked them. She was looking at Alula when she said it. She did not look the least bit worried, not like the main character might in one of those old black-and-white science fiction films where the aliens came intent on taking over the planet or destroying it if it didn't shape up.

Those movies always made Alex's father laugh, but they frightened Alex. Now he understood why his father found them so funny, and why he always told Alex not to worry. Alex was young, but old enough to realize there was no way his father could know that for certain. Of course, Alex didn't realize at the time that the earth was already getting visitors and his father knew their intentions.

Alex wished now that he had pressed his father harder as to why he was so sure. Perhaps he would have told Alex if he had.

"You mean like has she come in peace?" Alex responded. "Alula has lived most of her life here, and I was born here."

"No, not those intentions. I meant how do you want to proceed in terms of the press conference. How do we let the world know about the planets and you? How do you want the world to meet you?"

Amber looked at Alula again. They both did.

"You could be standing next to me on the podium when I reveal the information about Trappist One. Or you might want to appear remotely on a screen the first time. Initial reactions can be funny sometimes...even a little scary."

"I think the world will be fine with it," Alula said, "especially when they learn how many of us are already here."

"Perhaps...that could cause some consternation," Amber said.

"I agree," Alex said. "Some people will think Home has been colonizing Earth to take over."

"A rather strange way to try to accomplish that," Alula said, "considering we've been here for hundreds of years, and no one has ever noticed."

"Very true," Amber said, "fear is not always rational."

"That's exactly what I've been saying," Alex chimed in.

"Will the other settlers identify themselves?" Amber asked. "What if some of them or their descendants are in positions of power? Like congressmen or senators."

"It could turn into a witch hunt with neighbors accusing neighbors," Alex said. "It always happens like that in the movies."

"You're both being ridiculous," Alula responded, literally waving away their concerns with her hand. "There is nothing to be concerned about. We don't even know who or where the other settlers are. We have no way of communicating with Home, and Home has no way of communicating with us. Settlers spread out all over the globe, and they're on their own. This becomes our planet...our only planet. We are supposed to blend in and become Earthlings like everyone else.

"Over time the settlers marry other Earthlings and assimilate into the population. There must be almost two hundred thousand descendants by now, and I doubt more than a handful have any idea that one of their ancestors may have come from another solar system. If they've heard old stories passed down over the years, I'm sure they don't believe them."

"Alex does have a point," Amber said. "It's still a risk, which is why I think it would be better if you're not at the news conference. First, give the world a little time to digest the news about you."

While Alex nodded vigorously, Alula covered her mouth as if she wanted to think it over, as if they had not already discussed this very same point ad nauseum over the past three months. On one hand, Alula did not want to lie about anything or make it look as if she had anything to hide. On the other hand, she did not want her message to get lost in the uproar.

"Alula has already agreed to wait a month or two after the Trappist-One announcement before popping out of her jack-in-the-box," Alex said.

"A month is better."

Alex slapped the table, and a few of the nearby patrons looked over for a moment as if they were expecting to witness a breakup. Instead, they saw Alula reach out and rest her hand on top of Alex's.

"But you still need to tell the world about me at the news conference," Alula said.

"That you're the source of the information," Amber added.

"Yes, they learn about the planets and how you found out about them...then a little while after, they get to meet me...us."

Alula looked over at Alex, who nodded and sighed at the same time.

The three of them sat quietly for a while sipping their coffees. It was a lot to take in, sitting there in Starbucks, planning out the best way to change the world.

"No names and no descriptions at the press conference," Alex said, breaking their reverie, "nothing that would give us away."

Amber nodded. "The world gets to know you exist and look exactly like us, but I hold onto the details until you're ready."

"The people on this planet are not known for their open eyes, open hearts, and open minds," Alula added, "so hopefully a month will help with that."

"Or two," Alex said.

"Or two."

"This way when and how we come forward," Alex added, "will be up to us. I think we should begin by making a video to distribute to the major TV networks and follow that up when the time is right with you at a news conference."

Alula bit down on her lower lip, never a good sign.

"I'm willing to go slow, but I won't wait too long, I don't want people to think we have something to hide."

"Can I tell them all about Alcor and the settlement program?" Amber asked.

"Absolutely."

"They'll put enormous pressure on you to say what we look like." Alex looked around to make sure no one was listening. "What will you say?"

"I'll say I don't know. No one has to know we've met."

"You would lie like that?"

"A white lie necessary to keep you two safer...until you're ready to come forward, absolutely."

"Keep in mind," Alex added, looking up as a couple passed by with their coffee, and lowering his voice to a whisper, "once you tell the world how you made your discovery, they'll be more interested in Alula than the planets."

"Which is the whole purpose of this," Alula said before Amber got a chance to reply. "It's time the earth realized it's not the most advanced species in the universe, not by far, and that if we're not more careful, we can wind up extinguishing all life here, the way it's happened on other planets."

"I'll show them the emails," Amber said, "tell them that we've talked over the telephone, and that you assured me you look exactly as we do. There could be no settlement program otherwise."

"And the reason we're coming forward at this time," Alula added. "They have to understand the urgency of the moment."

Amber shook her head.

"But no names, no ages," Alex said, closing his eyes like he was going through a mental checklist, "no descriptions, not even where we've been living. We could have contacted you from just about anywhere."

"That's not a problem."

"We're going to leave Seattle before the press conference," Alex said. "It'll be much safer if we're not anywhere nearby, so we'll need some advance notice when you set a date."

"Of course."

Alula looked over at Alex as if to remind him what she had been saying a lot lately— stop worrying, because there's no stopping it now. She liked to joke that they were traveling into the future faster than the speed of light.

"What's the timetable for the news conference?" Alula asked.

"Four weeks or so to finish verifying the orbits and getting them peer reviewed. Right now, the other astronomers think it was just a hunch...something I stumbled on. You know, women's intuition...one of my colleagues actually called it that." Amber smiled. "The paper doesn't mention you. Your role will come out at the press conference. I'll give you a heads-up when we're ready to go live."

"Great."

They all stood up. Amber gave Alula a big hug. Then she hugged Alex and whispered into his ear.

"You two are going to change this planet forever...for the better."

"I hope so," Alex whispered back. He was not really thinking about the planet. He did not see any of this turning out well for him and Alula. He imagined all the things the authorities would do once they got hold of them. Would they search for all the other settlers and their descendants? Put them into internment camps like they did to the Japanese-Americans during World War II?

Could they identify all the aliens through their DNA? Could they DNA the entire planet?

Would anything they did make a difference in the long run? Alex hoped so, but he had his doubts. Instead of turning their attention to the earth, a lot of people will want to start preparing for a potential invasion by spending enormous amounts of money on weapons in space. A lot of politicians will jump on the defense spending bandwagon because it is always popular with the voters.

Why should anyone worry about a future that they, their children, and their grandchildren would not likely be around to see?

Alex and Alula were lying in bed later that night both wide awake.

"I'm feeling the desire again," Alex said.

"For me?"

She turned to him, moistening her upper lip with her tongue, a habit Alex loved, but Alula didn't have to read minds to know he wasn't referring to that.

"For drugs," he said.

"I know...it's because of me."

"No...well, maybe. You're the reason I've come this far without them. I'm afraid everything is about to change...and not for the better…not the way you're hoping. I'm afraid it'll all come crashing down on top of us."

"Whatever the outcome, nothing will change for us. We will always be together, I promise."

"How can you promise? It's not in your control."

"How it ends is…when it comes to us."

"Right," Alex said, "the old transformation and rebirth, the return to stardust."

Alula snuggled up against him. "As long as we keep our eyes open, our hearts open, and our minds open, we'll be fine."

Alex lay there, his hands behind his head, trying to see through the ceiling to the stars. Unfortunately, all he could see, even with his rediscovered imagination, was the darkness pressing down around him.

"I couldn't do this without you," Alula said.

Alex sighed. She could, but it was still nice to hear, especially since he knew she really meant it. Her heart was always open. She did not lie about things like that. She was more in touch with her feelings than anyone he had ever met, certainly since his father. Alex did not know what else to say, neither did Alula, and they lay there in silence until sleep eventually overtook them.

Nothing happened over the next five weeks. They checked the email account Alex had set up, which he hoped would be impossible to trace, especially once they left the Seattle area and destroyed the laptop. If it was traceable, it would hardly matter at that point.

In his reborn imagination, Alex saw them leaving Seattle—fleeing really—and disappearing into the heartland. At least for a little while since Alula had made it clear she was not willing to remain out of sight for long. She had this fantasy about Amber introducing her at a second news conference a month later with everyone in the room rising up to give her a standing ovation.

Alula still believed the world would welcome her with their eyes, hearts, and minds opening to the significance of a greater living universe and the insignificance of their own petty differences. People everywhere uniting to take immediate action for the sake of the planet and each other—to protect the climate, eliminate war, and end poverty. A world eager to join the universe's family of planets and to take its place among those advanced interstellar civilizations who have left war and inequities behind.

Alula saw a new world bursting with love and reaching out to embrace life everywhere, more than just life but everything in existence, whether they be trees or mountains. It was more of a fantasy, as far as Alex was concerned, than the one he thought Alula was suffering from the first day they met in art class.

"I thought you were a student of Earth's history," Alex said to her one night in bed. "Look how people have reacted over the past two thousand years when they felt threatened and afraid. Look how we've treated people with different-colored skin and different gods. It doesn't seem to me your eyes really are open."

"Open to the light and its possibilities," Alula replied. "If you cannot believe in the universe's endless potential for growth and change, why bother to exist. Why not simply transform? All things eventually will."

"Maybe you need to add two more commandments to the big three," Alex whispered, "wishing and hoping."

"Already there—that's what it means to keep your heart open."

Alula took his hand and squeezed it tight.

She never appeared the least bit concerned or afraid. She always seemed so confident and content. Alula was constantly reminding Alex how exciting it was to be the first ones to take this giant step. Someone needs to be first, she liked to say, and if they did not make it across the finish line, the next brave souls would.

"You have to believe in dreams," Alula said, "if you expect any of them to ever come true."

"Like Tinkerbell."

"Exactly."

At the beginning of the sixth week, the email they had been waiting for arrived.

"All confirmed," Amber wrote. "Peer reviewers are off the wall. No mention yet about the source of my interest in Trappist-One. Everyone thinks it was intuition or dumb luck. I will not reveal the truth until the news conference. Date to be set soon. Shall we meet once more before it?"

Alula was ecstatic. They arranged to meet for coffee the next day.

Amber brought along a copy of her paper.

"The press conference is scheduled for next Monday," she said. "It's being called a major scientific discovery. Right now, everyone is focusing on the three planets. They keep asking me why I picked Trappist-One, and I keep answering because no one had studied it like that before and because of some anomalies...slight irregularities in the light I noticed when I was at the UW observatory. They think I'm brilliant, but I've been asking everyone to hold off their judgment until the news conference. It's going to blow them all away."

Amber looked down at her coffee. She was thinking, *Everyone but Greg.* Greg knew the truth. She saw no reason to bring it up now since in a few days it would hardly matter. She wished now that she had not said anything to Greg. But what choice did she have once she showed him the first email, and it would have been difficult to get the other observatories on board without his help. Difficult, not impossible.

At least Greg had no idea she had been meeting with her alien and what she looked like. She had kept that secret.

"Once I tell them the truth, the entire focus will shift to you," Amber said. "The existence of some habitable planets nearby will seem insignificant because you will be the irreputable proof there is life out there."

"A certainty as opposed to a statistical likelihood," Alula said with a big smile, "which is exactly what this planet needs."

Alex asked them to keep their voices down.

"I agree," Amber whispered, "but you both need to be prepared for the bright lights that are coming."

"And it won't be like we're movie stars," Alex added, turning to Alula. "It'll be more like we're the enemy. People will have a thousand reasons to be afraid and want us locked up."

"Maybe at first, their knee-jerk reaction," Alula said, repeating the same argument Alex had already heard a thousand times, "but give them time to think it over and get to know us; they'll come to their senses. A smile can work magic."

"Maybe on a television sitcom."

"People can change," Amber interjected. "They will adapt to the truth when there's no other choice."

All Alex could do was grunt in response.

"You know," Alula said, looking over at Amber and raising her finger to her lips like she had a great idea, "I think we should keep it even simpler at the press conference. You can tell them about me and how long I've been here and the settlers...but don't mention Alex."

Alula turned to him. "I think we should keep you out of it for the time being."

Alex slapped the table, which got the attention of a few of the patrons. "No way," he whispered after their eyes turned back to their phones and their coffee.

"Think about it for a minute," Alula said. "If they're looking for me...just me...a single woman traveling alone, it'll be easier for us to move around as a couple and stay out of sight."

Amber nodded. "She's got a point."

"You have a long history here in Seattle," Alula reminded him.

"You mean with drugs?"

"You haven't stayed off the grid like I have."

"Meaning you haven't been arrested and fingerprinted."

"That too, but it's only for a little while...thirty days...until we make the video."

Alex took a sip of his coffee while they both stared at him.

He realized that it did make sense. This way they would not be looking for a couple. It was not what Alex wanted, but it was only for a month or two, and he knew how difficult it was to change Alula's mind once it was made up.

Alex nodded.

Amber wanted to run through her plans for the news conference one more time.

"I'm going to hand out copies of the emails and explain that it's your intention to come forward soon after the world has had a month or two to get accustomed to this new reality. I'll tell them we spoke on the telephone twice...once at the beginning and once shortly after the news conference."

"How did you call her?" Alex asked, as if he was a reporter.

"I didn't; she called me."

"They'll check your phone."

"She called my office through the University switchboard. They must get a thousand calls a day."

Alex liked the fact that Amber had ready answers.

"When will you guys be leaving?"

"Tomorrow or the day after," Alex said.

He already felt exhausted and it wasn't even noon. He had not been sleeping much since Amber's email announcing the date of the press conference.

"I'm still concerned it won't be enough," Alula said.

"What won't be enough?"

"The discovery of the planets is easy for you to prove and for the world to accept. It won't be so easy when it comes to me. A few emails are not going to convince many people."

Amber looked as confused as Alex.

"I've been thinking a lot about it the last couple of days," Alula explained. "What if they think you're making up the emails and the calls?"

"Why would I do that?"

"To hype your discovery, to get more attention and press coverage."

"I hardly need to do that. The discovery of three habitable planets relatively nearby in a similar orbit to the earth is more than enough."

"Maybe…maybe not."

"I can't imagine very many people will think like that," Amber added.

"She's right," Alex added. He was afraid Alula was about to change her mind and insist on appearing at the press conference to prove herself by making someone else's burns disappear. "I don't think we should be making any last-minute changes to the plan at this point."

"There will always be doubters," Amber said, "even when it comes to our calculations about the orbits. There will always be some scientist who says we got the numbers wrong or misunderstood them. I agree with Alex, we should stick with the plan."

"I'm not trying to change it," Alula said. "I have something else in mind. It's just a little tweak."

"How come you didn't mention anything about it to me," Alex said, unable to hide his annoyance.

Alula smiled back.

"Because I only came up with it this morning as we were about to walk out the door. What if I can give Amber some proof…some irrefutable proof?"

"Like what?" Amber spoke quickly, her eyebrows practically jumping up to the ceiling.

"What are you going to do, give her an x-ray?" Alex asked. "The fact that your internal organs are reversed doesn't prove anything. I looked it up. It's called situs inversus, and it happens in one out of every ten thousand people."

"The result no doubt of DNA passed down over the centuries from other Home settlers," Alula said.

"They're reversed?" Amber asked.

"Yes, everyone on Home, but that's not what I had in mind."

"Then what?" Alex said.

Alula reached into her pocket and brought out a small white crystal rock about the size of a walnut. "This."

She handed it to Amber, who looked it over.

"One of your diamonds?" Alex asked.

"It's not a diamond," Amber said, looking up at Alula, "but it's not anything I recognize. I'm far from being a geologist. What is it?"

"You won't find it on Earth or anywhere else for that matter because it's made on Home...you can't chip it or scratch it. You can't change its temperature or damage it in any way, not even with a laser."

"They'll say it came down in a meteor," Alex said.

"Look closely, you can see the maker's mark in the center."

Amber stared into it, as did Alex.

"It looks like a series of dashes and dots."

"It's the date of manufacture. They give out samples to schoolkids. I hid a couple of them in my bag before we left."

"I guess I'm not the only one in this relationship who breaks the rules," Alex said with a smile of relief.

Alula smiled back. "Your scientists can examine it by passing light through it, but that's all they can do. Otherwise, it's indestructible."

"Come on," Alex said, "indestructible? How about a nuclear blast?"

"Indestructible."

Amber held it up to the light.

"How do they make it?" Amber asked.

"I have no idea. I know it's a slow process."

"What's it used for?"

"Intergalactic transportation and mining."

Amber put it carefully down on the table, and Alex picked it up to examine it more closely. His father liked to collect rocks. He had one that looked a little like this one that he kept on his dresser alongside his keys and loose change. Maybe a lot of kids took theirs with them as a keepsake when they left to settle. His mother tossed out his father's rock collection after he died. Alex wondered if it might still be there somewhere in the backyard.

"Show them this at the press conference," Alula said. "Let one of your geology professors examine it beforehand. They'll be stumped."

"You may be opening up a can of worms," Amber whispered.

"May?" Alex spoke a lot louder, turning a few heads nearby.

"I don't see how we can avoid it." Alula kept her voice low. "Not if we want the world to be absolutely convinced what you're saying is true."

"Having the ability to make something indestructible might make some people even more afraid," Amber said. "Particularly the generals and politicians. They'll fear a civilization advanced enough to bring you here, but they'll be terrified of one that can also make something indestructible like this."

"Interstellar travel is proof of how advanced Home is and what it can do. Traveling faster than the speed of light took a lot longer to figure out...and it was a lot harder to figure out than this."

Alula took back the piece of quartz from Alex—which is what it looked like—and held it in her palm.

"If Home was intent on taking over the earth or any other planet, it could have done it a thousand years ago when all the earth had were bows and arrows, instead of coming as settlers and being careful not to interfere with Earth's development."

"Until now," Alex said.

"I'm not interfering. I'm just informing the earth that it's not alone...something it will find out soon enough on its own, even if I didn't say anything." Alula looked over at Amber and then back to Alex. "Unfortunately, the earth can't wait however soon that might be. Time is of the essence. People need to understand and trust that goodness and kindness always win out in the course of evolution...given enough time."

Amber nodded as she took the piece of quartz back from Alula.

"Now you have the irrefutable proof you need," Alula said, leaning back in her chair and smiling at Alex. "You okay with it?"

He nodded. What choice did he have at this point?

Amber put the piece of quartz in her bag.

Alex leaned forward and whispered, "I think we should get a bigger head start and leave tomorrow."

"If you want," Alula responded. "I'm okay with that."

Alex pushed his chair back, ready to get up.

"Wait," Amber cleared her throat, "there is one more thing I should tell you. There is another astronomer, a colleague who teaches with me...we've been going out a while...who knows. I showed him the first email before I responded because I thought it was a prank. He saw your response. I needed his help to get access to the other observatories. He doesn't know anything about us meeting, before or today."

"You trust him?" Alex asked.

"He promised not to say a word without first getting my approval."

"Promises are cheap."

"He's honored it so far," Amber said, "and we are in a relationship. Besides, what can he do now? We are going public in four days, and what he knows won't matter. He doesn't know what you look like or your names. He doesn't even know there are two of you. He thinks it's just Alula. I've kept him in the dark as much as I could."

"It's fine," Alula said. "Soon enough everyone will know what he knows."

"And we'll be long gone by then," Alex added, still unsure about where they should be heading other than east. "They won't know what we look like; they'll be looking for a single woman. They'll never find us, not until we're ready."

Alex turned to Amber.

"They won't know what we look like, right?"

"Absolutely," she replied, looking a little insulted as she stood up. "Let me know when you're ready."

"We will," Alula said, standing up and giving Amber a big hug.

Amber and Alex exchanged nods.

With that they all left, Amber turning toward the university, Alula and Alex toward the coffee shop. Alex felt bad quitting without notice—the owner had been very kind and supportive—but he had no choice. He was planning to tell him his aunt in Texas was very ill and he would be there for at least three months.

Alula decided to turn off into the park a couple of blocks before the coffee shop. She wanted to spend some time walking alone and thinking. Alex understood that feeling very well.

CHAPTER 6
BOYFRIENDS CAN NEVER BE TRUSTED

Greg played along with Amber. He did not pepper her with questions or rummage through her desk when she was in the shower on the nights he stayed at her apartment. He did not need a doctorate to know she was holding something back. He was certain Amber was talking regularly with her alien, although she insisted there had been only one call. He also suspected she had been meeting with her. He decided to keep his suspicions to himself until the time was right.

When she left his apartment early in the morning, much earlier than usual, he was sure Amber was meeting with her in advance of the upcoming press conference. He was not worried about something happening to Amber like being kidnapped or turned into a pillar of salt—he chuckled at the thought of that—but he did feel the need to protect her from herself. He also had to do what was right to protect the world. Amber was playing with fire; who knew what would happen once she made her announcement at the press conference.

He needed to know everything she knew in case, as his father used to put it, the shit hit the fan.

What if the government decided to go after Amber and took her into custody? Locked her up until the alien came forward? What if she refused to cooperate? Did she think the authorities would understand and send her back to class with a slap on the wrist and a warning? If they didn't arrest her, they would tap her phone and bug her apartment before the news conference was twenty-four hours old.

Amber was naïve like most women Greg had met and did not fully understand the gravity of the situation. She wasn't thinking enough like a man, a man from a big city like Chicago, a man of the world like Greg. He knew the government's response would not be nearly as rational and scientific as Amber expected. It would be much more than a summer storm, as she described it one night during dinner, where the thunder, lightning, and torrential rain passed quickly followed by calm blue skies.

They would want to interrogate her alien—more than anything they had wanted since the Cold War—and Greg did not have to be a student of history to know the government always gets what it wants, however long it takes, even if it takes force and torture. Amber would eventually have to tell them everything she knew, and if he could make it easier for her by knowing more than she wanted him to know, that was the least he could do.

Wasn't that what a relationship was all about?

When Amber said she had some errands to do in town without being more specific or asking him if he needed anything, as she usually did, he knew there had to be another reason. He wanted to have a description of the alien in his back pocket. It was the best way to protect her. The government was practiced at making life miserable for witnesses who refused to talk. They could claim national security, suspend habeas corpus, and lock Amber away until she cracked. They could get her fired and drag her through the mud. She would not be able to find a minimum wage job after that.

As her boyfriend, Greg could be dragged into it right along with her. Tainted with the same brush. The government would never believe he was not involved and did not know everything Amber did. Greg's own job could be in jeopardy. He had to protect himself, as well as humanity. Skepticism is what every scientist should bring to the table every day, and in Greg's opinion Amber had abandoned hers.

So, he followed Amber after she left his apartment. Greg put on a shirt and jacket she had never seen him wear before, as well as an old baseball cap he found at the bottom of his closet. There were always a lot of people walking around the campus in the morning, making it easy to stay out of sight, and the area of town where she headed was already crowded and easy to blend into. Amber had no reason to suspect anyone might be following her, not before the press conference.

She did not turn around once to look behind her. Amber was a Midwest farmer's girl, the trusting, naive type who, in truth, was the only type of woman Greg could put up with or who could put up with him. Unfortunately, there were not many of her type to be found on campus; all the more reason Greg needed to do something to preserve their relationship and routine.

Amber met her alien in a Starbucks, which did not surprise him since she was addicted to coffee, and what more inconspicuous place was there in Seattle. What did surprise him was that there were two of them—a young man to go along with the young woman. Greg assumed they were both aliens because coming down as a couple in a pod made more sense. The fact that Amber did not trust Greg enough to tell him there were two of them troubled him.

Of course, she had not told him she was meeting with the aliens either, which was even worse.

If you asked Greg, their need to keep secrets was a basic part of their nature and the reason women remained second-class citizens. They needed secrets as much as the flowers need the sun, and every secret needs a string of lies to protect it. Things like that held people back in Greg's opinion.

Greg wondered what else Amber could be lying about. She should have brought him along, certainly to this last meeting. Maybe this was all part of her plan to cut him out and keep all the credit for herself. So much for love and trust. This kind of secret, which goes to the heart of the matter, did not bode well for their relationship going forward.

In the end, Greg realized, he had to do what was right for God and country. To hell with his promise; it was meaningless now. What if Amber was too starstruck to realize the aliens' true intention? What if the information he provided saved the planet from an invasion? He would be hailed for his foresight and bravery. Who was to say the aliens, realizing he was spying on them, might not zap him?

Greg pushed the daydream out of his head to better focus on what was happening.

The alien couple looked to be in their mid-twenties. She looked like every other girl in Starbucks, but she was the prettiest in the room. She could have been the heroine in any one of his favorite movies growing up. She had a white heart-shaped face with eyes so round and bright, they were like a couple of spotlights, especially compared to Amber's face, with its gray pallor and deep-set eyes always hiding behind the shadow of her brow.

The female alien seemed way more otherworldly than her companion. He looked like every other college pothead who walked around campus sure every problem in the world could be fixed with a little grass, and the best way to attend class was stoned.

The girl was clearly the one in charge, the one who was making the tough decisions. He could see it by her posture. She had a strength and confidence about her, as if she had no fear, as if she knew there was no one in the room who could touch her, no one she could not incapacitate with a killer look.

Greg wondered if she had x-ray vision that could incinerate him like the aliens always did in the comics.

He looked up at the board like he was trying to decide what he wanted. He did have to step up and order so as not to appear too conspicuous, but he used the far register and kept his head down and turned in the opposite direction. Once he got his coffee, he retreated to the far corner of the Starbucks and leaned against a column where he was barely visible.

Fortunately, he was wearing his sunglasses and hat.

When the alien talked, all her features—her bright eyes, her full lips, a dark crimson through his sunglasses, her perfect nose, the kind you would find on a Greek statue—all moved in unison as if they were tied to a puppeteer's string.

It would really be something, Greg thought, if it turned out she was not alive, but an android controlled from the mother ship.

The boy did not seem like anyone special. If anything, he was more likely the android sent along to serve and protect her. He was tall with a long, thin face that looked flat and creased from a distance, almost as if it were the result of an origami project. In truth, he looked like most every other male student on campus, unhappy and angry about something he could not explain no matter how hard he tried.

In Greg's experience those two emotions—unhappiness and anger—went hand in hand when it came to boys that age. He refused to consider them young men. A young man was someone like him, who could think with more than his penis and was always looking at the bigger picture.

A girl like that would never be with someone like him unless she had to.

Greg tried squinting, hoping he might be able to read their lips, but it didn't help. It was clear from the boy's expression that he was not happy about something the girl was saying.

Greg's view was partially obstructed by the tables in between, which were filled with people ignoring each other as they focused on their phones and laptops. He thought about moving closer, close enough to take a photo, but it was too risky. What if the boy had some sensor on the side of his head? He did look around from time to time like he was indeed more a bodyguard than a companion.

Greg thought about how rich he would be if he could bring a robot like that to Apple or Microsoft to reverse-engineer.

He made mental notes of their descriptions so he could write them down as soon as he could on the small assignment pad that he always carried with him. He never knew when a great idea would pop into his head. Usually, it was just another addition to his to-do list, but sometimes Greg had an idea—a really good idea—that surprised even him.

In truth, neither of the aliens looked dangerous. If he had seen them walking hand in hand across the campus, he would not have given them a second look, except for her for obvious reasons. Even though she was sitting, he could still tell she was hot. Sometimes the figures on the girls in his undergraduate stars class made it difficult for him to concentrate. The clothes they wore, particularly when it was warm, were inappropriate, like they were trying out for a chorus line rather than attending a lecture.

When they came up with a question after class, it was all he could do to keep his eyes from giving them the anatomical examination they clearly wanted. Why else dress like that? Unfortunately, the faculty rules were clear, get involved with a student, especially one in your class, and you are out—no ifs, ands, or buts. It had to be almost impossible to find another teaching job after that, not at a respectable university.

It was different back in his father's time. Men were freer to follow their natural instincts. Greg shook his head slowly from side to side. There should be a dress code in class. It was unfair to tempt a professor like that.

Greg decided it was too risky to continue leaning against the column and staring in the same direction, even if he tried to look bored and disinterested, so he left Starbucks, crossed the street, and waited for the aliens to leave.

Greg still could not understand why they would have contacted Amber and not him, or someone else on the faculty, someone with more credentials and seniority. Greg still had his doubts—until now—thinking that perhaps Amber had stumbled on the idea that there might be planets orbiting Trappist-1 and created the alien story to get more attention and trick him into helping her. She could never have verified any of it without his assistance.

Women can be very devious that way, particularly a female instructor hoping to become a professor.

Greg had always imagined that the first contact would be very dramatic, like a large spaceship hovering over the White House or a broadcast from outer space. If they wanted to start with an astronomer, why not someone whose thesis was devoted to their very existence? Picking someone like Amber, who focused more on black holes, made no sense. Alien life was superfluous to her research.

Still, it was exciting to be part of the first contact. Amber's connection was his as well since they were practically living together. Indeed, he was the second person on the planet to know of the aliens' existence. Greg was sure the reporters would want to spend time interviewing him as well—no doubt putting a photo of the two of them on the covers of *Time* and *People* magazines—and he would talk about everything as if it was a joint effort from the very beginning, which for all practical purposes it was.

What if he walked back into Starbucks, right up to Amber, and pretended it was a big coincidence? He could tell her he had come into town to buy some toiletries at Walgreens and decided to stop in for a cappuccino. He would ask her to introduce him to her friends. Perhaps she would say they were students in her class who she happened to bump into, although she would know instantly from the look on his face that he did not believe it.

"Welcome to Earth," Greg would whisper as he sat down, officially and forever becoming an integral part of the first contact.

Greg thought it over for a few minutes, but he knew Amber would never buy it. She would know he followed her and break it off like all the other women who thought him overly possessive, narcissistic, and chauvinistic, traits he possessed in small quantities like every other male on the planet, the only difference being he didn't pretend otherwise.

Greg had to be careful because he wanted the relationship to continue for a while, at least until his place in history was secure, putting him in line for his share of the grant money and awards. Perhaps the head of the astronomy department at a big university. Amber was not the type to hoard all the credit for herself. How could she? All she did was respond to an email with Greg's encouragement and assistance.

They stayed talking in Starbucks a long time. Fortunately, Greg did not have a class until the afternoon. He intended to follow the aliens after they left Starbucks to find out where they lived and the names they used. With that kind of information, the authorities should have no trouble finding a photo of them on some street camera and catching them.

Greg decided he would wait for the right moment before providing the information, keeping it in his back pocket for now. He would make sure the aliens were treated right—he would be very vocal about that—which should endear them to him, her especially. That would give him his own press platform so he wouldn't have to piggyback on Amber. They would both be stars, either one of them able to appear on television or call a press conference whenever they wanted.

If Greg played it right, Amber would never have to know he was the one who helped the government catch them. He would make the authorities promise to keep the source of the information secret. It should not be hard to convince them since all governments prefer to take sole credit for their successes and blame everyone else for their failures.

Greg pictured himself as the liaison between the government and the aliens, doing the hard work interacting with the press while Amber went around speaking to women's clubs and high school students interested in astronomy.

The more Greg thought about it, the more convinced he was that the right thing to do was to hold onto whatever information he learned and use it as leverage when the time was ripe. When he could ride in like the cavalry to save the day, particularly if it turned out, as he expected, that Amber found herself in trouble. She was way too trusting for her own good.

As a scientist—and an Earthling—you should never assume the aliens' intentions are one hundred percent honorable.

Amber's meeting with them lasted over an hour, and the only one who looked unhappy when they left was the guy. In the light of day, he could have passed for one of those drug types who stand on the corner in certain parts of town with their hand out, swearing they need money for food. A good disguise as far as Greg was concerned, suggesting that the aliens had been well prepared for their visit.

Greg was not one hundred percent sure he bought the story about thousands of aliens coming here to settle over the last two hundred years—not hook, line, and sinker the way Amber had. It sounded too cute to him, a clever way to lull everyone to sleep.

Amber headed back to the campus while the boy and girl, holding hands to look like ordinary young lovers, walked in the opposite direction. Only the boy looked behind him after they left. It was easy for Greg to stay out of sight on the other side of the street. After a while he must have been satisfied that they were not being followed because he stopped checking.

Greg chuckled to himself as he followed them. Did the guy really expect to see a spook in an overcoat wearing a fedora with a soft brim and indented crown like they did in the old movies?

After six blocks they split up, the girl turning in to the park and the boy walking straight ahead. For some reason Greg decided to follow the boy. The girl slowed her pace as she entered the park, like she was taking a stroll to think something over—perhaps to get instructions from the mother ship—while the boy walked on with a purpose, as if he had something important to do.

The boy walked another four blocks before entering a coffee shop on Eighth Street. One of those small, independent places that dot the poorer neighborhoods in Seattle where Starbucks would never consider opening. Greg never found their coffee as good, or at least not as consistent. Amber preferred them to the bigger chains.

It was part of her politics, small better than big, local better than national. Always trying to be politically correct. She was too damn liberal, but Greg had never complained about it. He knew better. That kind of change took time, and he had to be subtle about it. Most people become more conservative as they get older and assume a more established position in society. He was sure Amber would move in that direction in time as she rose to assistant professor.

Certainly after they got married and she came to accept more and more of her husband's views. It was inevitable. He witnessed the same thing growing up, even if it was more of a silent nod than vocal support.

Greg found it hard to believe the guy needed another coffee so soon after Starbucks. Perhaps that was how he stayed thin and why he seemed so jumpy. Maybe it was not drugs, but too much caffeine. He was in there a while, and Greg thought about going in to buy some coffee but thought better of it. It was too risky. What if he had noticed him in Starbucks? What if he was a robot with face recognition software? What if he had some advanced weapon that could zap his memory in an instant like *Men in Black*?

He waited patiently, not easy for Greg, but he was rewarded when the girl came back and went into the coffee shop. Five minutes later they both walked out, neither of them carrying coffee, and went into the next building. There were apartments there, Greg could see that, and he did not have to be a private detective to realize it was where they lived.

Greg figured the guy probably worked at the coffee shop and went in to give his notice because they planned on fleeing Seattle well in advance of the press conference.

Greg gave them ten minutes before walking up to the building and opening the door. Buildings in neighborhoods like this did not have buzzers or locks on their entrance doors, at least not ones that worked. There were three mailboxes inside with their names handwritten on white tape. He knew instantly which one was theirs. Alex Rigel, the seventh brightest star in the night sky.

He wrote it down, as well as the other two names just in case, and walked back to the campus. It was a very successful tailing, if that was the proper way to describe it. Greg was proud of himself. This was not the type of bold action expected from an astronomy professor. He thought it was heroic.

Greg wondered if one day, ten or twenty years in the future, they would make a movie about the first alien contact and put in a scene based on what happened today. He pictured the hot young star of the moment, handsome and popular with the ladies, playing him and saving the day by giving the authorities the information they needed to protect the Amber character and save the planet.

Not that Greg wanted there to be trouble or expected the aliens to have evil intentions—not purely evil intentions—but there were bound to be some problems and misunderstandings. He had to believe that in helping the authorities identify the aliens, he would save the earth a lot of anxiety and aggravation, and in the end earn the aliens' respect and gratitude by encouraging them to come forward and be more transparent.

Three nights later as they lay in bed—this time in Amber's apartment—Greg asked her if she was ready for tomorrow's press conference.

"About as ready as I'll ever be."

"This is going to be a big deal, you know that. You're going to join Galileo and Sagan as astronomers the world will always remember."

He left himself out of this pillow talk, but he fully expected to be standing there beside her with his name just as renowned, like Masters and Johnson or Pierre and Marie Curie. He hoped Amber would have no objection to one day taking his name. He was a big believer in tradition when it came to things like that.

"I doubt it," Amber said, sounding more frightened than excited about the prospect of fame and fortune.

"Granted, finding a few habitable planets forty light-years away might not do it, but meeting with one of its inhabitants, well, that's historic. Up there I'd say with Columbus discovering America."

"She's not from the Trappist-One system."

"I know...Alcor...I was speaking figuratively."

How did Amber not get that Greg wondered or understood the full significance of what was about to happen?

"Alcor is much farther away."

Greg had to bite his tongue to keep from saying something snarky. He did not want to rock the boat until his key role in this little drama was securely established.

"Traveling that far," Greg said instead, "requires an incredible leap in terms of physics."

"Based on what we know now."

"They have to be a million years ahead of us scientifically... assuming it's even possible to travel faster than the speed of light."

"She's proof of that," Amber said. "How else could she be here?"

"I suppose they could have figured out a way to open up some kind of dimensional doorway in the vacuum of space."

"Which is possible according to quantum physics."

"Theoretically."

"It's so Star Trekkian," Amber said.

Even Amber sounded excited by the prospect.

Greg nodded. Amber was a big fan of that show, Greg not so much. He thought it was too much like a soap opera, although sometimes science fiction did get some things right. Some science fiction writers were a little like visionaries. Science fiction writing would have been Greg's second choice after astronomy, albeit a distant second. Not much to discover sitting in a chair in front of a typewriter.

"Did your alien ever hint about how they managed to travel so far?"

Greg was hoping the alien might have said something to Amber about space travel, something she might not have realized the importance of, which he could announce to the scientific community.

"No."

"To travel faster than the speed of light using quantum physics," Greg explained, "would require a wormhole or some other anomaly, some doorway we can't even fathom."

"I know."

"It never came up?"

Amber shook her head slowly from side to side.

"I told you we only spoke briefly over the phone."

"That's a shame," Greg said, but Amber was only half listening. He could tell her mind was somewhere else. Greg hated it when she got like that. All the women he had ever been with would tune him out from time to time. His mother was the same way with his father.

"How many times did you speak on the phone again?"

"Exactly what I told you...twice...once early on after the first emails and then again last week to discuss the press conference."

"Did she ever talk about what life was like on her planet?"

He needed more information, as much as Amber had, whether it was to bring to the authorities or include in his speech one day when he stood beside her accepting the Nobel Prize.

"No."

"What else did you talk about on that first call besides Trappist-One?"

"Not much. How the world might react. She denied it, but I think she was a little nervous about it...understandably."

"Not nearly as nervous as the rest of the world will be."

They lay quietly for a while. Greg could tell Amber was still awake. Her breathing always slowed down when she was drifting off to sleep. She always fell asleep first. Sleep did not come easily to Greg. It had not for as long as he could remember. Even as a child he remembered lying in bed listening to his father lecture his mother about something that happened or shouldn't have happened.

These days the quiet disturbed him just as much. He always took whatever was on his mind to bed with him—the slights and disappointments, the words he wished he could take back, the ones he wished he had said, the looks he was not supposed to see. The world could be very unfair sometimes.

Greg decided it was time to be bold and step up. With the press conference the next morning, Amber needed to know he wasn't as naïve and accepting as she might believe and that, as his father used to say, she had a lot to learn.

"You met with her the other day, didn't you?" Greg said.

"*What?*"

He could feel Amber's body tighten.

"You went to see her last week after the press conference was scheduled."

"What makes you think that?"

"You left early in the morning, way before class...said you had errands, but you didn't ask me if I needed anything. I figured it out, you were going to meet her."

"You should have been a detective," Amber said.

She did not sound amused, but it could not be helped. Did she really think he was an idiot? It was getting too late for subtleties. It was time to put up or shut up, another one of his father's favorite expressions.

"Isn't that what astronomers are, detectives?"

Amber sat up in bed and looked over at him, her face empty of expression—not the kind of look a man expected from his woman in bed—before she turned away to stare out the window. He might have told her the whole truth if the press conference was not the next day.

"You're not going to tell anyone, are you? You promised."

"Of course not," he responded when what he was really thinking was *It depends.*

Amber shook her head up and down without looking away from the window.

"Because I'm not going to mention anything about it tomorrow. I've agreed to keep her description secret until she's ready to come forward."

"I get it, I won't say a word," Greg said, thinking to himself, *At least not yet.* "What have you decided to say?"

"What do you mean?"

"I'm sure you've worked out a script."

"I'm going to tell the world the truth. That's what she wants."

"That you got the information about Trappist-One from an alien from another galaxy?"

"Yes, I'm going to show them the emails and point out the star where her planet orbits."

"But it's not the whole truth," Greg said with all the warmth of the bad-guy interrogator questioning a reluctant witness. "You've met her; you know what she looks like."

"No, that will come soon enough, sixty to ninety days, I already told you that. But I'll tell them how long she's been here and about the settlement program."

Greg knew he was making Amber a little uncomfortable, but it could not be helped, not if he was going to protect her from herself. This was not the way he imagined—or believed—an advanced civilization should present itself. They should present themselves right away, in person, eager to take questions. It almost seemed as if the alien did have something to hide.

"But you are going to tell them that she looks exactly like us?"

"Yes."

"And how will you say you know that?"

"Because she told me so, and it wouldn't make sense otherwise considering they've been sending settlers here for hundreds of years."

"Assuming that's true."

Amber looked over at Greg. Some expression had returned to her face, but it wasn't loving or even pleasant. She clearly did not like his tone.

"Don't get upset," Greg said. "I'm just playing the devil's advocate. Some reporter is going to ask you a question like that."

"And my answer will be 'Why would she lie? What could she possibly gain by it?' She is going to come forward and plans to send out a video soon and appear at a news conference in the next thirty to sixty days. She wants to give the world a chance to digest all this before meeting her."

"What about her honorable intentions? What if some reporter asks you how you can be so sure based on the emails and a couple of calls?" Greg tried not to sound too confrontational this time. "How will you answer that question?"

Amber got out of bed before responding and sat down on the chair by the window. There was no mistaking her annoyance at this game of twenty questions the night before her big press conference. Greg had seen the same look plenty of times over the last ten years. It was not long after it that the girl would announce she was breaking it off. It never surprised him when they did, and it never upset him all that much because he realized they were not his type, and it would never have worked out anyway.

His expectations were always too high, as it should be for a man in his position.

Greg couldn't help wondering sometimes if marriage was the right thing for him. He had always been pretty content keeping his own company. An astronomer is never alone; he always has the stars. They are forever loyal, always quiet and accepting, eagerly waiting every night for his return, satisfied with whatever attention he can spare.

"If their intentions were anything other than honorable," Amber said, "it would have been clear by now. They are so far ahead of us, they could have done anything they wanted. Why keep up this charade if their intentions were otherwise?"

"I'm sure you're right... and Lord knows I trust your judgment... but what if you're wrong? What if they have been coming here all these years to build up a critical mass to take over? What if they have been migrating from their planet, not because it's too small, but because it's dying? What if their sun is burning out? What if your sweet and gentle alien hasn't been told the truth and doesn't even know that her stepping forward is the next step in the process?"

"What process?"

"Taking over the earth."

"You're being ridiculous."

Amber's face was turning red.

"Don't get upset," Greg said. "It's called the scientific method, you know that. You have to look at every possibility...weigh every potential outcome."

Amber didn't respond.

"A lot of people won't believe she's harmless until they get to meet her and hear for themselves."

She looked away from him and back out the window.

"Some people won't believe she exists until you produce her. They'll think you're making her up to bring more attention to your discovery. Finding other planets in habitable orbits is no real surprise, but a living, breathing alien already here on Earth...well, that will make you the belle of the ball."

Amber jumped up and began pacing back and forth in front of the bed. "You think I'm making her up?"

If this was not her apartment, Greg was sure she'd be getting dressed and heading out the door.

"Of course not, that's not what I'm saying. I'm saying there are going to be some people...a handful...who might think otherwise. The kind who can be loud and vocal. I'm just trying to help you prepare for tomorrow...trying to imagine some of the questions, or worse, the accusations you might face. It's going to be an earth-shattering announcement, and you have to expect the unexpected."

Greg smiled at Amber, who didn't smile back.

"Humor me, how will you respond to an accusation like that?"

Amber sat back down and took a breath. "I'll say that I don't need to hype a discovery like this. Just look at the peer reviews. The existence of the planets alone this close to Earth is frontpage news."

Greg saw Amber glance over at his clothes. He wasn't going to let her ask him to leave this close to the big announcement. He needed history to tie him tightly to the big reveal.

"Listen, Amber, I'm sorry if I'm coming on a little too strong. You know me, I worry, and I'm compelled to challenge every assumption. It's the way I was trained."

Amber nodded, a bit reluctantly in his opinion.

"There's going to be a lot of pressure on you tomorrow to provide more information...some real proof. You need to be prepared for the questions and the doubters."

Amber rubbed her eyes while she took a deep breath. When she opened her eyes, she whispered, "I do have some proof...some real proof."

"Really?"

"Yes."

"That's great. What is it?"

Amber told him about the gem—which is what she had started calling it—that she had left with one of the geology professors to examine. He was going to bring it to the press conference.

"It's not really a gem; it's more like a cross between a diamond and a piece of quartz. But it's like nothing we've ever seen before, and it's manmade."

Greg remembered the three of them looking at something when they were in Starbucks, but he couldn't make out what it was.

"Who did you show it to?"

"Professor Allan."

"I know him. Good man."

Greg had not said more than two words to him in three years. Allan was a little older than Greg was, but already a full professor, and very popular with the coeds. Not surprising, considering he was tall, built like a block of granite, and looked a little like Superman in his Clark Kent disguise.

"Is he married?"

"I don't think so."

"Maybe I'm thinking of Professor Roberts," Greg said. "What did the rocks man have to say?"

"That he'd never seen anything like it. He couldn't scratch it with anything, not even with a diamond-tipped drill. He's going to do some more tests before tomorrow's news conference."

Greg let out a breath he did not realize he was holding. He did not like the way this was shaping up. Why did she tell Professor Allan about it, but not him? He pictured Professor Rocks coming to Amber's rescue when the questioning became too intense.

"What's the plan?" Greg asked.

"Use it at the end…if it becomes necessary."

"Which it will."

"Professor Allan will come up and talk about his findings."

"How are you going to say you got it, if you're not going to tell them you met with her?"

"I'm going to say I found it in an envelope by my office door."

He doubted an experienced FBI agent would believe that.

"If it is indestructible, the government will confiscate it."

"I expect so. She doesn't care."

"They'll try to reverse-engineer it. It could throw the balance of power out of whack. Start another arms race."

"She said there is no way we could duplicate it because it's way beyond our present science."

"The thought of something indestructible like that," Greg added, speaking slowly and in a deeper voice to show just how serious he thought this new development was, "will cause panic in every government on the planet. The generals will go ballistic."

"She says it's not a weapon and has never been used as a weapon; it's for mining and intergalactic travel."

"What she says isn't going to cut it."

Amber shrugged. "At this point it can't be helped."

"They'll search every block in Seattle," Greg said. "They'll go door to door within a mile of the campus."

"She's already gone. The email account deleted. She'll be hard to find."

"Hard is not the same thing as impossible."

"She realizes that, but it's only for a month or two. She'll be coming forward long before they can find her."

"How will you contact her?"

"I can't, she'll contact me."

"This isn't going to be easy," Greg said, envisioning Amber being dragged away in the middle of the night, locked up for national security reasons and used as bait to draw the alien out into the open. They would cite the danger to national security of having some technically advanced alien running around the country with an indestructible projectile. The country could not afford to let the Russians get her first.

"It'll turn out all right in the end," Amber said. "It's the price you pay sometimes for progress."

Spoken like a truly naïve, unworldly young woman, Greg thought, but instead of saying what he was thinking, he just nodded as if he agreed. Clearly, Amber did not grow up watching the old science fiction movies like he did. *The Day the Earth Stood Still* was about an alien who was sent to Earth with supposedly good intentions to threaten us with extinction if we did not shape up. We had to behave according to their rules or be incinerated.

Good intentions do not always mean good outcomes. His father used to say that all the time. Greg did not realize back then just how right he was.

What did a farm girl know about the real world, especially one who went directly from the farm to outer space?

He had to protect her from herself, and more importantly, Greg owed a duty to the country and the world. He would have to give serious consideration to making an anonymous call to the FBI—perhaps a day or two after the press conference, depending on how it went—with a detailed description of the two aliens or the alien and her android bodyguard.

Greg wondered whether the alien was the same as an Earth girl in every way. She looked normal enough sitting there in Starbucks and walking down the street, harmless as well, but you should never judge a book by its cover. If there was a truer idiom, he did not know what it was.

Thank God he followed Amber the other day; otherwise, he would have nothing to offer.

The press conference the next morning went pretty much the way Greg thought it would. First came the scientific proof about the planets orbiting around Trappist-1, three of them the approximate size of the earth with orbits that would support water and an atmosphere. It had been confirmed by using three major observatories, and every astronomer who worked on it agreed—euphorically—there it was very likely there would be some form of life on at least one of them.

There was no reason why we should be the only planet where that spark necessary for life occurred.

"If we can detect three planets in habitable orbits forty light-years away," Amber said, "imagine the number of planets in similar orbits around the countless other stars we haven't yet studied or are too far away for us to observe."

That would have been more than enough to make the front page of every newspaper around the world and spread across the Internet like a super-virus. But there was more to come, the real zinger.

Somebody asked, perhaps someone planted by Amber, how she became interested in Trappist-1 in the first place.

Amber glanced over at Greg before she responded.

"It wasn't luck or any insight on my part," she announced, covering her mouth for a moment before the big reveal, as if she were stifling a yawn. "I was directed there by someone who already knew about the planets."

"Who already knew? Who was that?"

It was as if every reporter in the room called out in one voice.

"An alien who came here from another planet…not from any of the ones orbiting Trappist-One."

There was an eerie silence, a moment that seemed to stretch out a lot longer than it did. Greg could practically see everyone in the room replaying the words in their heads to make sure they had heard them correctly.

The quiet pause was followed by pandemonium. It took ten minutes before the room quieted down enough for Amber to be heard. She explained how she had first been contacted. She passed out copies of the emails and projected them on the screen behind her, the same screen she had just used to show the location of the planets orbiting Trappist-1.

In response to the questions being screamed out by every reporter, Amber confirmed she did not know the alien's identity, nor what she looked like, although the alien had assured her that she was a female and looked exactly like one of us. Amber projected a picture of the Big Dipper onto the screen and pointed to the spot where she came from, a small planet orbiting a star we called Alcor.

Amber confirmed she had no idea where the alien was currently or where she was when she made the first contact.

Greg sighed. He had always hoped to be the one to say those words to the world—*the first contact.*

"Is this some kind of scam," one reporter called out. "A way to hype your discovery and make you famous?"

He hoped Amber caught a glimpse of him nodding ever so slightly.

"You have no real proof of any of this," someone else called out. "Anyone can make up an email."

Murmurs and nods of agreement spread throughout the room.

"The odds I would have stumbled onto the planets orbiting Trappist-One on my own are astronomical. There are countless stars visible to our telescopes that I could have picked. Her communication was the only reason I chose Trappist-One. It took three observatories located in different parts of the world to confirm what she already knew…and shouldn't have."

The buzz in the room made it clear Amber's answer did not satisfy anyone. Reporters require facts and proof as much as scientists do, if not more.

"You people have been desperate to find extraterrestrial life for ages," someone called out.

"You people" being astronomers, meaning scientists with inferiority complexes.

"I'm sure you expect this charade to boost your funding," someone else called out.

The words and questions kept bubbling up like lava foreshadowing the big eruption.

"I do have proof," Amber finally interrupted, raising her voice so she could be heard.

Her words sucked the air out of the room, rendering it almost as silent as a graveyard, the only sound now being the turning of heads expecting someone in a green costume with antennae and webbed feet to come walking through the door.

"She sent me this," Amber said, reaching into her pocket and pulling out the gem.

The silence was replaced with laughter.

"A piece of quartz?" a chorus of reporters sang out.

"It's not a piece of quartz and it's not something that can be found on Earth…it's a manmade substance."

"You brought a piece of plastic as proof?"

This came from one of the reporters front and center, as if he had been delegated to speak on behalf of the others.

"No," she told the skeptical assembly of disbelievers, "it's not a piece of plastic. It is unlike anything we have ever seen before…and it's completely indestructible."

At this point she brought up one of the University of Washington's most prestigious geologists, Professor Allan, to confirm it. He explained how the Geology Department went about examining the object, which he called a crystalline-type substance that was clearly manmade.

"How do you know that?" someone called out.

"There is a printed code visible at the center of it," he explained, putting up an enlarged projection of the gem on the screen. He pointed to the series of dots and dashes visible in the center. "I would assume it's a source code for the manufacturer to trace the date of production in the event of a failure."

"A failure at what?"

"I understand it's used for space travel."

"They travel in transparent ships?"

"I don't know," Professor Allan answered. "Perhaps they have a way of colorizing it or making an opaque version."

He went on to explain how it was unlike anything anyone in the Geology Department had ever seen in nature or anywhere else for that matter.

"For one thing it does appear to be indestructible, which I suppose is why it's used in space travel."

He held it up for everyone to see.

"Pretty ordinary-looking, but nothing we tried could scratch it, not a diamond-tipped drill or a laser…and it didn't react at all to extreme heat or cold. What I find even more amazing is that light passes straight through it. Glass bends light somewhat—even air does. It's imperceptible to most of us. But this medium, whatever it is, does not affect light in the slightest…it doesn't bend it even a fraction of a degree, so it doesn't slow it down."

The room grew quiet again.

Professor Allan explained there was no way at this point to determine its composition or the structure of the atoms composing it.

"We don't have the capability of making anything like this. It's way beyond our science."

He suspected it would take years, maybe decades, to make any progress understanding it or reverse-engineering it, assuming that was even possible.

"I am sure it must contain hydrogen and helium atoms since those two elements are found in all the stars."

Professor Allan handed the gem back to Amber, and in the ensuing pandemonium, she and Greg managed to sneak out the side door.

The press conference was the lead story on every news program. The next morning it was on the front page of the *Seattle Times*, along with just about every newspaper around the world. Before Amber and Greg had a chance to finish their morning coffee, the authorities came knocking on her door to seize the gem pursuant to a warrant authorizing them to take it to the Army's Argonne National Laboratory for analysis. The FBI agents who came to collect it also seized Amber's computer so they could trace the emails. They had already executed a search warrant on her office.

The agents questioned Amber about the alien, in Greg's presence, as he had spent another night in Amber's apartment listening to her recount the press conference, as if he had not been there and heard every word. She confirmed with the agents that she had spoken briefly with the alien over the telephone on two occasions, once shortly after the initial contact and the other about a week before the news conference, which is when she told her about the gem. Amber said she had no idea who delivered it to her office.

"It appeared in front of my office door in a plain manila envelope addressed to me."

"I need to see the envelope," the lead agent demanded. It was not a request as much as an order.

Unfortunately, Amber told him, she had not thought to keep it.

"Handwritten address?" the agent barked out.

Amber nodded.

"Sealed?"

She shook her head again.

"When did you throw it out?"

"When I got it, after I opened it."

"Where?"

"In my office trash. It has to be long gone by now."

The other agent shook his head from side to side while he wrote it all down.

Amber knew there were no cameras in the hallway where their offices were located. While the University of Washington blanketed the campus with cameras, including all the public areas, the faculty offices were off-limits for reasons of privacy.

After the agents left, Amber assured Greg her alien was long gone from the Seattle area by now, as if she thought he would be relieved. He smiled and pretended that he was.

"Without a picture, a description, or a name," Amber said, "I don't see how they can possibly find them."

"*Them*?" Greg stepped back and threw his hands up like he was completely surprised.

He had been waiting for Amber to slip up. She had been very careful to this point to refer to the alien as "she." Greg knew it was only a matter of time before she let her guard down.

Amber covered her mouth for a moment before lowering her hand.

"She has a boyfriend whose father was a settler."

Greg watched her bite down on the corner of her lip, a habit he detested. His mother used to bite the inside of her cheek whenever his father caught her in a lie. If they were already married, he would raise his voice like his father and tell Amber it was time to tell him the truth, the whole truth, and nothing but the truth.

When a woman marries, she has to tell her husband everything. Rule number one according to his father. Why should it be any different if a woman sleeps with you? It should be a hard and fast relationship rule.

"You didn't have to keep it from me," Greg said, trying to add disappointment to his look of surprise. "We are in this together. You know you can trust me."

"I know…it's just that I made a promise. This way they will be looking for one person, instead of two."

"That won't change. I'm not going to tell anyone." He paused for a moment to let his words sink in before adding, "Is there anything else I should know?"

He waited, hoping Amber would do the right thing and tell the truth to the man she supposedly loved about her meetings with the aliens and what they had discussed. It would be hard for him to forgive—or forget—if she did not.

She took her time thinking it over.

"Well?" he said, pressing her as if he were the FBI agent asking the question.

"I can't think of anything else."

Greg turned around to hide his displeasure. Why would he want a woman who kept secrets from him, especially one as important as this? He couldn't imagine many who would.

Greg looked down at the business card the agent had handed to him before leaving. He had left one for Amber also, and she had told him she would call if she remembered anything else or heard from the alien again. Fat chance of that.

Greg had no doubt any calls or emails Amber received from now on would be closely monitored. His as well.

Greg replayed the agents' visit in his head. "This is a matter of national security, Ms. Garrigan, and if you don't cooperate, the consequences…well, I'm sure I don't have to spell them out for you."

Amber assured him she intended to fully cooperate. She sounded very convincing; even Greg might have believed her if he had not just heard her lie to the FBI when the agent pressed her to give him her best guess as to what the alien looked like.

"Based on her voice…did she sound thin, fat, tall, short?"

"I have no idea," Amber replied.

"Was her voice husky or soft? Did she sound young or old? Did she have any accent?"

"No accent, youngish, sweet sounding, but she did assure me she was a very ordinary-looking woman. No different than anyone you might pass on the street."

Greg had to look away and suck in his lips so as not to call Amber out on that lie. The alien was as far from ordinary as Alcor was from the earth. She was as pretty—if not prettier—than any of the models he saw in the advertising supplements that fell from the newspaper every Sunday.

Amber could have given them a complete description and told them to look for two people, not one, but Amber chose to lie and break the law. Greg remained silent, but in his opinion that was not quite the same thing. He had no choice if he was to remain on the inside, where he could learn things the FBI could not. He would be much more helpful this way in the long run.

Greg really needed a drink after the agents left.

Amber had no idea what she was getting herself into. She might be super-intelligent when it came to galactic nuclei and black holes, but she did not have much common sense. If she did, she would realize that lying to the FBI was a serious crime, and once the aliens were caught—which was inevitable—the truth would come out about her meeting with them.

The government would not be forgiving. It never was.

Not telling him the whole truth was also a crime in Greg's opinion—a crime against love.

The FBI agents did ask Greg a few questions as well, though not very many. He confirmed Amber had shown him the emails and he had helped her with the observatories. Fortunately, they did not ask him the same kind of questions they asked Amber, not after he confirmed he had no contact with the alien—which was true—so technically he did not have to lie. Tailing someone and watching from a distance was not nearly the same as having contact.

"You do know," he whispered to Amber that night, "lying to the FBI is a crime."

Amber did not respond. She just lay there, hands behind her head, looking up at the ceiling.

"You know what she looks like...and you didn't tell them about the guy."

"I promised."

"You could go to jail. You could lose your job...everything."

"It's the price you have to pay sometimes to do the right thing...to advance knowledge and help save the world."

Greg almost choked after Amber said the last part—saving the world. She sounded like a little girl who believed in fairy tales.

Amber sat up and looked over at him. "You're still on board, right? You're not going to say anything? You gave me your word."

Greg nodded.

"Yes?" Amber asked again, not satisfied with a gesture.

"Of course, yes."

Amber lay back down and looked up again at the ceiling. What did Greg know anyway? Not much. That there were two of them instead of one. Big deal. He had no idea what they looked like, but he could make things a lot more difficult for her, as well as Alex and Alula, if he told the FBI she had met with them a few days before the press conference.

She wondered what Greg would say if she told him that it was not the first time.

She glanced over at Greg, who also looked lost in thought.

Amber did not know Greg long enough or well enough to be sure what kind of stuff he was really made of. Some things he said from time to time did raise doubts in her mind. She knew he was a bit of a chauvinist, but most of the men she met in the science world tended to be the same way. Could she depend on him if things got dicey? His remarks lately, as well as the way he looked at her, like she was one of his denser students, or a child, had made her a little uneasy.

Amber had been thinking for a couple of weeks now that it might be time to cool things down for a while, maybe permanently.

Amber was not sure what love felt like, but she figured it had to be more than this. Comfort and convenience, someone to eat with and to attend faculty functions with hardly rose to the level of desire she always imagined and saw in the movies. This seemed more like a new routine than a burning passion, like another class added to her schedule.

Amber decided not to take any chances by breaking it off now. This was not the time to rock the boat, not with Greg knowing what he did. She would wait until after the video came out. She might even change her mind by then. Maybe Greg would come through in the end. It would be nice having someone to share all this with and to bounce ideas off, someone who loved the stars as much as she did and believed in the great potential of extraterrestrial contact.

Greg looked over at Amber. Her breathing was beginning to slow down. She was falling asleep. He was tired as well, but he could never fall asleep until she did. He did like Amber. He never had a relationship develop such a quick intimacy before or last this long, almost six months. He figured relationships had to get easier once you hit your thirties and lowered your expectations.

He could not say for sure if it was love because he did not read fiction or watch chick flicks. Greg did not have much prior experience to help him out. His parents never looked at each other the way couples did in the movies, and they were never affectionate, not even with him. They came from the same social strata, and as far as Greg could tell, their marriage was arranged by their parents.

Greg sighed again before rolling onto his side. Amber had no idea how ruthless the government could be. It did not take no for an answer. He knew the FBI agents would be back again and again. Whatever it took. They would never accept Amber's initial answers as the complete truth. They would keep digging and digging and crush her, even if they didn't have to, if only to teach her a lesson. They could get her fired at the snap of a finger and make sure she never found another teaching job again.

Amber could wind up giving star tours at the planetarium.

Without him for sure.

With that, Greg fell asleep and had his favorite dream, the one where he was on a big pool float drifting through the universe from one planet to the next. On some of the planets, the inhabitants waved at him, while on others they stood and saluted as if he were a god. He had had that dream or a version of it many times since starting high school and falling in love with astronomy.

CHAPTER 7
THE NEWS CYCLE THAT NEVER ENDS

Amber made the cover of *Time*, *Newsweek*, and a dozen other national magazines. Her picture was on the front page of the *Seattle Times* four days in a row. She was booked on a half-dozen talk shows ostensibly to discuss her discovery—the planets in earth-like orbits around "nearby" Trappist-1—but after a few minutes the conversation always turned to her alien and the indestructible gem.

By now most of the country had seen an enhanced photo of Alcor in the handle of the Big Dipper. The photo already had over two hundred million hits on the Internet.

Amber made it clear during every television appearance that she had no doubt whatsoever about the alien's peaceful intentions, notwithstanding the indestructible object her planet was able to manufacture.

"I understand it's used solely for space travel and mining."

The follow-up question was always the same. "How can you be so sure?"

"Because I've spoken with her," Amber explained, "and like any scientist I have to look at the circumstantial evidence. Think about it, she looks like us, she sounds like us, and she has been here for fifteen years. She's grown up here, and there have been thousands of others who have come before her over the past two centuries to settle and live peacefully among us. What better evidence could there be?

"Their planet is simply too small and overcrowded. Wouldn't we do the same if we got to that point here on Earth, assuming we had developed the same capacity for interstellar travel? Would a civilization so far advanced, a civilization without war, disease, or hunger, come to Earth with anything in their hearts other than peace and love? If they wanted to take over, they could have done it hundreds of years ago."

"Peace and love," Greg repeated to the television one afternoon while he watched Amber's performance. She sounded more like an informercial salesman than a scientist. Was the earth's existence supposed to depend on one woman's intuition? What if their planet's resources were not simply insufficient, but almost completely exhausted? What if they were running out of food, water, and oxygen? What if their plan was to relocate every inhabitant over time? What if the real purpose of the settlement here on Earth was to eventually take over the planet and isolate the surviving Earthlings in Australia, or worse, turn them into slaves or food?

Amber had blinders on—or her imagination had deserted her—because whenever Greg brought up that possibility, all she did was laugh. She refused to consider anything other than her "candy-land" version of events, which is what he called it one night over dinner. Greg saw the fire in Amber's eyes after he said that, and he quickly backed off.

Greg wondered if he should ask to accompany Amber to one of the TV interviews, as the co-discover of the Trappist-1 planets, and instead of sitting there nodding the whole time like the ultimate yes-man, he would surprise her by starting a fuller discussion—a point-counterpoint-type of discussion—which would make for lively television. She might be forced to come back down to earth after that.

Fortunately, Professor McNamara did bring up the other possibilities. Having been proven wrong—at least it seemed like it—about the absence of intelligent life anywhere else in the universe, he was now warning everyone that aliens would not travel millions and millions of miles for a space tour or an alternate lifestyle unless they had to, unless they were trying to escape, whether it was from a dying planet, a dying sun, a famine, a plague, or war.

"Who knows," he said during an interview in the campus newspaper, which got picked up by the wire services, "perhaps they were terrorists on their own planet and decided they would be better off with a planet of their own."

He assured any reporter who would listen to him—and there were enough of those around the campus these days—there had to be more than one reason for a species to journey across the known universe, and he had no doubt at least one of those reasons had to be somewhat sinister.

"Life on Earth from the smallest amoeba to mankind proves one rule time and time again," Professor McNamara explained, and he had one of those professorial faces that looked as if it would shatter if he tried to say anything untrue. "Life is always about the survival of the fittest. Self-preservation is at the core of every living organism on Earth...without exception. Why should it be any different anywhere else in the universe?

"Even if they have an unlimited source of renewable energy and ways to manufacture food out of thin air," Professor McNamara continued, "red stars like Alcor are prone to giant flareups. They may be millions of years apart, but perhaps their advanced science enables them to predict when one is coming. When it does flare up, the planet will be burnt to a crisp. There is nothing their scientists can do about it, which means they need to get away long before it happens. Or Alcor could be at its end stage of its lifecycle and about to turn into a cold star, which would be even easier to predict.

"An advanced civilization is not going to wait until the last minute. It will start preparing centuries in advance by sending out settlers to various planets before deciding which one is the best to colonize. Clearly, we are high up on the list if they are still coming...a less advanced, violent, polluting species, they might consider beyond redemption and worth sacrificing for their greater good. They may even feel as if they're doing our planet a favor by substituting themselves for us...considering how badly we've been treating the earth."

Professor McNamara did concede it was all speculation, but he warned the world against wearing rose-colored glasses and considering only one story, which he called the Santa Claus narrative, where the aliens come to Earth with bags filled with goodies.

Greg had to admit the professor did present himself well and made some sense. Amber called him disgusting. She called it "pure nonsense" and said no one in their right mind should listen to him.

"I'm the only one on the planet," Amber said, "who has met her and looked into her eyes. I saw what was in her heart."

A line Greg thought only a woman could say. Billions of lives resting on the infallibility of her gut based on some eye contact in a crowded Starbucks. Could anything be any less scientific?

"Assuming you're right," Greg replied, reluctant to agree with Professor McNamara on anything, "isn't it possible that she doesn't know all the reasons for the settlement program? Maybe keeping the settlers in the dark is part of the plan. Why would their governing bureaucrats be any more up front and honest than ours?"

"Meaning?"

"If they knew the whole truth...the real plan to take over...and their loyalties turned after spending years on Earth, they might warn us. Help prepare the world for what's coming. As a scientist, you have to consider all the possibilities."

Amber refused to discuss it. She said she was not going to dignify Greg's weird, mindless conspiracy talk with a response.

Still, like most women Greg had met, Amber could not remain silent for long. "Why would any advanced civilization want to destroy a planet's native species?"

"We do it all the time."

"Which is why we're not anywhere near their level of evolution."

Greg sighed. He did not see the point of trying to reason with a woman being held down by her emotions.

Professor McNamara's theory did inform and inflame the conversation on some of the more conservative news outlets, and the authorities were more determined than ever to catch the alien as quickly as possible. These popular talk show hosts warned that a civilization able to manufacture an indestructible piece of plastic could easily create a weapon able to wipe out humanity. Our nation, they screamed, indeed the world's nations, needed to prepare for the worst-case scenario.

The only time Amber and Greg talked about anything having to do with the aliens now was when they were walking through campus. Greg said they had to be careful because he was sure both of their apartments had been bugged, as well as their phones. More importantly, he did not want the authorities to think he was in on the conspiracy. It was bad enough he had not come forward yet with the valuable information in his possession.

"Do you think she really wants to reveal herself?" Greg asked Amber about a month after the press conference as they walked through campus.

"I am sure of it. She said she would send out a tape after thirty days."

"Which is in two days."

Amber nodded.

"You haven't heard from her...them, have you?"

He would not have been surprised if she had and was holding out on him yet again. Greg figured he would be able to tell by the tone of her voice if she was hiding something.

"Are you kidding, how could they get a word to me? I feel as if there's a camera pointed at me twenty-four-seven...look over there."

Amber gestured at the two men walking parallel to and a bit behind them, about thirty yards away on another path across the green. They were pretending to be college students in their matching jeans and baseball caps, but their neatly pressed button-down shirts gave them away, as did their ages. They had to be in their mid-thirties. Their posture was too straight and their gait too deliberate and determined. They might as well have had "FBI agent" tattooed on their foreheads.

"I haven't seen those two before. They change them all the time."

Amber nodded.

"The way they're hunting for her," Amber continued, "and those disgusting talk show hosts...I hope she stays put for a while and holds off on the video. She said her purpose was to let the world know it was not alone, and she's done that. What's gained if they catch her and lock her away?"

Greg lowered his voice. "Perhaps she has things to tell the authorities she couldn't tell you...things she wasn't supposed to tell you."

Amber frowned. "You've seen too many science fiction movies."

"Well," he said, "you can relax, because without a description they'll never be able to find them."

"Thank God."

Greg glanced over at their two shadows and could swear one of them nodded back at him. They did not seem to care if he and Amber saw them. Perhaps they preferred it that way because it made their job easier.

"A lot of people are scared...panicky...you can see it on the news," Greg whispered. "A recent poll found that eighty percent of Americans want the authorities to catch her to find out her true intentions."

"We already know her true intentions."

"They're worried about that indestructible piece of plastic."

"They should worry more about global warming," Amber said.

"And they want to find the other settlers," Greg added, "assuming they exist. Sixty percent don't believe there are any others."

"And you?"

"I don't doubt it for a minute," Greg said, although he did. "Almost fifty percent doubt she's really from another planet."

"The same people I suspect who still believe the sun revolves around the earth."

"Congress is about to allocate a billion dollars to reverse-engineer the gem."

"The hysteria will eventually pass when nothing happens."

"What if something does happen?" Greg said. "What if you're wrong?"

Amber looked away and sighed. She had been doing that a lot lately, turning away when what he suggested did not fit into her neat little narrative. Why even talk with him if all she wanted to hear were her own thoughts? What kind of scientist was Amber turning into?

"I'm not saying you are wrong," Greg added. "I'm just thinking out loud. Trying to put myself in the minds of middle America."

Amber kept walking, eyes straight, drifting a bit farther apart than they had been just a few moments earlier. Greg realized he had to watch what he said, or Amber might break it off just as suddenly as the others. It was too soon at this point. After the aliens were caught and debriefed would be a better time. He did not want history to remember him as the guy who once dated the astronomer who made the first contact.

Greg was beginning to dislike Alula and her half-Earthling boyfriend, even though he had never met them. In his experience, dislike and distrust were like kissing cousins. The first was almost always followed by the second.

A couple of days later, Amber was arrested, not arrested according to the FBI's press release, but taken into protective custody in the interest of national security. The release said that the FBI had reason to believe that Ms. Garrigan knew more than she was telling them. The government always assumes that, and in most cases it's right. The FBI spokesman said they would be testing her for residual radiation on the theory she did meet with the alien, notwithstanding her denials.

They left Greg alone, and although he was not allowed to visit her, they did let him call Amber. She was not allowed to speak with anyone else. The press made a big deal about it since Amber was no longer accessible, which made the rumors worse and increased the general hysteria and panic.

Why would the government arrest an astronomy instructor if it did not have a good reason?

Sightings of alien ships were being reported everywhere from Alaska to Argentina.

At this point, Greg decided it was time for him to do something. It turned out that the name on the mailbox, Alex Rigel, was real. It was not hard for him to track down the house where he grew up on the outskirts of Seattle. His mother answered the door dressed in an old housecoat. She was not drunk, not this early in the afternoon, but she seemed well on her way.

Greg introduced himself, explained who he was—people were always impressed by professors—and that he believed her son was traveling with the alien. She doubled over with laughter as if it was the funniest thing she had ever heard. The last time she had spoken to Alex was about six weeks earlier when he told her he had met someone, and they were heading to Mexico for a couple of months of vacation.

She laughed at that as well.

"Vacation from what, making coffee? I hope she has some money, because he never does."

"Did he say where in Mexico?"

"No, I'm sure it's someplace where they can buy pot on every corner."

"Did he mention her name?"

"I don't remember. If he did, I wouldn't have paid any attention since he's never had a girlfriend last more than a month or two."

She insisted Greg come in and sit down.

"You know," she added, "I've never met any of his girlfriends. He's never brought a single girl home. I'm sure he's afraid I'd embarrass him. Big deal, so I drink—tell me how that's any different from getting high all the time. I'm not the one who's been in rehab three times."

"Is he coming back to Seattle?" Greg asked.

"He always does as soon as he runs out of money. He couldn't have saved much working in a coffee shop."

Greg wrote everything down like the FBI agents did.

She offered him a drink, which Greg was tempted to accept, but it was too early, and he politely declined.

"I'm sure he would have mentioned it if she was green and had a couple of antennas on the top of her head."

She laughed so hard this time she said she almost peed in her pants.

"Sure you won't have a drink?" she asked again as she poured herself another one.

"No, thank you."

Greg could not imagine that outing Alex Rigel would cause much of a problem for his mother. She might even enjoy the attention.

She chuckled to herself as she sipped her drink.

"She'd have to be from outer space," she said, staring into the glass that she was holding at eye level, "to hook up with Alex."

She put the glass down and looked over at Greg.

"Maybe she can understand him, because I can't. His father was a hardworking mechanic, never missed a day of work."

"Where is he now?"

"Dead...killed in an accident with a tire iron. Turned out he wasn't as good as he thought he was."

"There's something else," Greg said.

"You're from another planet too, and you've been sent to bring her back?" She chuckled at her own joke.

At least she was a happy drunk.

"Not quite," he said, before telling her what he had heard about Alex's father being from the same planet as the alien.

"One of the settlers," he added, "if you've been following the story on the news."

She picked up her glass and swirled the ice around it without spilling a drop.

"Come to think of it, I think Alex mentioned that when he got out of rehab."

She chuckled to herself before taking another sip from the glass.

"Imagine... my husband traveling here... from... another... planet." She could barely get the words out as she alternately chuckled and cleared her throat. "To take a job...what, fixing cars. Seems like he could've come up with a better way to make a living after traveling a million miles."

"It's a lot farther than that," Greg said.

She opened her mouth as if she had something more to add but raised her glass instead, tilted her head back, and emptied its contents into it like it was a funnel. Then she placed the glass back on the coffee table, carefully covering up the ring that looked like it had been there for years, before sitting back and sucking on the ice as if to get every last drop.

Greg had never seen anything like it before since his mother was a teetotaler and his father limited himself to one scotch and soda at dinner, two on Saturday nights. Greg was also very disciplined when it came to that. No more than two glasses of wine with dinner, no exceptions. Perhaps a nightcap on those occasions when the moment warranted.

She chuckled again to get his attention. "I suppose it could be true."

"Why do you say that?"

"Lord knows, my husband always had his head in the clouds. You find me another man who would rather watch the stars at night than the television. Didn't give a damn about sports. He used to go out back almost every night...even when it was cold...alone in the beginning and then with Alex. He knew the names of every star and had crazy stories about lots of them. He could trace all the constellations with his finger. Said it was his hobby as a kid. Pretty strange hobby if you ask me."

"But he never actually said anything to you."

"About being from another planet?" She forced a laugh this time as she poured some more scotch into her glass. This time she didn't bother getting any ice.

"He told me he and his parents moved here from Philly."

"Ever meet any of his family?"

"Just his parents. No brothers or sisters."

"What were his parents like?"

"Like everyone else. His father had a small hardware store. His mother was a homemaker. You know what that is?"

Greg nodded.

She picked up her glass, but this time she just stared down into it.

"Did I tell you we met in high school?"

"No."

She looked back up with a little smile and proceeded to tell him about the first time they kissed.

"He didn't have any kind of accent, and you'd think he would if he came from another planet. He spoke English the same as me. Nothing strange about him, and let me tell you, I knew every inch of him."

She took a sip of her scotch and made a face as if all this thinking and talking was ruining the taste.

Greg thought Amber would be very interested in his observations if only he could tell her. She was always telling him things she noticed about her students, and when she asked him about his classes, he never had anything comparable to say. They all seemed the same to him, class after class, year after year. What would be the point of telling her about this term's crop of pretty coeds? Unfortunately, he could not say a word about meeting Alex's mother, not yet anyway, probably not ever.

"Wouldn't that be a hoot...I mean if it was true. He seemed like every other guy...if you know what I mean. His blood was red, I can assure you of that."

"Was there anything unusual about him...besides his interest in the stars?"

"For me, yeah. He never raised his voice or his hand, not once, and I'd known men before him who did that as often as the clock struck the hour...you know what I mean?"

Before he could nod, she added, "Like my father."

She sat there staring at him, her face showing shades of anger, sadness, and confusion. Greg imagined it must hard for a woman like her, an alcoholic among other things, to maintain any subtlety of emotion—everything always hanging out there for every visitor to see. He couldn't imagine she got many.

"Do you think they might have gone back east to Philadelphia?" Greg asked.

"Who?"

"Alex and his friend."

"What for? He has no family there. It was one of the reasons his parents left."

"Do you think he'll call you, let you know where he is, how he's doing? I'd love to know if you hear from him."

She laughed.

"The only time I ever hear from him is when he needs money or is going back to rehab...and I already told him I don't have any more money to waste on him. I've got to hold on to what I got. I can't go back to work. Who would hire me? I haven't worked in thirty years."

She raised her glass as if making a toast to those past years before taking another drink.

"I'd go visit in a minute if I could. What's the planet called again?"

"Home."

"That's the name?"

"That's what they call it."

"How funny is that? I'd love to check it out... This planet is nothing to brag about. Maybe they'd let me in because I married one of them."

She laughed again. She sounded much drunker now than when Greg first came in.

"Any way of getting there?" she asked.

"No, not that I know of."

"Too bad."

Greg thanked her, got up, and left. She made no effort to show him out. At least he was sure now about Alex's name and the fact that he worked at the coffee shop next to his apartment. They would undoubtedly have a camera there with pictures of both Alex and Alula.

Greg had quite a lot now to offer the authorities. If he was going to free Amber—winning her undying gratitude—and become the hero of the next chapter of this historic story, he had to act quickly before Amber caved and started talking or the aliens went public.

Amber did say they were treating her well. She was in a comfortable little apartment on some military base hidden in the mountains, and she said the food was edible. She would start complaining soon enough once the days stretched into weeks and the weeks into months. Women like Amber do not like to be held back for long, whether it's by force or reason.

Greg decided to sleep on it one more night before calling the FBI agent.

The next morning, he had no doubt it was time. He would offer to tell the FBI everything he knew provided they let Amber come home. He was going to call from his office right after his morning class, but by the time the class was over, the campus was already buzzing about the video Alula had sent into the Seattle NBC affiliate. It was all over the Internet.

She stood there like the prettiest weather girl on the planet pointing out the exact location of Home on a deep space star chart.

"It has two moons, black, fragrant trees, and a small red sun not quite as large as yours."

She should have said *ours*, Greg thought, if she truly wanted the world to believe she was now one of us.

Then she provided more information about the planets orbiting Trappist-1, describing the different dinosaurs roaming on the one nearest to that sun and the people who lived on the middle one.

"It's a primitive civilization of cave dwellers and hunters who look like us, except for bigger brows, broader and flatter feet, and longer arms. Naturally, they are still evolving."

It was the world's first look at her, and she was adorable. Cute and perky, completely unthreatening. She could have been selling timeshares and vacation trips to Disney World or starring in one of those television sitcoms Greg was hooked on as a teenager, like *Friends*.

How could anyone be afraid of someone like that?

Of course, they would not send one of their generals or a giant ten-foot robot to offer greetings to the earth, particularly if they had some hidden, sinister intention and wanted to allay any suspicion.

Alula held up another crystal, smaller than the one she had given Amber.

"You will eventually create a substance like this. It's perfect for space travel since nothing can penetrate it, not any of the small meteors you often run into along the way. It's also great for mining. Let me assure you, it is not a weapon and has never been used as one."

In fact, Alula explained, her planet had no army, no offensive weapons of any kind, and like all the other advanced civilizations in the universe—and she assured everyone there were quite a few of those—they respected the organic development and privacy of all life-forms on other habitable planets.

Greg took note of the fact she said Home had no offensive weapons. She did not mention defensive weapons, and it was hard to imagine a defensive weapon that could not easily be turned around and used offensively. She again referred to Home as her planet when the earth was now supposed to be her planet.

He could not be the only one to have noticed that.

Alula explained that Home was a small planet and had no choice but to send out settlers to live and assimilate. They didn't want to overburden the planet's resources and atmosphere. No one ever interfered, and they lived alongside the native population, blending in over the years through marriage and childbirth.

"Our goal is and has always been to assimilate and become Earthlings over time."

She went on to explain this had been going on for over 250 years, and there must be hundreds of thousands of descendants by now, almost all of them with no idea where one of their distant ancestors originally came from.

The only reason for revealing herself now, Alula explained, was because sooner or later the earth would discover it was not alone, and sooner seemed very important considering the condition of our planet—this time she got the "our" part right. The earth was facing a terrible climate and pollution crisis, she said, among other challenges. Alula hoped that knowing we were not alone would inspire everyone to take better care of Earth and each other and begin working toward the day when we could take our place among the other more advanced civilizations in the universe.

"Advancement is not simply a technological step forward," she said. "Advancement comes in terms of culture and community as well."

The universe is teeming with life, Alula confirmed, some more advanced than Earth and many far less advanced. She hoped—as an Earthling now herself, again hitting the right note—that one day soon the earth would reach the state of peace, sharing, and caring which is every planet's destiny.

"There are many examples of planets that did not make it," she said, looking gravely into the camera, "that used up their resources, rendered their climate and atmosphere uninhabitable, or destroyed their ability to sustain themselves through endless wars."

Alula mentioned a few of those planets...Relgis, Phandum, Carbino...planets that once had thriving civilizations not much different from Earth and which were now barren.

"It doesn't take much to render a planet uninhabitable," she explained. "It's a delicate balance, and the earth is getting close to upending theirs.

"We get to choose our planet's future by how we act going forward," Alula concluded at the end of the video. "I care as much about the earth as you do because this is my home now...my only home."

Instead of holding onto her solemn look, Alula punctuated her conclusion with a big, warm smile, bigger than any he had ever seen before on any television informercial or news show. Greg would have given anything to be with a woman who could smile at him like that.

That was her message. Wake up, recognize we are one species regardless of our different shapes and colors. Recognize that our similarities far outweigh our differences. Protect each other and the planet. Do it for our grandchildren and their grandchildren, and for the generations to follow. Stop living for the moment—and locally—and start looking toward the future and the greater universe.

Greg wondered how many people realized it was a scene right out of his favorite 1951 science fiction movie, *The Day the Earth Stood Still*. Except unlike the alien in the movie, who was stern and serious—and scary—Alula looked as American as apple pie, as cute as a prom queen, and sounded just as sweet and unthreatening.

Alex obviously shot the video. He did not appear in it. Smart to keep him off the radar for now. Let the world still think she was running alone. Not that it would matter much now that the whole world knew what she looked like. With all the facial recognition cameras around, it wouldn't take long to catch her.

If Alula thought her video would help diminish the panic and anxiety many were feeling, she was wrong. If she thought there was too much anxiety about Amber's revelation before, it was nothing compared to what followed. Now, in addition to those who were sure she was a Trojan Horse and that her smile was masking an imminent attack, there were those who were afraid she was wrong, and it was too late to save the planet. Perhaps because they knew what she didn't that the world's politicians did not have the resolve to think beyond themselves and the moment, and that learning the earth was not alone was not going to change their it's-all-about-me-and-my friends perspective on life.

Alula also riled up the authorities who do not like to be toyed with. Now they had a photo and the entire planet for their eyes.

"If she means no harm," the FBI agent in charge of the nationwide search said, "why doesn't she turn herself in for questioning?"

The one good thing to come out of the video was that they released Amber the next day. They did not need her now because they had Alula's photo. They no longer believed she was in contact with the alien or knew how to find her. Amber was able to resume teaching, although she was followed everywhere on campus by the press and fringe protesters with signs saying things like "Alien Lover" and "Traitor to the Earth." Campus guards had to stand outside her classroom to keep them out.

It was not easy for her or their relationship, and Amber started spending every night in her own apartment, asking Greg to stay away—for his own well-being—which is when Greg decided it was time to call the FBI and tell them what he knew about Alex. Knowing there were two of them and having Alex's description would be very helpful. They could get a photo of him from his mother or the coffee shop. The sooner the two of them were off the streets, the better it would be for him and Amber.

Maybe they could go on a lecture tour together, Greg thought. What university would not be eager to pay them a large stipend to give a few lectures and take a few questions?

They were tied together now by all this—forever really—at least the way Greg saw it, even if they never did become a couple.

CHAPTER 8
THE CHASE

Alex brought back dinner. They were not looking for him, at least not that they were letting on, but he knew it wouldn't be long before the art instructor at the rehab center recognized Alula and connected her to the painting with the two moons and red sun. She would remember how chummy she was with Alex, and his name, address, and photo would be easy to obtain. The rehab center had all his information.

Patient privacy was not going to stop the FBI.

If it were not the art instructor, then it would be one of the other baristas at the coffee shop. They knew Alula as well since she came in all the time when Alex was on break or finishing up for the day.

Finding the two of them would be easy considering there had to be cameras everywhere these days, whether it was a train station, a bus depot, a city street, or a supermarket, which is why they both wore hats when they went out and kept their heads down. Alex figured most of the street cameras were connected to a central computer with facial recognition software. It would be impossible for them to hide much longer without some help.

In Alex's mind, they were as good as caught.

They had not stopped anywhere for more than two nights since taking the bus out of Seattle. They switched to the train to get to Chicago, but public transportation was making him nervous, and Alex bought a cheap, used car with some of the money he had saved. The seller included some phony plates, which he said would trick the out-of-state cops.

They left the car in New Jersey before taking the train into New York City. Alex figured if they couldn't hide in New York City, they couldn't hide anywhere. They found a cheap motel by the airport in Queens. He thought they should be near the airport in case they needed to catch a quick flight somewhere. Alex figured they could fly to Bangor or Miami and try to disappear there for a while.

He had to grit his teeth every time he thought about Alula's video, which the news played a lot. She insisted on making it and sending it to the Seattle TV station once they learned Amber had been taken into custody. Alex begged her to wait, but he knew how stubborn she was once she made up her mind. It was as if she wanted to be caught, as if she were sure in the end that everyone—including their captors—would come to their senses once they got to know her better.

Alula clearly was not a student of history. From the Salem Witch Trials to Nazi Germany, people do not usually come to their senses until it is way too late, until the only thing left to do is mop up the blood.

Alex had gone out to buy food. Alula was no longer safe out on the street, which is why he went alone. She was watching TV when he got back.

"Has the world turned to love yet?" he asked.

He was not expecting much more than a chuckle in response.

"It appears I am uniting the world...at least the world's governments...in their hunt for me. I've been sighted on just about every continent."

"Pretty girl, long hair...you're everywhere."

"Someone in Canada thought they saw me flying through the sky like Superwoman."

Alex set out what he bought, some packaged turkey, cheese, and bread for him, a salad for Alula.

"I think you should cut your hair," he said, "and dye it a different color. Maybe we could buy you some bigger clothes to hide your figure...use layers to make you look a little fatter."

"What about you?" Alula said, turning off the TV.

"That's what the beard's for."

He had been growing one for the past two weeks, but it didn't look like much. His father did not have a lot of facial hair either. Maybe it was a Home thing.

Alula sat down at the little table by the window.

"This looks great," she said.

"A regular Thanksgiving feast."

He reached down into another bag by his feet.

"I bought this too," he said, pulling out red hair dye. "I think you'll look good as a redhead."

"You too," she responded. "We could travel as siblings."

"I'm sure they know who I am by now. They're probably keeping it under wraps, so I don't get spooked."

They ate a while in silence. Alex liked it better when the news was not blaring at them. He wondered what Alula was thinking. Did she regret any of this? Was she thinking it might be better for Alex if she turned herself in?

She had to be listening to his thoughts because she turned to him, looking as serious as he had ever seen her look, and said, "I'm considering it. They can question me all they want. I have no secrets…nothing to hide. They're not going to learn about any invasion plans."

"They'll examine every inch of you."

"Let them. Eventually they'll get tired of it and let me go…and you'll be there waiting."

"I'll be there with you," Alex said. "If you're going to turn yourself in, we do it together."

Alula smiled.

"It's all wishful thinking on your part if you ask me. They will never let us go."

"They can't hold us forever," Alula said, still smiling.

"Don't bet on it."

Alula finished her salad.

"What if they torture you for the names of the other settlers?" Alex asked.

"I don't know any of them."

"You knew about my father…and me."

"Only because my father's family knew your father's family back on Home…and your father helped us get settled after we got here."

"How did he do that?"

"He helped my father get a used car."

"That sounds like him."

Alex wondered how much different his life would have been if his father had told him and his mother the truth. Would they have become friendly with Alula's family? They never had any close family friends when he was growing up. It would have been nice, particularly after his father's sudden death. Maybe he wouldn't have felt so alone. Maybe his mother wouldn't have taken up with the bottle.

"It's against the settlement rules," Alula said.

"What?"

"Settlers have to spread out after they arrive. We're not supposed to become friends or stay in touch. We can blend in better that way."

"Does that mean you're breaking the rules by being with me?"

"I think fifteen years apart is long enough."

"Now you're a rule breaker too."

They both laughed.

"You know," Alex said after finishing his sandwich, "whatever you do know they'll get out of you."

"No, they won't."

Alula looked over at him with one of her winsome smiles. The one that hit him like a warm summer breeze and felt like a declaration of love. It always made him completely forget whatever was bothering him.

"I forgot to tell you they released Amber," Alula said. "I knew they would once we sent out the video."

"How did you find out?"

"I heard it on the news…right before some army general announced they were close to reverse-engineering the crystal."

"Can that be true?"

"No."

"The truth never matters when it comes to our government," Alex muttered, "any government really."

"He said being able to neutralize it was essential to the earth's safety because otherwise it could be a devasting weapon."

"How?"

"He thinks Home would use it to build unstoppable tanks and bullets."

"They all grew up watching too many war movies."

"Why would we do that?" Alula asked, genuinely perplexed. "What would be the point? If the earth doesn't want any more settlers, Home can send them somewhere else. There is an inexhaustible number of planets to choose from. Those are the types of questions they should be asking themselves."

Alula shook her head slowly from side to side.

"Why destroy a planet or its inhabitants? No one on Home would ever think like that. If it wanted to destroy a planet or its inhabitants, it could do it instantly. It wouldn't need to build indestructible tanks. They could do it the same way Home pulverizes asteroids when they wander too close."

"How?"

"I'm not sure; it's some kind of anti-matter laser."

"Sounds scary," Alex said.

"If you're an asteroid. The point is when you advance that far scientifically, you advance just as far culturally and ethically. We care about every living creature and every object…every plant, rock, mountain, as well as the planet… We are all related, all stardust. If you ask me, that's a much more difficult and significant advance to make than being able to manufacture an indestructible piece of plastic."

"Unfortunately," Alex muttered, "Earth is not anywhere near that kind of advance."

"No kidding."

Alula got up and lay down on the bed.

"This is a funny civilization. All the leaders care about is advancing science and technology…being stronger than their neighbors. They have very little respect for those who devote their lives to kindness and compassion, or those struggling through no fault of their own. They hardly care about how they'll leave the world after they've transformed."

Alex climbed onto the bed and lay down beside her. He did not see how he could rise to the defense of Earth's politicians.

"Hardly anyone here spends time looking up at the stars," Alula said, "trying to imagine what could be."

She had said the same thing to Alex a number of times before.

"Our politicians worry about their jobs. The future is someone else's problem, not theirs."

"If we're not going to turn ourselves in," Alula said, "perhaps we can open up a dialogue with them through Amber."

"They'll be monitoring every call and email she gets. They'll find us an hour after we try to contact her."

"We can't do this alone."

"Do what?" Alex asked.

"Hide, communicate, change the world. We need to be heard."

Alula's voice was devoid of the fear and anguish Alex was feeling. If only he could think of death as a transformation the way she did.

"Any suggestions?" Alula asked.

Alex looked up at the yellowing ceiling, the tiles slashed in places as if they had been the victims of a knife fight, imagining he could see through it to the stars. He could almost see the Big Dipper. Not Alula's star—his father's birthplace—but it did give him an idea.

"What if we try the same thing we did before?"

They could contact an astronomer again, but this time in New York City.

"Maybe someone at Columbia University," Alex said, "who can help us figure out a way to get more of your message out there."

"Our message."

"Yes, our message."

This was not Alex's first choice; running and hiding was his first choice, disguising themselves and living in the remote mountains somewhere was his first choice, but he knew it was not what Alula wanted, assuming it was even possible to evade the authorities anywhere on the planet.

"I like it," Alula said, rolling over and wrapping her leg around him. The rest of the night was pure bliss. Alex felt like he was floating in space.

The next morning Alex went to the library to use the Internet to look for a good candidate, not that there were a lot to choose from since Alula preferred a female astronomer.

"Men on Earth tend to be more about themselves," Alula explained. "Women are more about others. They're kinder and more open to change…and if you ask me, they're more trustworthy and would make better leaders."

That was not true in the drug world where Alex used to travel. You couldn't trust anyone, whatever their gender.

The one female astronomer at Columbia in a department of twelve was Rose Milton. She was over eighty, Professor Emeritus of Astronomy, specializing in galaxy dynamics, interactions, formation, evolution, something called the intergalactic medium, and the Milky Way.

Alex printed out her CV with a black-and-white photo. Alula liked her face. She liked all the wrinkles. She thought they made her look kind and wise. Alex thought they made her look old and tired.

"She's not afraid of anything, I can tell…not even death," Alula said, as if she could read faces easier than thoughts.

Alex called her early that afternoon, and by late afternoon they were sitting in Rose's office in Morningside Heights—her door closed—sipping tea.

"I can't tell you how honored I am to meet you, Alula, and you, Alex. You truly are a dream come true for an old astronomer like me. We've been reaching out to the stars for millennia; it about time they started reaching back to us."

Alula smiled. Alex remained impassive, the way he set himself when they left the motel. At the last minute, he tried to change Alula's mind, suggesting they head upstate instead, find some rural community in the middle of nowhere, and rent a small house in the woods. He could find a job at a convenience store, and Alula could write her story, which they could send to the *New York Times*.

Alula shook her head, smiled sweetly, and walked out the door. He followed behind her, unable to shake the feeling this was a big mistake and the beginning of the end.

"You haven't told anyone about us?" Alex asked a little too loudly.

It was a simple question, but it sounded almost like an accusation.

"No, of course not."

"I'm afraid of what the authorities might do to Alula," he added in a much quieter voice.

"I'm not," Alula said, resting her hand on Alex's arm.

Rose said she shared Alex's concern.

"There is a frenzy out there," she explained, "particularly on the Internet. The world needs time to work this through. It is hard to hear the truth when the loudest voices are shouting that the world is ending. In time the naysayers will scream themselves out and the voices of reason, the more prescient ones, will be heard."

Alex was afraid it might take a lifetime, their lifetime.

"You're safe within the scientific community," Rose added, "particularly among the astronomers."

Unfortunately, astronomers have never had much clout in politics or society.

"I have a house in the woods in the Catskills," Rose said. "You'll be safe there. I'll take care of everything."

She wanted to involve one of her graduate students to help.

"I would trust Miriam with my life," she added, turning to Alex. "She can bring up supplies and help me interview you so we can write your story. I know someone at the *New York Times*... Once we bring the two of you out of the shadows, things will change, you'll see. We can be very welcoming once we get past our fears."

"We will never have a normal life together," Alex said.

It sounded more like a whine than an observation.

"It's all relative." Rose narrowed her eyes as if she were trying to make a quick assessment about Alex. "How many people live completely normal lives? Very few as far as I can tell, and I have been around for over eighty years. Certainly not if you're the wrong color or gender."

Rose took a sip of her tea as if she needed to center herself during this remarkable moment in her long life.

"It'll be normal in some ways, but not in others," she said after a few moments. "You will be famous...an object of curiosity...the paparazzi will follow you everywhere you go, but you'll learn to live with it. You can find happiness in whatever space and time you can find, if you let yourself."

Alex hoped she was right because he feared much worse. In his irrational moments, he was afraid that after they were caught and held incommunicado for years, Home would decide to send soldiers to free Alula and take her home, but not before teaching the world a costly lesson. That was how it always happened in the old movies, but this was not a movie, and Alula had repeatedly made it clear Home would not be coming to her rescue.

In his more rational moments, Alex imagined the two of them living the rest of their lives in a zoo opened only to visits by generals and government scientists.

Alex figured they had to accept Rose's offer because they had no choice. Otherwise, they would soon be caught and disappear into the system.

Alula and Alex left to get their things from the motel and arranged to meet Rose at the George Washington Bridge bus terminal, where she and Miriam would pick them up and drive them to her mountain house. She assured them it was located in the middle of the woods with no neighbors for miles.

"You're not worried about her telling anyone?" Alex asked Alula as they left the motel.

"No, she meant every word she said."

"You read her thoughts?"

"Open eyes, open heart, open mind. It works both ways. She trusts me and I trust her, don't you?"

"I suppose," Alex said with a shrug.

Alex had not been in the trusting business for many years. His mother could not be trusted after his father died, and there was very little trust in the street when it came to drugs.

"And if we're caught, so what," Alula added. "It might be better in the long run."

"I doubt that."

Now it was Alula's turn to shrug, although she always did it with a tender smile, as opposed to Alex's usual grimace.

Rose's cabin was in the middle of the woods bordered on three sides by state-owned park land. They had to drive a half mile down a narrow, private dirt road at the end of which Rose's house sat in front of the Neversink River, which she said was well known for its trout fishing. While Rose did not fish, she did keep fishing poles on the back deck. Not that it mattered since Alula would not eat fish and could not bear the thought of seeing one caught on a hook. Just talking about it sent a shiver down her spine.

Alex had never been fishing. His father never took him to the Pacific Ocean or any of the mountain lakes around Seattle like some of the other kids, which Alex understood now, although he didn't back then. His father did assimilate in part by allowing himself to eat meat, hot dogs being one of his favorite foods.

The cabin was over one hundred years old, Rose said, but she renovated it about twenty years earlier, and it looked as if it belonged on a postcard. It was the nicest place Alex had ever stayed, and it was five miles from the nearest town. Without streetlights, the view of the night sky was incredible, especially through the telescope in the little observatory Rose had built behind it.

Alula liked Miriam right away, as did Alex. She was their age and almost as calm and composed as Alula about everything, including the prospect of interviewing Earth's first visitor from another planet, at least the first one to go public. She and Rose started interviewing them right after dinner for the article they planned on submitting to the *New York Times*. Since Miriam and Rose had to return to Columbia during the weekdays, they figured it would take at least a month before they had anything worth sending.

The first thing Alula did after it got dark was give them a tour of the night sky—as Alula saw it—introducing them to stars and planets they could not see or verify. Alex listened and stared up at the stars while Rose and Miriam took notes. It was a beautiful night, the temperature ideal, and not a cloud in the sky. There were more stars twinkling above than Alex could recall seeing since he was a little boy.

Alula told them about a planet in the Sunflower Galaxy located in the northern constellation of Canes Venatici. The galaxy got its name because it looked like a sunflower.

"M63 on the star maps," Miriam said, and Rose nodded.

"The air there is traceable like a whiteboard, and the inhabitants make art wherever they go. Every movement is like a ballet," Alula said with childish glee. "It fades after about thirty seconds."

"Have you visited?" Miriam asked.

"No, we learned about it in school."

"That galaxy is about thirty million light-years away," Rose added.

"And it has almost four hundred billion stars," Alula added.

"Wow," Alex exclaimed before Rose or Miriam could say a word.

Alex was learning a lot about the stars, not just from Alula, but from Rose and Miriam as well. After a few weeks, Rose suggested he consider enrolling as a student in her graduate program, even though he did not have a college degree. She said she would figure out a way for him to get both at the same time. Rose also promised to make it tuition free. Children of faculty members get to attend for free, and since she had no children of her own, Rose said she was owed one.

"How long would it take?" Alex asked.

"With someone like you...with your curious mind...two years...three tops. Depends on how much time you're willing to devote to it."

Six months earlier, Alex would have laughed at the prospect. He would never have considered his mind curious back then. Addictive, yes, thirsty for knowledge, no.

"Unfortunately, I don't think we're going to be around for that long," Alex said.

"I could stay here forever," Alula said, "if they'd let us."

"You're more than welcome to."

Rose intended to leave the house to the Columbia University Astronomy Department, but she said she could amend her will to give them both a life estate.

"Which means?" Alex asked.

"It's yours as long as you want to live here."

Alex could be happy with that as well. He couldn't imagine the world would let them.

While the news about Alula died down a bit after a couple of weeks, they all knew the government was still out there searching for them. The authorities probably asked the press to move the story off page one so the alien would begin to feel overconfident and thus more likely to slip up.

They never mentioned Alex, not in any of the newspapers or television interviews, but Alex knew the authorities were aware he was traveling with Alula because he did get a message to his mother through Miriam, who traveled to Ohio to visit her family and used a burner phone to contact her. His mother said she had been visited by some professor, as well as a couple of FBI agents.

Alex let her know they were safe and living somewhere in Canada, but he doubted the government would buy that diversion for long.

Rose was also contacted by the FBI. They were working their way through all the astronomers in the country to see if any of them had been in contact with "Stargirl," as they sometimes called Alula. Alex figured they were starting with the female astronomers.

"I wish she had," Rose told the agent. "I'd give anything to speak with her."

Rose figured they might follow her around for a while to make sure, so she stopped visiting. Miriam brought up the supplies. Alex suggested to Alula it might be time for them to move on.

"I'm done running" was her response.

She said it was time for the world to get to know her.

"We have to get the hard part over with," Alula said, "if we're going to have any chance of getting married and having a child."

Those words almost stopped Alex's heart. He never saw himself as a father. He never saw himself as a husband either until he met Alula. Now he would welcome it and any boring routines that came along with it. He would gladly fix cars or do carpentry if it meant spending the rest of his life with Alula.

"They'll interrogate us, poke up, and prod us," Alex muttered, "like we're specimens in a biology lab."

"Eventually they'll have to let us go."

"The government doesn't have to do anything it doesn't want to do."

"We haven't done anything wrong."

"Except illegally immigrate," Alex said, wondering how Alula could remain so optimistic and naïve.

"There is no way to get visas from Home," she said with a chuckle before taking Alex's hand and assuring him that everything would work out in the end.

"One way or another."

Alex did not like the sound of that.

"I wish I could believe you," he said. He paused to take a deep breath. "I know you can read thoughts sometimes, but that's not nearly the same as seeing into the future."

She squeezed Alex's hand. "You're a citizen, you were born here. They can't change that."

"You weren't. What if they keep you confined forever, you know, for national security reasons? Put you in that jail in Cuba…what's it called…Guantanamo."

"Then I'll join the stars."

"They'll be watching you twenty-four seven."

"They can't stop me. It's part of my telekinetic power."

"Killing yourself?"

"Transforming."

"Can you do that to me as well?"

Alula nodded.

Not long after that conversation, in the middle of their second month in the Catskills, Rose and Miriam showed up for the weekend with a trunk full of food and wine, and a copy of the latest edition of the *New York Times*.

There had been a lot of stories lately about the planets around Trappist-1 and a lot of speculation about the kind of life that might exist there. According to the polls, half the people believed there was life on at least one of the planets, and the other half didn't. The breakdown in the polling was almost the same with Alula. Half of the country believed her story about the settlers, and the other half thought it was all a hoax.

The disbelievers demanded more proof. They were not satisfied with an indestructible piece of plastic. Those naysayers said the gem could have been stolen from a research lab at a big multinational corporation or a top-secret government facility. It's the type of thing they probably work on all the time.

It was the kind of discovery a scientist might stumble upon without understanding how or why he got there, making it hard to duplicate. The kind of discovery every government on the planet would keep secret.

"You're not going to believe this," Miriam said, handing the paper to Alula. Alex walked behind Alula to read over her shoulder.

"This could be good," Alex said, meaning for him and Alula. He had been getting a little cabin fever lately. He was not craving drugs as much as he was a good latte.

The headline read *Secret Government Lab Affirms It Made the Indestructible Gem and the Alien Claim Is a Hoax*.

The article went on to explain how an unnamed government source had confirmed the gem was stolen from a top-secret government military lab and was not actually indestructible.

"There are ways to break down its chemical composition and render it unstable," the source said, "which are known only to the military."

The reporter confirmed it was still in the research stage and intended solely as a means of protecting valuable military and civilian assets.

"There are no plans to utilize it for any offensive purposes."

Apparently, the reporter wrote, a few pieces had been stolen by a former employee. He did not come right out and say it, but the implication was clear—Alula was the former employee and thief.

"How can they lie like that?" Alula asked, more bemused than anything else.

"The better question," Alex asked, "is when do they ever feel compelled to tell the truth."

"Only when they're caught red-handed in a lie," Rose answered, "and then they'll blame someone else or lie again if they can get away with it."

Alex read the next part out loud.

"The United States Attorney in Seattle has charged Amber Garrigan, an instructor at the University of Washington Astronomy Department, with fraud. Sources say the indictment, still unsealed, alleges she conspired with her friend, the alleged extraterrestrial, to make up a story to bring more attention to her discovery of the planets orbiting Trappist-1.

"Unnamed sources have confirmed that the woman in the video is an acquaintance of Ms. Garrigan who had been working at a secret military installation in the Northwest where she stole two of the prototypes. Ms. Garrigan was hoping that the publicity, along with the discovery of the planets, would fast-track her appointment to full professor. She is being held on one million dollars' bail."

"What does it mean?" Alula asked.

"It means the authorities want everyone to calm down," Rose said, "forget about the alien invasion, and go back to believing we're the only ones in the universe. This way they can continue searching for you under the radar and keep it quiet when they do find you."

"Making sure we disappear without a trace…forever," Alex said, looking more horrified than anyone else.

"How can they put Amber in jail like that," Alula said, settling into one of her rare frowns.

"If they find us, they'll keep it under wraps and never let us go," Alex added, his eyes narrowing toward a future he could see clearly now on the horizon. "They'll keep us hidden somewhere on a remote army installation where they'll prod our bodies and pick our brains until there's nothing left to prod and pick…and no one will ever know because they won't admit they ever caught us. They'll say we fled the country and supposedly died somewhere in the Amazon jungle. We'll be one of those unsolved mysteries like Amelia Earhart."

"That will never happen," Rose said, "because we will know, and I can make sure my colleagues do as well. There are too many of us to silence."

Alula sighed and looked up at Alex. Her eyes said all he needed to know. He did not have to be a mind reader to realize this was not what she wanted, and she was prepared to take the next step.

"None of this is acceptable," Alula said, "if it means everyone goes back to believing we're alone in the universe and it was all a big hoax. I don't want to wait another minute. Let's drive down to one of the big network television stations in New York City and give them an interview."

"They'll arrest us before we get a chance to go on air," Alex said.

"We need to do something to expose the government's lie and help Amber."

They all nodded, even Alex. He knew they had gone too far to turn back now.

"Any other suggestions?" Alula asked, closing her eyes and leaning her head back.

Rose and Miriam stood there staring off into space while Alex walked over to the window. There were trees everywhere obscuring the sky, making the world seem a lot smaller than it had a few minutes earlier.

No one spoke for the longest time.

"I have an idea," Alex said, breaking the silence.

They all turned to him.

"What if Alula does go on television for an interview, but it's not live and with little advance notice of the air date. One of those national news programs that do secret interviews all the time…like *Sixty Minutes*."

"We can trust a show like *Sixty Minutes* to be truthful and let the viewers decide," Rose added, "without giving you up to the authorities…and I know one of the producers."

Alula walked over to Rose and took her hand. "I don't want to cause you any problems."

"At this stage of my life, darling, I have plenty of problems I don't want or need. This is one I'd love having. You and Alex are the kind of problem I've been looking for my whole life."

"Let's do it," Alula said to Alex, who could not help but smile in response.

It sounded better to him than being hunted, captured, and tortured in secret.

"How is an interview going to prove anything?" Miriam asked. "How different can it be from the video you sent out? Particularly now that the government is saying you stole the crystal."

Rose nodded slowly while she covered her mouth with her frail, wrinkled hand. She could not hide the tremors. Alex had seen them before. They were most noticeable when she was thinking— more like agonizing—about something.

Alula reminded Miriam and Rose about her telekinetic powers.

"What can you do in the space of a one-hour news segment?" Rose asked.

"I can heal someone's scars."

"Like she got rid of my burns," Alex said, holding out his arm. "I was covered with them from the cappuccino machine."

"How about a broken arm?" Miriam asked.

"A simple, non-displaced fracture," Alula said, "but it would take more time and require a doctor and an x-ray machine to verify it."

"I think we go with the burns and scars," Rose said. "Something that doesn't require a third-party expert...something the audience can see happening before their eyes."

Rose's producer friend at *60 Minutes* was eager for the story and assured her they were very experienced at keeping interviews secret. They did the same thing with El Chapo, the notorious drug kingpin, and many others. Since Rose did not think it was a good idea to give up their safe house, they agreed to come to the show's studio in the city.

The producer wanted something dramatic, something visual the audience could see in terms of Alula's healing power. They agreed on a young child, a family friend of the producer, whose face had been badly scalded by an accident with a pot of boiling cooking oil.

"Do they believe you or the government?" Alex wondered out loud while they lay in bed the night before the interview.

"Doesn't matter," Alula responded, "they will believe me soon enough."

Rose and Miriam came with them the day of the taping. They did not have to disguise Alula's face since it was all over the news from the video. They offered to disguise Alex's face, but he declined since he was sure the government had his photo by now and thought it was time the world got to know about him as well. The set was closed, the cameraman and crew sworn to secrecy. They intended to air the interview the next day on Sunday, bumping some golf story. It was too timely to wait for an open slot.

They treated them respectfully, but in truth Alex did not get the feeling the crew really believed Alula. He suspected most of them thought it would turn out to be another hoax, right up there with Howard Hughes, Bernie Madoff, and unicorns.

The interview was relatively straightforward. Alula told her story about emigrating from Home at the age of eight. She talked about what it was like traveling through space and how they settled outside Seattle initially before moving to the Midwest. Her parents moved again some time ago and changed their names. They had kept off the grid, she explained, and did not even have a phone.

She explained how she sought out Alex to help her, knowing his father was from Home. She told the interviewer how they decided to contact a female astronomer at the University of Washington and picked Amber Garrigan at random. She told them all about the indestructible crystal and assured the television audience that the government's claim to the contrary was a lie.

Alula did not hold anything back.

"They can't scratch it, let alone reverse-engineer it. Not with the current level of their scientific knowledge. It could take them a hundred years if I had to guess."

She assured everyone it had never been used as a weapon, but only for space travel and mining. They also had some large star charts on which Alula pointed out Alcor, Trappist-1, and some other stars with planets supporting life.

She came across as very believable, very likeable, and completely harmless, as much an Earthling as any other woman on the planet.

Then they put on a doctor who confirmed her organs were reversed.

"While it's considered a very rare and harmless variation, it's not unheard of and can be found in a certain statistical sample of the population."

"Of course," Alula responded, "that would likely be in people descended from Home settlers."

This is the point at which they brought out Brenda, the young burn victim whose face had been badly scarred and who was looking at years of plastic surgery. Her parents stood beside her, their expressions alternating between hopeful and skeptical.

It was cruel, Alex heard one of the production assistants whisper, to raise their expectations like this. He hoped Alula and her boyfriend got caught and spent the rest of their lives in jail.

Everyone was quiet as Alula walked up to the little girl and smiled. She got down on her knees, took her hands, and closed her eyes. The little girl did not look the least bit afraid. She must have been poked and prodded by so many doctors that another one hardly mattered, even if Alula was not a doctor, and it was all being done on camera.

Nothing happened for five minutes, but then her face began to change. It almost looked like an animation. The burns, the discoloration, the redness, and the thickened skin began to fade, as if they were merging into one another. Brenda's face softened and for a few moments her skin looked as if it was being bathed in sunlight. A few minutes later Brenda looked like any other young girl, not a line or crease, no burns or scars.

If it was quiet before, it was even quieter now. It stayed that way for what seemed like a long time for a television program—even her parents stood quietly, their mouths open and their eyes filled with tears—before everyone in the room finally started applauding and cheering, and Brenda's parents fell to their knees to hug their daughter.

Just like that, this coming Sunday, the world would get proof beyond any reasonable doubt. If he and Alula were feeling the heat before, Alex realized, it would be nothing compared to what would happen after the show. The government will have been embarrassed, caught in a lie, and will have to defend its honor.

They left out of a side entrance to return to Rose's Catskill house, careful to make sure no one was following. They took some unnecessary turns, stopped once or twice to check a tire, waiting for all the traffic behind them to pass. Unfortunately, neither Alula, Alex, Rose, or Miriam had any experience with espionage or subterfuge, and they were indeed being followed. One of the PAs had tipped someone off.

Fortunately, it was not someone from the government who was following them. If that were the case, there would have been a couple of SWAT teams storming the house instead of an old man climbing out of a Toyota Prius to knock on Rose's door.

Rose answered it, putting on a big smile to hide her fear and anxiety.

"Can I help you?" she said, Alex stood close behind her.

He looked like Rose, another member of the Greatest Generation, except he had that disheveled look of the absentminded professor in the old Disney movies.

"My granddaughter told me about the interview," he said, walking in as if he had already been invited. "I know she shouldn't have, but she didn't tell anyone else, I swear, and I won't tell anyone. You must be Alula."

He walked over to her and extended his hand. Alula shook it with a relaxed smile on her face.

She knew he was not a threat because she knew what he was thinking, although she said she would not have minded at all if it was the FBI now that the interview was in the can and scheduled to air the next day. Too many people had witnessed what happened to be silenced. She whispered those exact words to Alex during the car ride back.

"I'm Doctor Person." He chuckled after he introduced himself, extending his arm to shake Rose's hand and then Alex's. "I know, it's a funny name."

"Not any funnier than Alula Borealis," Alula said.

"Nothing funny about the stars."

"Doctor Person," Rose repeated, rubbing her chin.

"Do you know him?" Alex whispered to her.

"No," Rose said, "but I know *of* him."

"I used to teach at Dartmouth…physics. I was also part of a NASA team, a top-secret group working on deep space travel."

"Like Voyager One?" Alex asked.

"More secret than that. We were working on manned interstellar travel. Trying to come up with a way to travel faster than the speed of light."

"Did you?"

"No, we were disbanded about three years ago. They said we weren't making any progress. I think we were...theoretically, of course. Too many people believe it's impossible. I'm not one of them... Then you showed up."

Doc Person walked into the living room and sat down on the couch. They all sat down around him.

"Einstein's theory of relativity states that nothing with mass can travel faster than the speed of light, and as we all know," Doc Person said, patting his stomach, "people have mass."

"So how did Alula get here?" Alex asked.

"Empty space has no mass. It's a complete vacuum, which means it can expand faster than the speed of light. You just need to figure out a way to hitch a ride on the vacuum of outer space."

"Sounds very daunting," Rose said, and Doc Person smiled.

"If you have two electrons close together, they can vibrate in unison... That's quantum physics. If you separate those same two electrons...say by a thousand light-years of empty space, a total vacuum, they can keep that instant bridge of communication open. If I jiggle one, the other electron will immediately sense the vibration.

"Einstein's theory of relativity weaves space and time together. It explains the connection between those two distant electrons and suggests a way of breaking the light speed barrier through the warping of space time. It may be something like a wormhole that could theoretically let something...or someone...travel a vast distance in an instant, like that instant bridge of communication between the two electrons."

"Sort of like a gateway to the stars," Alex said.

It almost made sense to him.

Doc Person nodded.

"What would keep the wormhole open?" Alex asked.

"Ah, bright student...that's the right question. Some sort of exotic matter we have yet to discover that should exist thanks to the weirdness of the laws of quantum physics. We were trying to find that exotic matter when they disbanded us. We were looking for a way to create those wormholes…and keep them open so they could be used for instant travel whether it was across a continent or between stars, which is how I surmise Alula got here."

Doc Person looked at Alula, who wore one of those inscrutable smiles suggesting to Alex that he might be on the right track.

"We weren't close to an answer, but I think we were making some progress, small steps, but small steps are all you can make when you're trying to climb a mountain as steep as this."

Rose shook her head to acknowledge that truism.

"But you know bureaucrats. They think baby steps are a waste of time and money. They want great leaps, or they lose interest. I confess I had a few doubts myself until Alula came along."

Alula's smile was replaced by a steady nod.

"Can you help me?" he asked her. "Were we on the right track? How does one open a wormhole? How do you keep it open? What's it like traveling through one?"

"I left when I was eight years old. I didn't understand it then and I don't understand it now. I know it did involve some sort of gateway in space."

"How about your parents, do they understand how it works?"

"No, they were both agricultural workers, which is considered a very noble profession on Home. They don't send out scientists as settlers."

"Very wise," Doc Person said. "Civilizations need to advance at a measured pace. I can imagine how a sudden leap like that could lead right down into the abyss."

Alula nodded.

"Can you tell me what it was like traveling like that…faster than the speed of light?"

"There was quite a bump when we entered it and even a bigger one when we exited."

"What about the effects on your body?" Doc Person asked. "Even if we could create a wormhole or use one, I had my doubts whether an amoeba could survive passing through it, let alone a human."

Alula shook her head slowly from side to side. "I don't recall much. I was young and it seems so long ago."

"Come, Doctor Person," Rose said, "let's sit in the kitchen and have some tea while we talk about it."

We all followed Rose to the kitchen, where she made a big pot of tea. Miriam put out Rose's collection of mismatched mugs.

Doc Person could not take his eyes off Alula.

"Do you remember if you felt dizzy or had any sense of speed when you made that leap through hyperspace? Did they put you in a state of suspended animation?"

"I don't think so. I remember we wore oxygen masks, and they made me drowsy. Maybe there was something mixed in with it. I don't think I was ever completely unconscious. It was almost like a daydream or a lucid dream if that makes any sense."

Doc Person nodded.

"How long did it take from beginning to end?"

"I don't know. It felt like an instant, but it couldn't have been that quick because I felt very stiff after we landed, as if I'd been strapped into my seat for ages. What I remember most was feeling thirsty when we arrived, thirstier than I had ever been before. They gave us something to drink first thing...it was greenish and sweeter than water."

Doc Person rubbed his hands together like he had to warm them up.

"You don't know what this means to me...to know it can be done. It's absolutely amazing. It was all so theoretical before." He took a sip of tea. "I'd give anything for a week with your scientists, but I suppose a trip back is out of the question."

"No one ever returns. There's no turning back and no further communication. It's always been like that. We are on our own whether it works out or not. We either assimilate or we transform."

"Transform?"

"That's what they call dying," Alex chimed in.

Doc Person nodded like he understood perfectly. He looked disappointed.

Rose patted him gently on the back while she poured him some more tea.

"The one question I have," Rose asked, "is whether your granddaughter can be trusted to keep them safe."

"Absolutely, I have no doubt about that... Besides, she doesn't know where I am, and I'm not going to tell her."

Rose nodded at Alex and Alula.

"She did it for me," he said, "because she knows how much this means to me. It's been my life work, and I don't have long."

"Why do you say that?"

"I was recently diagnosed with pancreatic cancer, stage four."

Rose reached out again, this time to rub his back.

"Can you help him?" Alex asked.

"I don't know...that's a tall order. Can you stay a while?"

He nodded.

"I can try," Alula said. "I've never tried anything quite like it before. Even if I can, it will be a long, slow process. I don't know if I can find every malignant cell. They could have spread all over his body by now."

"Try what?" Doc Person asked. "What process?"

The *60 Minutes* show had not yet aired, and Doc Person's granddaughter had no time to tell him what happened, so Rose explained about Alula's telekinetic power and what she did during the taping.

After the show aired on Sunday, it was all anyone could talk about. The government came clean with some lame excuse that their prior story was not a lie, but part of their strategic plan—a trick really—to lure the alien out of hiding, which in fact had worked.

Although they had not captured her yet, the general in charge announced it would not be long now. The television appearance had confirmed what they already knew—she was not traveling alone. It had also provided them with a ton of clues, including the fact that the alien was hiding somewhere in the New York metropolitan area.

"All we have to do now," he said, "is follow the trail of breadcrumbs."

They obviously knew Alula had to be staying somewhere in the vicinity of the *60 Minutes* production office. They also had to know she was getting help, and since an astronomer had helped her on the West Coast, they renewed their focus on astronomy professors in and around New York City.

Rose had a big heart and a sharp mind, but she was not schooled in the art of deception. As careful as she tried to be, she did not fully understand the risk when Alula asked her to contact Amber—who had been released after the show was aired—to see how she was doing and to let her know she and Alex were safe.

Rose had read every word in the newspapers since Amber's announcement about the planets around Trappist-1 and knew all about her colleague and close friend, Greg Underwood. She knew what the press had reported about them being more than just friends. Rose figured it would be safer, even with a burner phone, to call Greg's office and get the message to Amber that way. She did not plan on identifying herself, which she figured offered another layer of security.

Greg told Rose that Amber was doing fine, and she told him to tell her that Alula and Alex were as well and very appreciative of everything she had done.

They talked a few minutes about the *60 Minutes* show, Alcor, and what Alula and Amber's discovery meant for the future of astronomy and the earth. When he asked her if she had any concerns about the indestructible nature of the gem the alien had brought with her—and he called her "the alien" instead of Alula—Rose shuddered and quickly ended the conversation. But by then it was too late because Greg had recognized her voice, having heard Rose lecture on more than one occasion at the American Astronomical Society.

Greg locked the door to his office after she hung up to think it over. He figured the FBI probably had a bug on his office phone as a person of interest. After all, he was still Amber's boyfriend as far as everyone was concerned, notwithstanding Amber's resistance to his presence and counsel since she had been released. He knew they would identify Rose's voice soon enough if they were smart and checked with someone at the AAS.

All he would do by coming forward now was speed up the process a bit, keep himself safe and above suspicion, and perhaps preserve and expand his opportunities in the future, whether it was participating in the debriefing with the alien or applying for government funding.

If they were listening—which Greg was almost certain they were—and he did not come forward, they would conclude he was part of the conspiracy, which could make him a target. Surely, some of the higher-ups in the FBI and National Security Council would argue he should have known better and immediately reported the call. It could mean serious consequences for his career.

They say the Justice Department could indict a ham sandwich if it wanted to. He had to take that possibility seriously. It would be incredibly unfair to him and Amber—the world as well—if he allowed this uncertainty to continue. Hadn't the alien repeatedly told Amber she wanted to come forward and make herself accessible to the public? Isn't the government the public?

They would call him a hero for coming forward, Greg had no doubt about it. Amber would have to understand it and accept it. What choice did she have?

Once he told the FBI agent the aliens were being hidden by Rose Milton, Professor Emeritus of Astronomy at Columbia University, they would pick them up within an hour.

He had already made one mistake, not coming forward earlier—before the video—when his detailed description of Alula and her companion would have been worth something in terms of favors and fame. He was not going to make the same mistake twice.

The next morning, without saying a word to Amber, Greg called that first FBI agent who had left his card. He told him about the call from Rose Milton. She did not give her name, he explained, but they talked long enough for him to recognize her voice and to conclude it was the old woman astronomer from Columbia University.

"I've heard her lecture a couple of times," Greg said, trying to sound innocent and surprised.

He told Amber what he had done later that night during dinner at her apartment. She did not jump up and overturn her chair the way he imagined she might. In his experience, women tended to overreact—at least initially—because they let their hearts take control of their mouths, the crying and yelling drowning out any reasoning or logic.

The fact that Amber did not cry or start choking on her pasta was a good sign. She just stared at him, her pupils narrowing as if she was trying to process what he'd done by putting herself in his shoes. Greg thought it was a good sign and sat back in his chair. Once Amber finished using the scientific training to weigh the facts, she would come to the inevitable conclusion that he was right and had no choice. All she had to do was think rationally—like a man faced with a tough decision—and consider what was best for the country, the planet, and their future.

Greg felt even more relieved as Amber continued sitting there silently, her expression more contemplative than angry. He had planned out what he was going to say once she stopped screaming and crying. First, he would demand she sit quietly for a few minutes and hear him out. He would be adamant about it and tell her she owed him that much considering all the time they had spent together and the fact that she would never have completed the Trappist-1 research without him.

He had used similar lines with other women he'd dated—reminding them how much he had helped them in their studies and how much they needed him—but it never worked. But this time it seemed different, Greg thought, looking at Amber sitting there, because she was a scientist, not an English major, a history major, or a business major like the others. Amber was trained in the scientific method. The other three women relied on their gut.

"I am glad you're taking this so well," Greg finally said, taking her prolonged silence as an invitation to explain himself, perhaps even a tacit form of acquiescence. "I knew you'd understand if you took a moment to think about it. It's clear I had no choice. It's not hard to explain."

"No need," Amber said, gently putting down her napkin, slowly pushing her chair away from the table, and standing up.

Greg smiled. It seemed Amber already understood and agreed. She looked down at him, standing there calm and composed, as if she were about to start cleaning off the table to make room for coffee and dessert.

Greg took a deep breath and let it go slowly. This was turning out easier than he thought. He smiled up at Amber, and in response her mouth snapped shut, her lips pressed so tightly together they looked more like a scar.

Okay, Greg thought, so she was not overjoyed, that was to be expected, but she still got it. She wasn't yelling and pounding the table. Her intuition was telling her that he had done the right thing, and as she had said a dozen times, doing the right thing is never easy. People in their position can't simply follow their hearts.

He looked up into her eyes and smiled, but they didn't smile back; they had turned to stone.

"Listen," Greg said, "you need to appreciate the risks I faced because of the call. I don't know why Rose Milton called me instead of you, but she did. If the FBI were listening, as I am sure they were, I could be risking everything by remaining silent."

He waited for Amber to nod or otherwise respond, but when she did neither, he continued.

"We both could have lost our jobs and, believe me, no school would hire us after that. My reporting it to the FBI was all about protecting our reputations and our standing in the academic world, as much as it was about protecting the country and the planet."

Greg could see the vein below Amber's left eye turning blue, as the rest of her face turned crimson.

"This is much bigger than the two of us, surely you must realize that by now. The time has come for us to step forward as citizens of the earth. We are scientists first and foremost, which means we must always remain skeptical and wary. The aliens should have asked our permission before coming here. They had no right to use our planet like a breeding colony. What they have done is illegal, plain and simple, and they had to know that. They're no different from the immigrants who sneak across our border every day."

He watched Amber start digging her fingernails into her palm.

Greg still figured it would pass if he kept talking and gave her time to process what he was saying.

"Their motives have to be scrutinized and challenged," he added. "Even if we can't simply send them back, we need to meet with them, perhaps segregate them while we investigate. If it turns out the story is true, we can be welcoming…but on our terms. We need to keep an eye on them, and we need to stop any further settling. We have enough people here as it is."

Greg sat back down. He had not even realized he was standing. He must have unconsciously risen after Amber did. He felt much better now that he had said his piece. The hard part was over. His throat was dry, and he desperately needed some coffee.

"Did you put up the coffee?" Greg asked.

"I'd like you to leave," Amber responded in her normal speaking voice, as if she was addressing an unruly student. Then she walked over to the front door and opened it.

"Were you listening to anything I just said? Surely, you see my point. It's so obvious."

"Out," Amber said, still using her speaking voice.

"Let's talk about it some more. You haven't taken the time to think it over the way I have. You owe me that much…you owe *us* that much."

"NOW," she said, this time loudly and firmly.

Still the teacher—no crying and no screaming. Greg had to admit this was very different from the way it had gone down with the other women. He stood up and moved hesitantly toward the door, as if she might change her mind if he moved slowly enough.

"You don't really want to do this," Greg said, trying to look surprised and hurt, which was not all that hard to do since he was surprised and hurt. He expected more from Amber, even if she was able to hold it together. In the end, she was like the others, just without the tears.

"You're being irrational and emotional," Greg told her. "You're not acting like a scientist."

"If you don't leave now, I will call the police," she said, softer this time but just as determined.

It's always the same with them, Greg thought. They were quick to forget the past intimacies. Women were always ready to move on to the devil they didn't know. That was one proverb they didn't take to heart.

Greg stepped through the door and turned around, raising his pointer finger like he was in front of the class and about to say something important. He was going to tell Amber she was making the biggest mistake of her life by letting this small, debatable point ruin everything they had built together.

"I don't want to hear another word," she said before Greg could say anything. "You broke your promise. Nothing else matters." She said it without any of the emotion words like that deserved; then she slammed the door in his face.

The next morning, Greg found everything he had kept in her apartment in two shopping bags in front of his office door with a note asking him to please return the favor. She added that they could be cordial at faculty meetings, but that would be the extent of their relationship going forward.

Amber called Rose from Professor Allan's office in the Geology Department to let her know what had happened and to warn her. Fifteen minutes later Rose and Miriam were in the car driving up to the Catskill house to pick up Alula and Alex and take them someplace else. Unfortunately, it was the worst thing they could have done since they were already under surveillance.

Back at the house, Alula was sitting quietly with Doc Person, holding his hands and doing her best to transform the malignant cells into stardust, as she put it. Unfortunately, there were so many of them. The cancer had spread beyond the pancreas, which made it much more difficult. She had never attempted anything like this before or used her telekinesis power this intensely for such a long period of time. She was exhausted at the end of each day, and Alex practically had to carry her to bed. Doc Person was exhausted as well and could barely get up from the couch after each session.

Still, they were making progress, Alula said. She could feel it.

Twenty minutes after Rose and Miriam arrived to tell Alula and Alex about Amber's call and discuss where to go next, the authorities arrived. There were dozens of them with enough weaponry and tactical vehicles to make it look like a small invasion.

They did knock first—forcefully as opposed to neighborly— and when Rose opened the door, she was greeted by a representative from NASA, a member of the president's National Security Council, two men who refused to identify themselves, and four FBI agents. A platoon of marines stood behind them, their guns held away from their chests to confirm how ready they were to use them. All but two of the soldiers waited outside while everyone else walked in without being invited.

The lead FBI agent looked sternly at himself in the hall mirror while the NASA representative politely introduced himself.

"You need to come with us," the FBI agent said, turning away from the mirror to stare at Alula. He said it with cool insistence, as if he had been practicing for this moment his entire life. There was no mistaking what he meant. If she did not come voluntarily, the next option would be less pleasant.

"You too, Alex," he said, making it clear they knew all about him as well.

"What about me?" Rose said, stepping into his line of sight.

"Everyone has to leave...now."

Only Alula and Alex were put in handcuffs. As they were doing that, Alula apologized to Doc Person.

"I'm sorry we didn't get to finish."

"I appreciate the effort."

"It's still there," Alula said. "It'll grow back."

"That's okay." Doc Person smiled. "I'm happy I got to live long enough to get answers to some of my biggest questions. At my age, if it's not the cancer, it'll be something else soon enough."

He waved, as did Miriam and Rose, as they were escorted to one car while Alula and Alex were escorted to another. Their car drove off in one direction, and the car with Doc Person, Rose, and Miriam drove off in the opposite direction.

"Where are we going?" Alex asked.

"You'll see" was the only answer he got. It was a tone Alex was familiar with from his prior arrests.

The rest of the ride—three hours—went by in total silence.

CHAPTER 9
THE INTERROGATION

"Welcome," their interrogator said the next morning when he came in to question them. "My name is Gerard."

He sat down at the table and placed the file he was carrying in front of him.

Two other men sat down behind him on the chairs against the wall. They were large men who seemed out of place. Gerard did not identify them. Clearly, they were not attorneys hired to represent them or interested scientists. They were the government muscle.

"Welcome to where?" Alex asked.

Gerard did not answer. Instead, he opened the folder and flipped through some of the pages.

It was a small room with one table at the center. Alula and Alex were seated on one side, their friendly interrogator on the other. There were no pictures on the wall and no windows. The room was painted a military gray, and the recessed overhead light provided a background hum that was as distracting as a large window, at least to Alex, who could not stop hearing it. The only thing missing, Alex thought, was a hot light shining in their faces, the kind they always used in the old movies to make the suspects wilt and confess, whether they were guilty or not.

As far as Alex could tell, they were in a military installation hidden somewhere in the Adirondacks. He could only guess since the windows in the back seat of the car were blacked out and a divider in front prevented them from seeing out ahead. The ride took about three hours, and he could smell the fresh mountain air when they left the car—blindfolded of course. He felt the crunch of twigs and leaves as they walked to the building and heard the birds and squirrels scampering about.

A military base in the Adirondacks was the only place he could think of that made sense, especially when he looked through the tiny window in the door and saw the soldiers standing guard. What better place for a secret military installation than the mountains and forests of upstate New York, where it could be hidden in the thousands and thousands of acres of government-owned park land.

Alex had yet to hear any of the soldiers who guarded them—there were four—say a word. Every fifteen minutes one of them looked through the little window in the door to make sure he and Alula were still there and had not beamed up to some spaceship sent to rescue them. They always stared at Alula for a long moment before moving away. They looked as concerned as they were enraptured, as if they were afraid that she might melt their brains with one angry look.

"Do we get food?" Alex asked the interrogator. "And coffee?"

"Absolutely, as soon as we're done here." Gerard continued flipping through his file.

"What more can I tell you?" Alula said, leaning forward in her chair. "Everything I know was in the video and the *Sixty Minutes* interview."

Alex realized she must be listening to his thoughts.

"I've watched both many times," he said. "It seems to me a lot of things are missing."

"Nothing is missing. I've got nothing to hide."

"Okay, then let's go through it all again…this time in person."

They did. After Alula finished with her story about the settlements and her decision to come forward, Gerard closed his eyes, rubbed his forehead, and sighed, as if he had the toughest job in the world.

"Not good enough," he said, writing something down. "Not nearly good enough. People are concerned and afraid, which means you have to do better."

Alex thought about shoving the table up against him. Alula reached out and gently rested her hand on his arm.

"What about you? Do I make you afraid?" Alula asked sweetly.

He smiled back like he thought it was joke, although Alex was sure that she did. The government feared anything it was unfamiliar with or could not easily control or intimidate.

"I don't answer questions. I ask them," he added.

The interview went downhill from there.

At one point, Gerard got up and stood behind his chair. He put both his hands on the back and leaned forward.

"Tell me about the gem…what is it composed of?"

"I don't know. I thought the newspapers reported you had reverse-engineered it."

Alex winced. He had enough experience with the police to know they did not appreciate being shown up. They wanted yes and no answers; they wanted downcast eyes and shaky voices. They wanted respect and apologies. They did not react well when you talked back or made a joke at their expense.

If looks could kill, Gerard's would have instantly transformed Alula.

Gerard pulled the gem from his pocket and held it up for them to see.

"Why do you think they let you take it with you?"

"I don't think they cared. They used to give out samples in school. I snuck it in my things."

"They had to know."

The government sees and knows all philosophy of those who spend their life working inside it.

"Or didn't care." Alula shrugged.

"Or wanted you to take it with you to prove how advanced you are…and to try to intimidate us when the time was ripe."

Alula smiled. "It's a trinket, a souvenir. You should be worried about climate warming, not a piece of plastic."

"It's a weapon," Gerard responded, slapping his hand hard against the back of the chair. "Home is a dying planet looking to resettle its entire population, isn't that the truth?"

"No."

"With plans to take over the earth."

"No."

"Of course, if you were only eight when you left, as you say, why would the authorities tell you or your family the real reason for sending you here?"

"Because Home reveres the truth," Alula answered without taking a moment to think about it. "Homebodies do not lie, not even the government. The more advanced a civilization becomes, the more it realizes how important the truth is…whatever that truth is, whether you like it or not. As one of your writers once said, if you always tell the truth, you never have to remember anything."

"Bill Cosby?" Gerard smiled.

"Mark Twain."

Gerard chuckled at that bit of naivete. Even Alex had trouble believing Mark Twain could ever have intended a statement like that to apply to the government. The government doesn't have to remember anything. It can always lie, piling one lie on top of another.

"No little white lies on Home?" he asked, glancing back at his bodyguards, who were trying to hold in their giggles like two little boys.

"Don't confuse courtesies and kindness with telling the truth."

"Okay, let's change the subject," Gerard said, sitting back down and turning a couple of pages in his folder. "I want to talk about your parents. Where are they now?"

"They were agricultural workers on Home. They don't know any more than I do."

"I assume they're capable of answering for themselves."

Alula did not respond.

"You can start by telling me where they live."

Alula sat back and folded her arms across her chest.

"Are you afraid?"

"Of you? No, not at all. They didn't choose to come forward, and I must respect their wishes. Since they can offer nothing more, I don't see the point."

"It doesn't matter whether you do or you don't. It's not up to you."

"It is up to me. I get to choose what to say, to whom and when."

"Perhaps," Gerard said with the hint of a smile. "You know, under the National Securities Act, we can hold you...and Alex...as long as we need to, and we will until we get the answers we want."

"Good luck with that," Alula said with a little smile back.

Gerard looked up at what Alex assumed was a camera hidden somewhere in the ceiling. Alex had no doubt Alula was making everyone watching angry.

"Until we know more about this substance, and the true reason you've been sent here, the anxiety level in the government and the military will remain very high, too high to consider letting you go or letting anyone know where you are."

"You can't do that," Alex said.

"We can."

"We have rights."

"And we have responsibilities."

"I can't help you with the government's anxiety," Alula interrupted, "but I can assure you that you have nothing to worry about from me or any of the other settlers. What you really need to worry about is the health of the earth."

"This will be a long, excruciating process," Gerard said, looking down at the folder, "if we don't get the right answers."

"I can't tell you what's not true."

Gerard shrugged like there was nothing he could do about it.

"Sometimes you need to accept things on faith," Alula continued as if she were reading his mind again. "Isn't that an important part of your culture?"

"Sometimes… Unfortunately, this is not one of those times."

Alex wanted to say something, but all he could think of were four-letter words.

"Just tell me where your parents live, and we can find you someplace a little nicer than this."

"I couldn't tell you even if I wanted to. They moved when I left a couple of years ago, after I told them about my plan to go public, so they could remain out of sight."

"There are many ways of extracting information…and some can be very unpleasant."

"And illegal," Alex added.

"Not when applied to an enemy combatant."

"She's not an enemy combatant."

"She is in our eyes."

"You can try whatever you'd like," Alula said. "Nothing you have will work on me."

"What about Alex?" Gerard asked.

"Or Alex."

"Okay, let's move on."

He flipped through a few more pages in his folder.

"Tell me about this philosophy that rules your planet."

"It's not a ruling philosophy."

"Eyes open, hearts open, heads open—what does it mean?"

"Eyes open, heart open, mind open. It's a way of life…a way of living life to its fullest."

"Right...minds open, not heads open...I guess splitting your head open is not a good idea on any planet."

Gerard turned around to look at his two bodyguards, who allowed the wisp of a smile to escape from their pursed lips.

"Tell me what it means."

"How much time do you have?" Alula asked.

The interrogator sat back. "We're not going anywhere. Take as long as you like."

"It means pretty much what it says."

"I'd still like to hear your definition. Start with eyes open."

"I think it's easier to understand if you start with the opposite, eyes shut, which suggests a person who is unable or unwilling to see what's in plain sight."

"Why would anyone do that?" Gerard asked.

"Some preconceived notion of what the world should look like, seeing things the way they want to see them. Eyes open means using all your senses to look at things from all different angles and points of view...even through the eyes of others."

"Simple enough," Gerard said, writing something down, "look where you're going so you won't walk into a telephone pole."

The bodyguards tittered softly behind him.

Alula looked at Alex and shrugged. He felt embarrassed by such a poor demonstration of intelligence, understanding, and respect from a highly placed and supposedly well-educated Earthling.

"What about hearts open?"

"Living with an open heart begins and ends with listening," Alula said.

"With your ears?"

"With your heart. The heart is another one of your senses. It can understand a lot and has a lot to say. It speaks in whispers that can often be hard to hear over the roar of our thoughts and prejudices. To keep your heart open means to be empathetic and compassionate. To be in touch with your instincts and intuition."

Gerard stared blankly at Alula before rolling his eyes up at the ceiling.

"What happens when it breaks?" he asked, which Alex assumed passed for a joke in his bureaucratic circle.

"If you live with an open heart," Alula continued, "there is always room inside it for the old and the new, for your failures and successes, and for forgiveness of others and yourself. An open heart will always heal; it always allows you to connect deeper and higher to who and what surrounds you."

"Meaning?"

"The universe. An open heart gives you the depth and height you need to find the light and the love."

"Sounds very poetic...the kind of things my wife's yoga teacher tells her. It's a lot of New Age mumbo-jumbo if you ask me...hardly the perfection I expect from a civilization after a million years of evolution...a civilization able to make an indestructible gem like this."

He rolled the gem around in his palm.

"Perhaps because it's too advanced for you to appreciate or understand. There is no perfection, no matter how far you evolve. There is always change. Change is the one constant in the universe. Welcoming it is the true sign of an advanced civilization."

"How about that last bit of wisdom, minds open?"

"I think it's the most difficult of all," Alula said. "If you're not open to other ideas and perspectives, to the universe of differences, you don't leave yourself enough room to learn and grow. Mind open means being willing to consider things that may challenge your longest-held belief. It means being tolerant of what you don't understand or believe in."

"Home is what, like thousands of years ahead of Earth?" Gerard asked.

"More like millions."

"And this is the best you could come up with. Haven't you guys pretty much agreed on everything by now? What's left to fight over?"

"They discuss on Home, they don't fight...not the way we do here on Earth."

Alex liked the way she used "we." The goons behind Gerard scowled.

"A person's color and shape are of no significance. All people deserve the same respect and opportunity to learn, whatever their ability or disability. The same right to exist and thrive applies to plants and animals...the soil...rocks...stardust in any form."

"Huh?" was the best response Gerard was able to muster.

Alex could not tell whether he was baffled by her concern for stones or trying for the right dismissive tone to impress his audience. His guess was the latter.

"Having different opinions is normal," Alula continued. "Vilifying those who don't hold yours is not. Having convictions and being passionate about something does not mean closing your mind to something else. Minds open means being empathetic to other people and their ideas...to other species...to all things, even the planets and the stars."

"So, what are we left with," Gerard said with a chuckle, "arguing over which side of the egg to crack? Is this the utopia you're offering Earth?"

"I'm not offering anything. I came here to live just as you do. All I'm trying to say in coming forward is that we're not alone in the universe, and we need to consider that in terms of how we take care of our planet and each other."

Gerard did not bother looking up. He was too busy writing something down.

"An open mind keeps you optimistic and mentally strong," Alula added.

"So does a good glass of scotch."

"To each his own." Alula looked over at Alex and smiled.

"Seems to me you'd like to turn us all back into kindergarteners."

"Would that be so bad?"

Alula reached under the table and took Alex's hand.

Gerard closed his folder, pushed back his chair, and stood up. "I think that's enough for today."

"For today?" Alex said. "How about period. When do we get to go home?"

Gerard looked down at him. Alex could not read his mind, but he could see the disdain in his eyes.

"Son, this is going to be a long, slow, agonizing process."

With that one of the goons knocked three times on the door, and a guard looked through the window before opening it.

"Don't I get a call?" Alex asked.

If they let him make one, he planned on calling the *60 Minutes* producer or the *New York Times.* The best way to protect themselves would be with the help of the press.

Gerard did not respond, he didn't even turn around, and there was no mistaking the sound of the door being shut and bolted behind them.

Alula kissed Alex on the cheek.

"I'm not worried," she said.

"You never are."

"There is an element of uncertainty in everything we do, every day we greet. Worry is never productive. I prefer mindfulness."

"Meaning?"

"Focusing on the moment, the day ahead. Visualizing a positive outcome."

"Even in the bleakest of circumstances?"

"Especially in the bleakest of circumstances."

"Unfortunately, I'm not like you."

"You can be."

"If I open my eyes, my heart, and my mind."

Alula nodded.

The only way this was going to have a positive outcome in Alex's imagination was if Rose, Miriam, or Doc Person could get the word out, which he doubted they would be able to. Or if the government made a mistake as it so often does. Someone might leak something because bureaucrats love to toot their own horn. A government official might call a reporter—anonymously—and whisper that they had captured the two aliens and were in the process of debriefing them.

That would get the press percolating. It was their best hope as far as Alex was concerned.

The next day they had a new interrogator, someone who said he was from the National Security Council and the Department of Homeland Security. If this were a movie, Alex would have considered this character the CIA spook. He was a giant compared to Gerard, at least a foot taller, and his face was wiped clean of expression. There were no pleasantries, just his name, John, followed immediately by his first question.

"What more can you tell me about your planet?"

"The earth is my planet," Alula said.

No reaction, not even a grunt or a roll of his eyes.

"The one you came from. Tell me about Home."

"Not much I can tell you that you don't already know. Red sun, two moons, smaller than Earth, less natural resources, smaller population, its civilization is far older."

"How old is far older?"

"Our ancestors first appeared about eight million years ago."

John nodded like he had already guessed that before moving on to his next topic, the risk to the earth of introducing alien DNA.

"If what you say is true," he said, "it means your DNA has been corrupting ours for over two centuries."

"Not corrupting it, perhaps modifying it a bit over time…or not at all… It depends on nature's selectivity. As I'm sure you know, DNA is a dynamic and adaptable molecule, and nucleotide sequences mutate all the time. Before picking a planet for settlement, Home's scientists first confirm that any likely mutations would be small and benefit the native species."

"Likely is not comforting enough. Adding a foreign species to any native population always creates a risk. I thought your planet believes in never doing harm."

"It does, which is why a planet isn't approved for settlement until there have been years and years of research and testing. Field studies as well. Home will never send settlers if there is any significant difference, or it poses any danger. They've been doing this for thousands of years without a single problem."

"That you know of," John responded.

"There are many inhabited planets throughout the universe. There is always another one to investigate if they identify any risk."

"We've tested your DNA…his too."

"My name is Alex."

John gave him a dirty look.

"There are variations we've never seen before," he added, turning back to Alula.

"Slight variations are normal. They exist throughout the universe just as they do throughout the earth. Neanderthals, Eurasians, Native Americans, North Africans, they wash out over time."

"How about your reversed organs."

"Insignificant as long as the doctor treating me knows in advance."

"And the telekinesis?"

"Coming our way, I suspect, in the next five hundred thousand years or so…assuming we're still around."

The conversation went on like that for a couple of hours before John suddenly stood up and ended it. He and his two mute bodyguards, different from the day before, left without responding to Alex's demand to make a call.

"The government's intentions are not honorable," Alula whispered in Alex's ear after they left. "They're not going to let us out any time soon, if ever, and they are not planning to let anyone know we're here. There will be no call. They want the world to think we are still free. They plan to discredit us again and make it look like a hoax. They figure it will be a lot easier if we disappear and the world can go back to believing it's alone."

"You were listening to his thoughts."

"Some of them. It was giving me a headache."

"What about Rose, Miriam, and Doc Person?" Alex said. "They'll go to the press."

"Unless they're still being detained and won't be released unless they promise never to say a word."

"They would never agree to that."

"Unless they believe something bad will happen to us if they do." Alula sighed. "It will be a long time before another Homebody steps forward."

Alex covered his mouth with his hand and whispered, "None of this sounds very good."

Alula put her lips to his ears and whispered back, "I think it's time we should leave."

"Fat chance of that."

Alula smiled. She had a plan, and it was easier than Alex could have imagined. He did not have to fake an appendix attack or complain about chest pains. As part of her telekinesis power, she had the ability to put people to sleep.

They whispered in each other's ears.

"It's easy as long as I can see them and they're not too far away."

"For how long?"

"About eight hours."

"Can you do that to me?"

Alula nodded.

"All those sleepless nights, I wish you had said something."

"No way, I like it when you're lying awake beside me."

"Okay, what are we waiting for?"

"The door is locked," Alula reminded him. "I can't do anything about that."

"Let me try."

Alex pounded on the door and said he needed to go to the bathroom. There was a bathroom across the hall, and they always stood inside watching him do his business, as if they feared he might be able to escape down the drain. Three soldiers stood there squeezing tight to their rifles while the fourth opened the door. In an instant they all fell to the ground.

"They're not dead?" Alex asked.

"They'll wake up in about eight hours, refreshed and ready to go."

They walked down the hall toward the front door, and as anyone approached them, some at a run, Alula looked at them, raised her eyebrows, and they fell asleep.

If there were cameras around, no one appeared to be watching because no alarms went off. Clearly, this army base was never intended to hold prisoners, its chief advantage being its location was probably unknown and in the middle of nowhere. When they got outside there were a dozen cars to choose from, and all of them had keys in the ignition.

The guards at the gate stood at attention as they drove toward them and quickly raised their weapons when they saw who was in the car. A second later they were asleep.

"Okay," Alex grinned, "mission impossible has been accomplished. Where do we go from here?"

"This is as far as my plan goes. Any ideas?"

"Well, we have eight hours at most before anyone realizes we're missing. Probably a lot less than that because someone is going to drive up and find the guards at the gate asleep. It won't take long to figure out we've escaped, and they'll know which car we're in by the process of elimination."

"So what do we do?" Alula asked.

Alex thought it over. They could try to switch cars at a rest stop. "Can you start a car without a key, you know, with your telekinesis?"

"No."

Alex wished he had watched more closely when some of his former drug buddies hot-wired cars.

"Then we need to go somewhere we can get to without traveling on the main highways, which all have cameras. Someplace not too far. I suppose it makes no sense going back to Rose's house in the Catskills."

"Probably first place they'll look."

"And we have to get to a phone," Alex said, "let the world know."

Alula nodded.

They discussed calling Amber or Rose's secretary, someone who could help get the word out. They talked about calling the *New York Times* or the Seattle newspaper.

"What about going to a local television station?"

"They might turn us in," Alex said. "They don't want to be on the government's bad side when they have to renew their license."

"What we need at the moment," Alula said, "is some time to make a plan."

"A motel would be too risky," he said. "They'll search every one of them for a hundred miles. Someone will spot the car. Besides, we have no money and no IDs."

"I know where we can go," Alula said after a few moments.

Alex looked at the gas tank. It was about three-quarters full.

"We probably have less than three hundred miles left in the tank, so it had better be closer than that."

"It is."

"Where?"

"My parents' farm."

"I thought they moved, and you didn't know where."

"They moved a long time ago, and I've been there many times."

"I didn't know you could lie like that."

Alula smiled. "I can when it's a harmless white lie...and for a good purpose."

"Okay, but only if you agree to let me stop somewhere and call *Sixty Minutes*."

Alula agreed.

Alex was able to get through to the producer and tell him everything that had happened. Where they had been staying, when they had been captured, and where he thought they had been held. Within a few hours the whole world would know they had been caught and had escaped by putting an entire army base to sleep.

Alex felt a lot safer after that.

Alula's parents had a small farm near the Finger Lakes, where they raised grapes for local wineries. It took them three hours to get there since they had to stick to the side roads. The gas tank was nearing empty by the time they hid the car in the barn.

The name of Alula's mother was Alasia, which she said was a star in the Serpens constellation, and her father's name was Mark, short for Markab, a star in the Pegasus constellation.

Alula looked exactly like her mother, which Alex found a little eerie since it was like seeing twenty-five years into the future. Both of her parents were thin like Alula, tall as well, with very few wrinkles and the same calm, contented way about them. They did not look surprised or upset about what had happened or might happen next. It was clear where Alula got her equanimity. If they were representative of the people from Home, the earth had nothing to fear and a lot to learn.

"I wish I knew how this was all going to turn out," Alex said, as they sat around the kitchen table drinking tea and eating the best chocolate chip cookies he had ever tasted. "I don't have a very good feeling about it."

"You never do," Alula said.

"One life, one encounter," Alula's mother said, patting Alex's hand much the way Alula did to reassure him.

"What does that mean?" he whispered to Alula.

"It means this form is transient," her mother explained, "like the magnolia blossoms on the trees out front, which is why we embrace the moment...this encounter and this life...because there will be others to follow."

Alex wished he could believe that.

"It's all about being mindful," Alula's father added, "of this exact moment, not the future."

"What if it doesn't work?" Alex asked, as Alula's mother refilled his mug.

"Being mindful?" her father responded.

"No, this great reveal. What if the authorities get rid of us and convince the world it was a big hoax? Or what if they believe us and no one cares? What if knowing the earth is not alone doesn't change a thing?"

Alula's father sat back and clasped his hands together as if he were about to lead them in prayer.

"Every journey begins with a single step," he said, "and each step leaves a footprint."

"A candle lights other candles even while it consumes itself," her mother added.

Those two bits of colloquial wisdom Alex understood.

"Your parents should be writing fortune cookies," Alex whispered to Alula, who smiled back.

"They can hear, you know. They both have excellent hearing."

Her parents chuckled in unison.

"I know what's coming next," Alula said, "because I've heard it a thousand times. It's one of their favorites. Go ahead, Dad, say it."

"You do the honor," he said, turning to her mother.

"If you insist. Back on Home, we have a saying...*starlight shines far.*"

"Meaning?"

Alula answered for them. "It takes one spark to create a star, and the light from that star can be seen from a great distance...whether it's measured in miles or years."

"And you're the spark creating the light that will reach into the future," Alex said.

"*We* are," Alula corrected him. "And that light will eventually become visible and bring change."

Alex had forgotten until that very moment what his father used to say about the first kiss with his mother. He liked to say it "shined as far as the stars."

"We've been settling on many planets for well over a thousand years," Mark said, "and the history books tell us there always comes a time when a planet learns it is not alone. Usually, they discover it on their own, but sometimes they get a little help. There is no formula for how or when it should happen."

"Does it always work out?" Alex asked. "Is it always for the better?"

"Knowing is always better than not knowing, although sometimes it comes too late, or it doesn't make a difference. Homebodies who settle know the risk."

"Is this the right time?" Alex asked.

"We've been talking a lot about that," Alula's mother said. "It's hard to know for sure, but it doesn't feel like the wrong time. We are proud of Alula for stepping forward, even if she only leaves a single footprint. She is our star, you both are, and your light will shine far, which makes us both very happy."

"No matter how it turns out?"

"No matter how it turns out."

Alex searched their faces and could not see the least bit of concern or fear.

"It's okay with me," Alula added, "however it turns out. Sometimes it takes a cluster of stars to shine bright enough to be seen far away."

"The universe is filled with stardust," Alasia said, still as cheerful as the moment they arrived, "so there will always be starlight shining far."

"What if it takes another million years?" Alex asked.

"A moment in star time," Mark replied.

"Hopefully, the earth will have that long," Alex added. Alula's parents looked a little doubtful.

"It's time for us to go," Alula told her parents after she finished her tea. Perhaps they had already read Alula's mind, because they did not make any effort to convince her to stay.

"Where are we going?" Alex asked.

Alula looked a little surprised by the question, as if she thought he might be able to read her mind as well. An old habit, no doubt, from being around her parents. Perhaps he had, which is why she waited for him to answer his own question.

"Back?"

She nodded.

"Not back to the military base or Seattle." He realized that as well and swallowed hard.

"Back to the beginning."

Alex knew exactly what Alula meant, not just from her words but from her eyes as well.

"How do we do that?" Alex whispered, the lump in his throat so large, he could barely get the words out.

"We make another tape, the two of us this time. Then we take the car. My father has gas in the barn." She stopped for a moment and looked out the window. Alex did as well. Even the sky looked a little sad and gray, as if it, too, knew what Alula had in mind.

"We deliver it to the local TV station in Syracuse, mail copies to the Seattle station, *Sixty Minutes* and a few others...then we go home."

Alula's parents remained silent; their arms wrapped around each other as they listened.

This is exactly what they did. They made a tape in which Alex told the world about their capture, interrogation, and escape. Then Alula warned of the dangers everyone on the planet faced from themselves, not from Home. She assured everyone there was still time and that sharing ourselves with the stars and the countless other life-forms in the universe was our destiny.

Alula promised we were not in danger from other more advanced civilizations, only our own, and while there was still time to save the planet, we had to act deliberately and without delay.

She spoke from one earthling to another.

They dropped the tape off at the NBC affiliate in Syracuse and sent copies to three other major stations in New York, Los Angeles, and Seattle, as well as to *60 Minutes*. They also sent copies to Columbia University and the University of Washington.

After that, they drove back to Rose's house in the Catskills.

"You know, they'll pick the car up on a camera somewhere along the Thruway," Alex said, but Alula already knew that.

They were done running and hiding. She had accomplished what she wanted to do. Alex felt surprisingly calm as well. No drug cravings and no fear. He was content in this moment—driving beside Alula while watching the world go by.

He knew what was going to happen to them—to their bodies—but it did not bother him. It was not like he was having a religious awakening, although it felt like something similar. He did believe everything was made of stardust and every transformation was an ending of one encounter and the beginning of another...a joining with the stars.

Understanding the nature of things—of stardust—brought a calm and stillness to his mind and heart unlike anything he had ever felt before, even when he was high on drugs, which might explain why Alex was already feeling a bit disconnected from his body.

Alula must have been listening to his thoughts because she reached out and squeezed his leg, whispering, "Exactly."

When they got to Rose's house, they tore away the yellow tape and used the hidden key to get in. Alex noticed the cameras the Feds had placed in the trees. He knew they would be there shortly.

The authorities showed up in force thirty minutes later. They broke in simultaneously through the front door, the back door, and three of the larger windows like they had been rehearsing for this moment for years. They wore special masks with dark lenses as if it might protect them from Alula's sleep ray, but they could not find either one of them. In truth, they did find them—they just did not realize it because they did not recognize them.

They were too focused on their own intentions and actions. Their eyes, hearts, and minds were not opened wide enough to see or feel the stardust or understand what had happened.

CHAPTER 10
WE ARE ALL STARDUST

I am everywhere and everything.

Not flesh, not blood, but no different in a cosmic sense.

I am Alex and Alula—together forever—joined with countless others. I am a turtle, a bird, a stone, a tree, the clouds in the sky, a breath of wind, a ray of sunlight, the moon, a comet, and a billion stars. As my father said, and Alula promised, I am part of everything, part of everywhere, and part of her…forever.

We are still together. I feel it as strongly as I did when I was able to reach out and touch her. Our atoms reverberate against each other, as they will for all eternity, no matter how far apart they drift, whether some of them become one with another star, a rock, or roam from galaxy to galaxy. We will always be together, always in touch because of some strange quirk of quantum physics that allows my vibrations to instantly touch hers.

In the instant before they burst through the door, I felt Alula reach inside me—as warm and as wonderful a feeling as I have ever had before—and touch something that set me free, scattering my atoms along with hers, allowing them to embrace and entwine as they rose to the stars.

In that instant, it felt as if we had lived a full life together, as I had come to understand it growing up on Earth. We grew old on the farm that had once belonged to her parents, watched our child grow up and go off on her own, and enjoyed our old age sitting together, holding hands, and looking up at the sky, astonished every night by how far the starlight shines.

Made in the USA
Middletown, DE
27 June 2022